POLICING THE CITY

POLICING THE CITY

An Ethno-Graphic

– Based on an original text by Didier Fassin –

TEXT

Didier Fassin with Frédéric Debomy

ART

Jake Raynal

– Translated from the French by Rachel Gomme –

OTHER

Other Press
New York

Originally published in French under the following title:
La Force de l'ordre by Didier Fassin, Frédéric Debomy, and Jake Raynal
based on Didier Fassin's work *La Force de l'ordre.*
Une anthropologie de la police des quartiers

Production editor: Yvonne E. Cárdenas

This book was lettered by Jake Raynal.

10 9 8 7 6 5 4 3 2 1

Printed in the United States of America on acid-free paper.
For information write to Other Press LLC, 267 Fifth Avenue, 6th Floor, New York, NY 10016. Or visit our Web site: www.otherpress.com

Library of Congress Cataloging-in-Publication Data

Names: Fassin, Didier, author. | Debomy, Frédéric, author. | Raynal, Jake, artist. | Gomme, Rachel, translator. | Fassin, Didier. Force de l'ordre.
Title: Policing the city : an ethno-graphic / text: Didier Fassin with Frédéric Debomy ; art: Jake Raynal ; translated from the French by Rachel Gomme.
Description: New York : Other Press, [2022] | "Based on an original text by Didier Fassin"—Title page.
Identifiers: LCCN 2021039950 (print) | LCCN 2021039951 (ebook) | ISBN 9781635422504 (hardcover) | ISBN 9781635422511 (ebook)
Subjects: LCSH: Police—France—Paris—Comic books, strips, etc. | Law enforcement—France—Paris—Comic books, strips, etc. | Ethnic conflict—France—Paris—Comic books, strips, etc. | Race discrimination—France—Paris—Comic books, strips, etc. | Minority youth—France—Paris—Caricatures and cartoons. | Youth and violence—France—Paris—Comic books, strips, etc. | Police-community relations—France—Paris—Comic books, strips, etc.
Classification: LCC HV8203 .F38 2022 (print) | LCC HV8203 (ebook) | DDC 363.20944—dc23
LC record available at https://lccn.loc.gov/2021039950
LC ebook record available at https://lccn.loc.gov/2021039951

To all those who undergo daily the harassment,
the humiliations, the baiting, and sometimes the violence
and the racism of the police, and who are finally
succeeding in making their voices heard.

The Aesthetics and Politics of an Ethno-Graphic

*In ways that I still find fascinating to decode, comics in their
relentless foregrounding seemed to say what couldn't otherwise
be said . . . I knew nothing of them but I felt that comics freed
me to think and imagine and see differently.*

Edward W. Said, *Homage to Joe Sacco*, 2001

This book was born out of a sociological study that aimed to better understand what the police do in low-income neighborhoods in France. It was the mid-2000s, and there was increasing evidence that the police's interactions with the public were a source of violent incidents, especially when they concerned young men from racial or ethnic minorities, as in 2005 in Clichy-sous-Bois and 2007 in Villiers-le-Bel, just two of many events in which several such young men died. But rather than these tragic events, what I sought to grasp was the everyday activity of the police and their relations with the people they dealt with. Ethnographic research was the best way to do this.

Ethnography is a social science practice woven from three strands. First, it is a method that involves sharing the everyday lives of those one is studying over a long period, in an attempt to better comprehend them. I thus spent fifteen months with an anticrime squad, on patrol in the low-income neighborhoods of a city near Paris. Second, it is the experience of a social world that the ethnographer gradually discovers, establishing relationships with those belonging to it. I participated in the officers' daily routine as an attentive observer, from conversations over coffee to interventions on the ground, interfering as little as possible with their actions and doing my best not to reveal my opinions, even when I found their behavior disturbing. Lastly, ethnography is a writing practice that may take the form of articles, books, films, or photographs through which the authors attempt to communicate what they have understood. Until recently, graphic books were not included among the possible vehicles, and the present work results from a desire to innovate in this respect. By depicting the boredom involved in police work, representing the ethnographer as a silhouette, and seeking out felicitous images to replace the words, we aim to render an account of these three strands of ethnography.

But moving from the four hundred dense pages of a social science text to the hundred or so plates of its graphic adaptation, from accounts of scenes and descriptions of places to panels that depict them, from the analysis of complex situations and theoretical questions to a succession of images accompanied by occasional speech bubbles and narrative boxes—in short, turning an ethnography into an ethno-graphic—was for me a challenge renewed at every stage of preparation of this volume, from the selection of sequences, through reconstitution of the historical background and sociological frame of analysis, to the design of each panel. I decided early on to keep to the facts rather than introduce fictional elements, as some have ventured in similar endeavors, and to develop the sociohistorical context, which a simple succession of anecdotes might elide.

Provided these essential parameters are borne in mind, using the graphic format to communicate ethnography has interesting potential on two levels. First, it opens the research to new audiences and novel exchanges: academic texts, even when they are written for a broad readership, fail to reach the majority of those they discuss and to whom they are most particularly addressed. Second, it opens the way to exploring new modes of writing that present researchers with unusual questions: it invites them to reflect on how best to present complex facts without simplifying their interpretation, how to remind the reader of the presence of the ethnographer in order to avoid the illusion of neutral objectivity, and ultimately how to develop a new way of expressing the realities of a social world. The term I propose to describe this new object, analogous with what the graphic novel is to the field of literature, is thus "ethno-graphic"—the hyphen representing the metaphorical bridge between the worlds of research and art.

But this project is more than aesthetic work; it is political. In the United States as in France and many other countries, it is acutely topical. The evolution of police practices, and of the law enforcement policies that make them possible, is especially disquieting because racism, discrimination, violence, and more generally the abuses perpetrated by the police become normalized as they go unpunished by the courts and remain denied by the authorities. It is therefore from civil society—from mobilizations of which Black Lives Matter is the most powerful example but which include many other less visible ones, from human rights organizations, and finally simply from citizens—that the demand for democratic police, whose abuses would no longer be protected and even encouraged, must come. If this ethno-graphic can contribute to this demand, it is doing so, in its small way, by exposing the social logics that enable what is claimed to be respect for public order to transmute into defense of the social order, and by providing some keys to understanding for those who, here as elsewhere, are fighting for a more just society.

D.F., August 2021

Acknowledgments

I am indebted to the police commissioner who took the risk of authorizing this research as well as the police officers who accepted the scrutiny of an outsider on their practices—whatever the implications would be. I am grateful to Bruno Auerbach, Séverine Nikel, and Louis-Antoine Dujardin for their support for the French version of this book, and to Judith Gurewich and the team at Other Press for their enthusiastic commitment to bringing this new version into being. My thanks go to Jake Raynal for his expressive drawings, to Frédéric Debomy for his judicious suggestions, and to Rachel Gomme for her attentive translation.

POLICING THE CITY

DECEMBER 31, 2006, 7:00 P.M.
?
B13 U

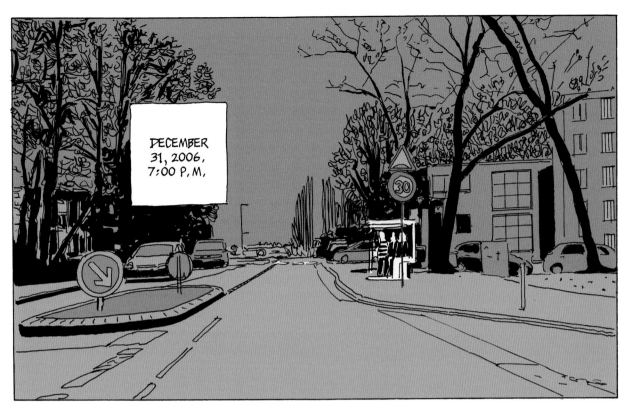

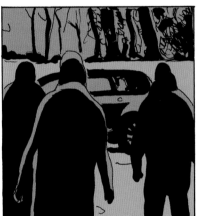

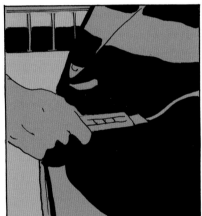

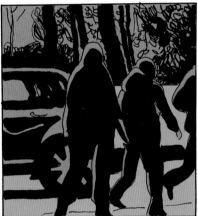

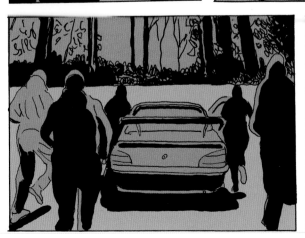

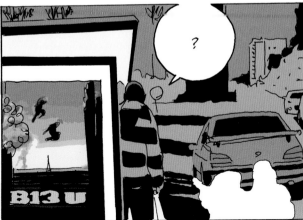

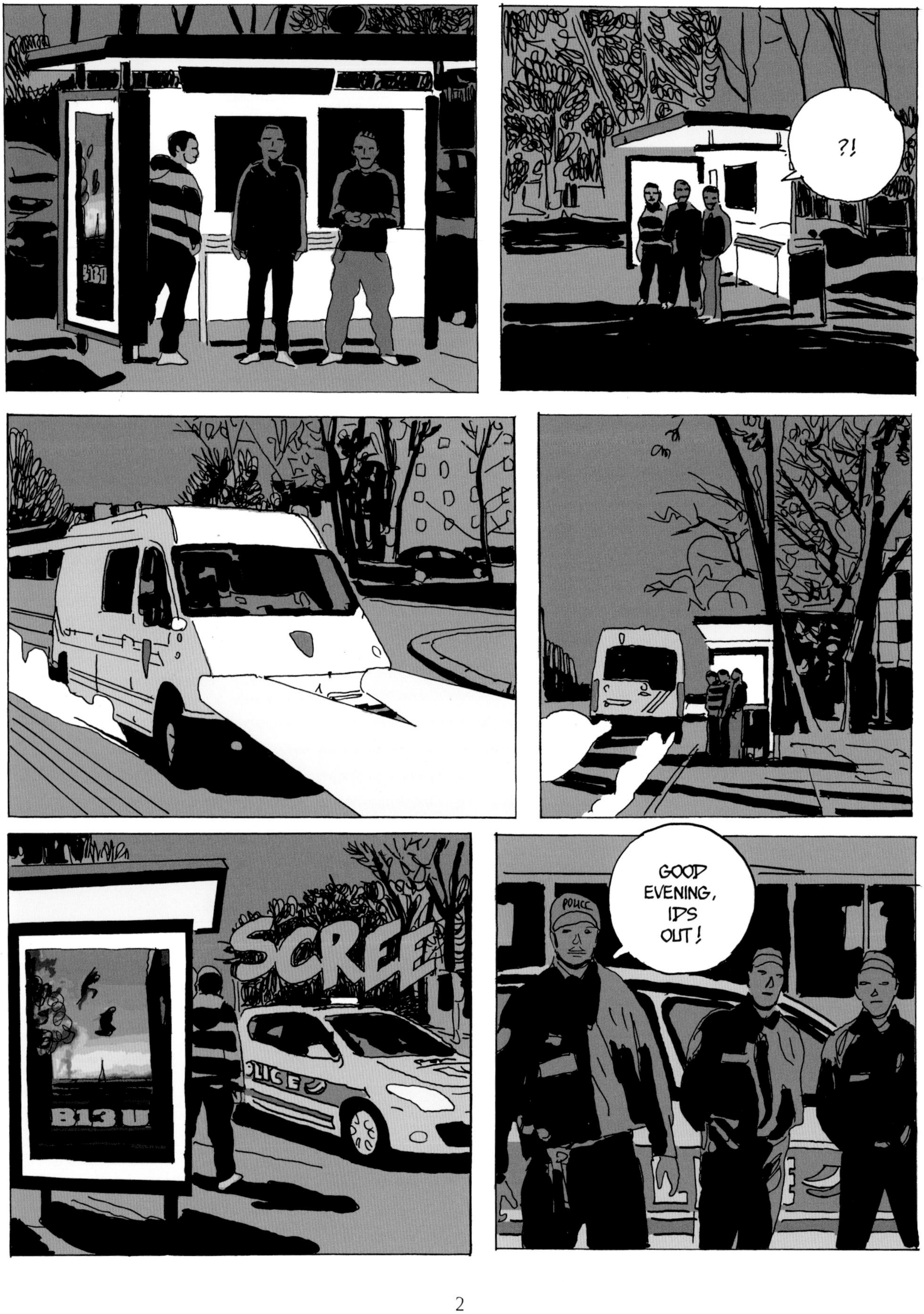
?!
SCREE
B13U
GOOD EVENING, IDS OUT!

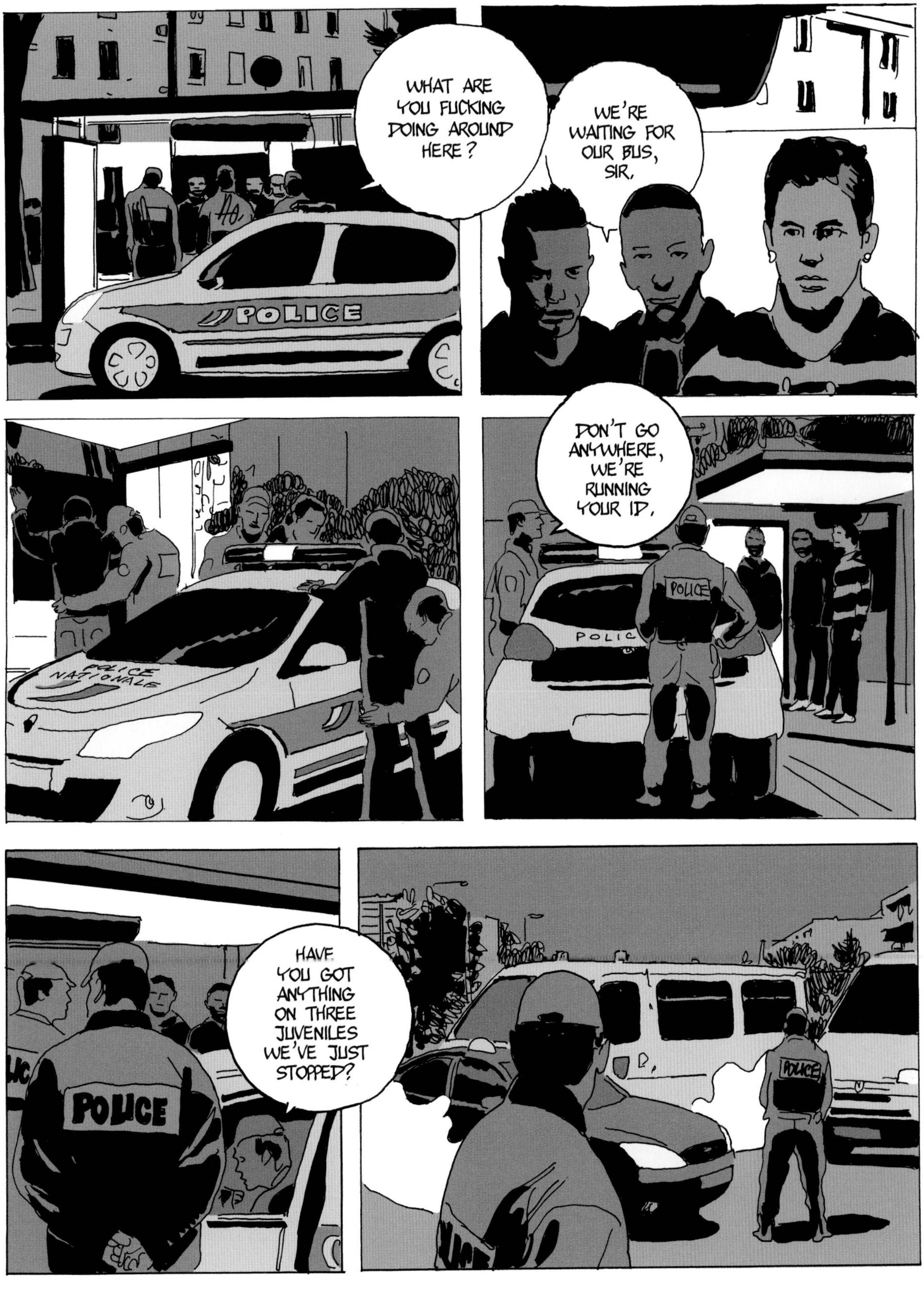

POLICE
WHAT ARE YOU FUCKING DOING AROUND HERE?
WE'RE WAITING FOR OUR BUS, SIR.
POLICE NATIONALE
DON'T GO ANYWHERE, WE'RE RUNNING YOUR ID.
POLICE
POLIC
HAVE YOU GOT ANYTHING ON THREE JUVENILES WE'VE JUST STOPPED?
POLICE
POLICE

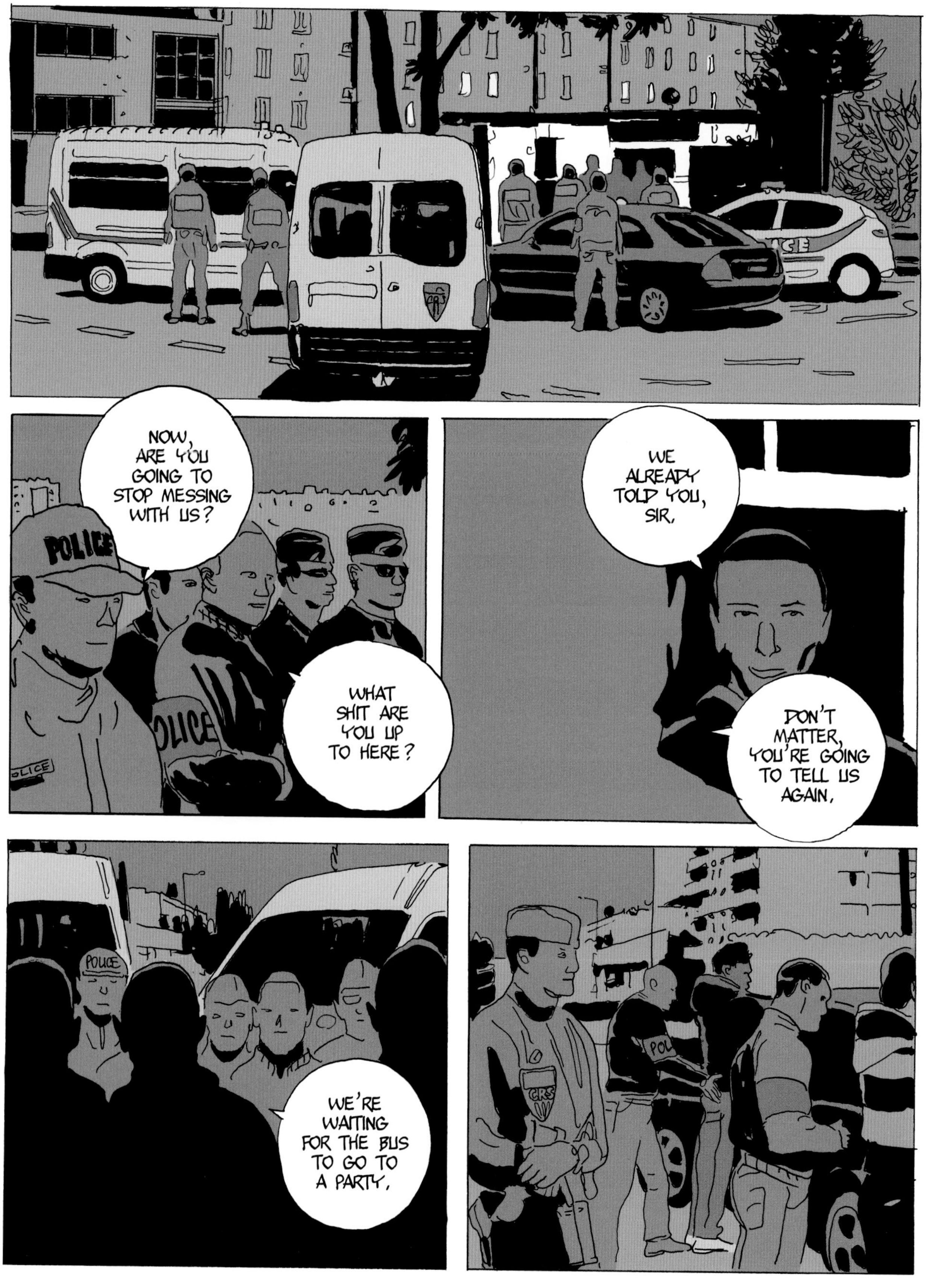

POLICE
NOW, ARE YOU GOING TO STOP MESSING WITH US?
WHAT SHIT ARE YOU UP TO HERE?
WE ALREADY TOLD YOU, SIR.
DON'T MATTER, YOU'RE GOING TO TELL US AGAIN.
POLICE
WE'RE WAITING FOR THE BUS TO GO TO A PARTY.

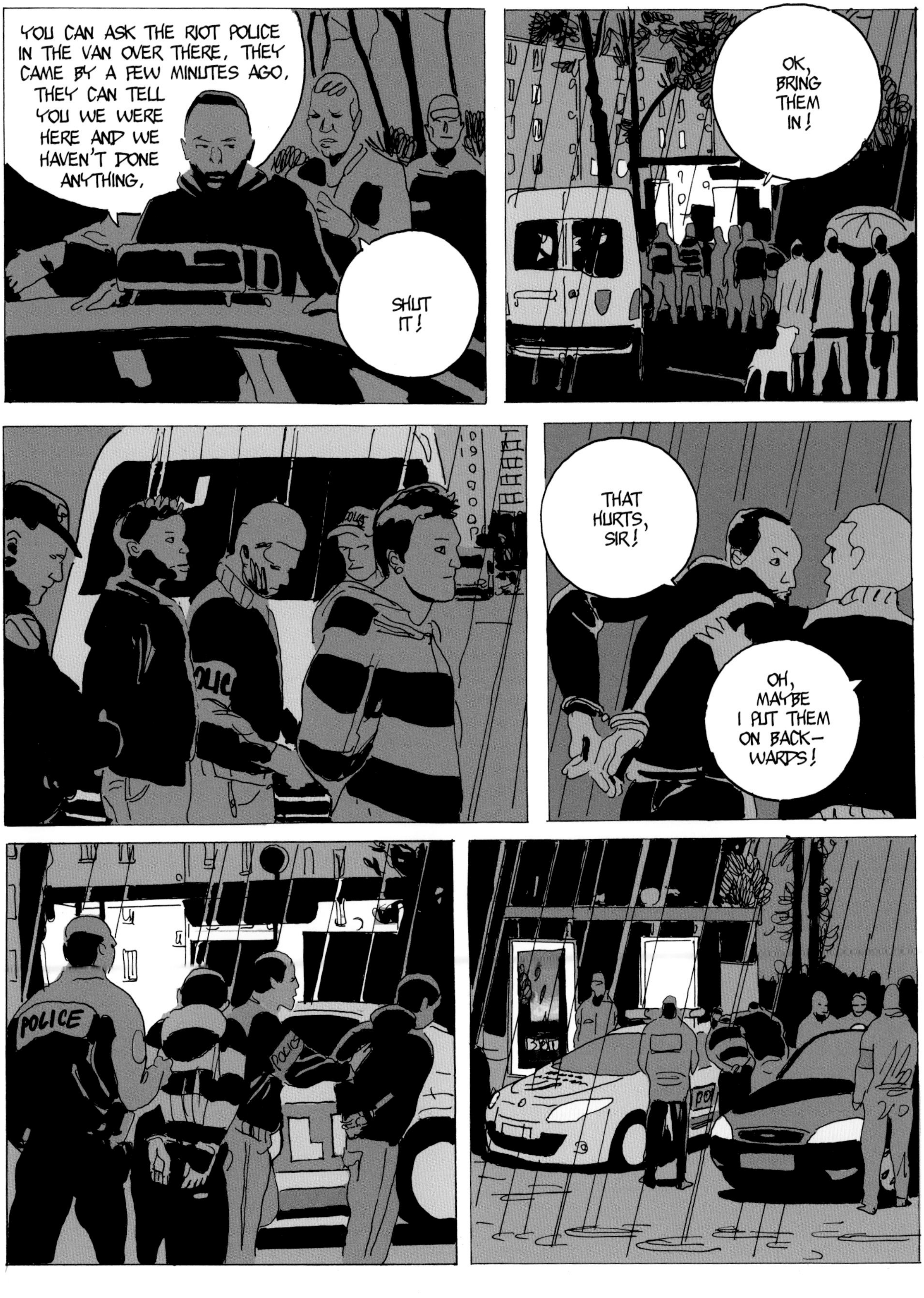
YOU CAN ASK THE RIOT POLICE IN THE VAN OVER THERE, THEY CAME BY A FEW MINUTES AGO, THEY CAN TELL YOU WE WERE HERE AND WE HAVEN'T DONE ANYTHING,
SHUT IT!
OK, BRING THEM IN!
THAT HURTS, SIR!
OH, MAYBE I PUT THEM ON BACK-WARDS!
POLICE

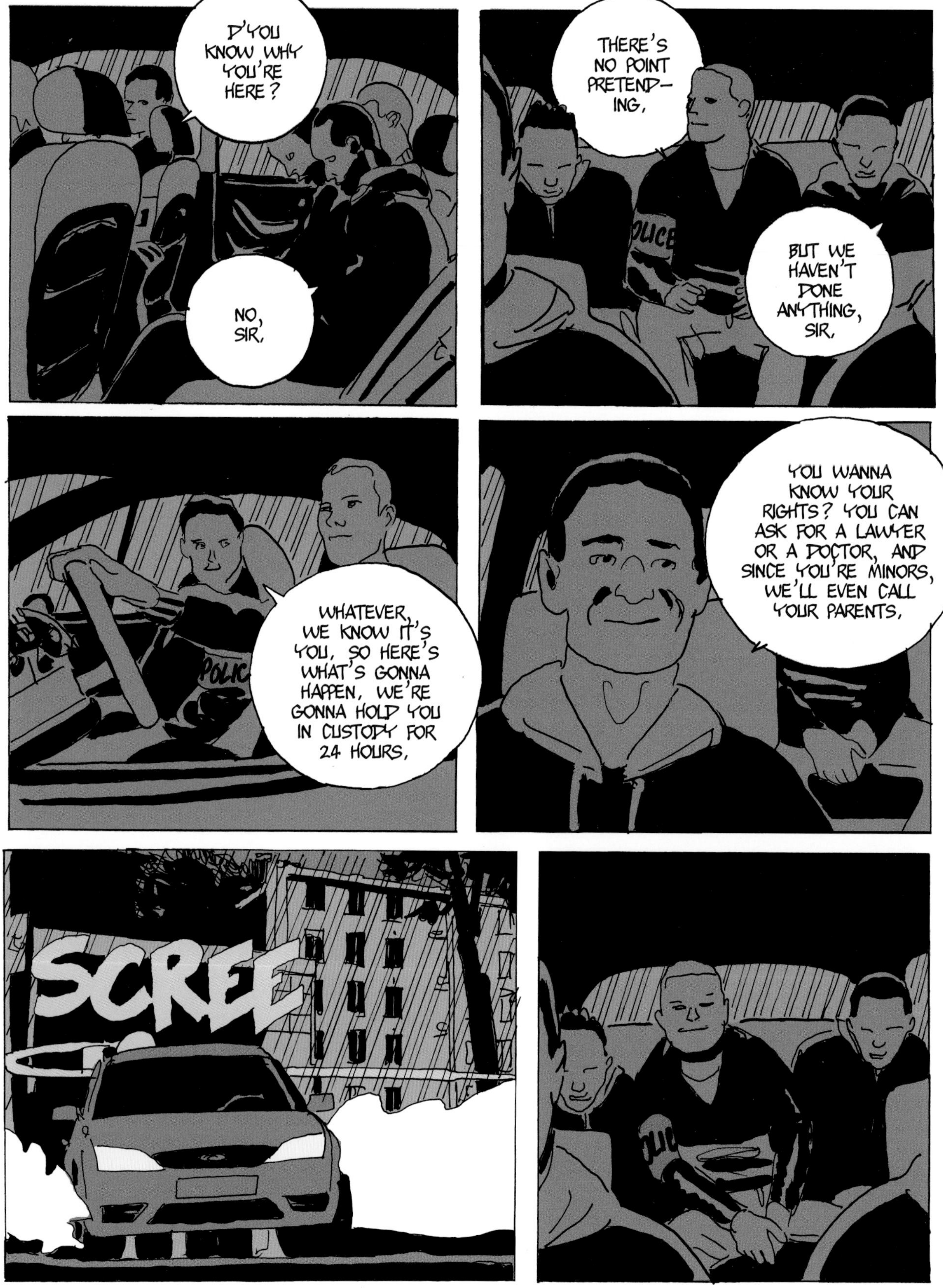
D'YOU KNOW WHY YOU'RE HERE?
NO, SIR.
THERE'S NO POINT PRETEND-ING.
BUT WE HAVEN'T DONE ANYTHING, SIR.
WHATEVER. WE KNOW IT'S YOU, SO HERE'S WHAT'S GONNA HAPPEN. WE'RE GONNA HOLD YOU IN CUSTODY FOR 24 HOURS.
YOU WANNA KNOW YOUR RIGHTS? YOU CAN ASK FOR A LAWYER OR A DOCTOR, AND SINCE YOU'RE MINORS, WE'LL EVEN CALL YOUR PARENTS.
SCREE

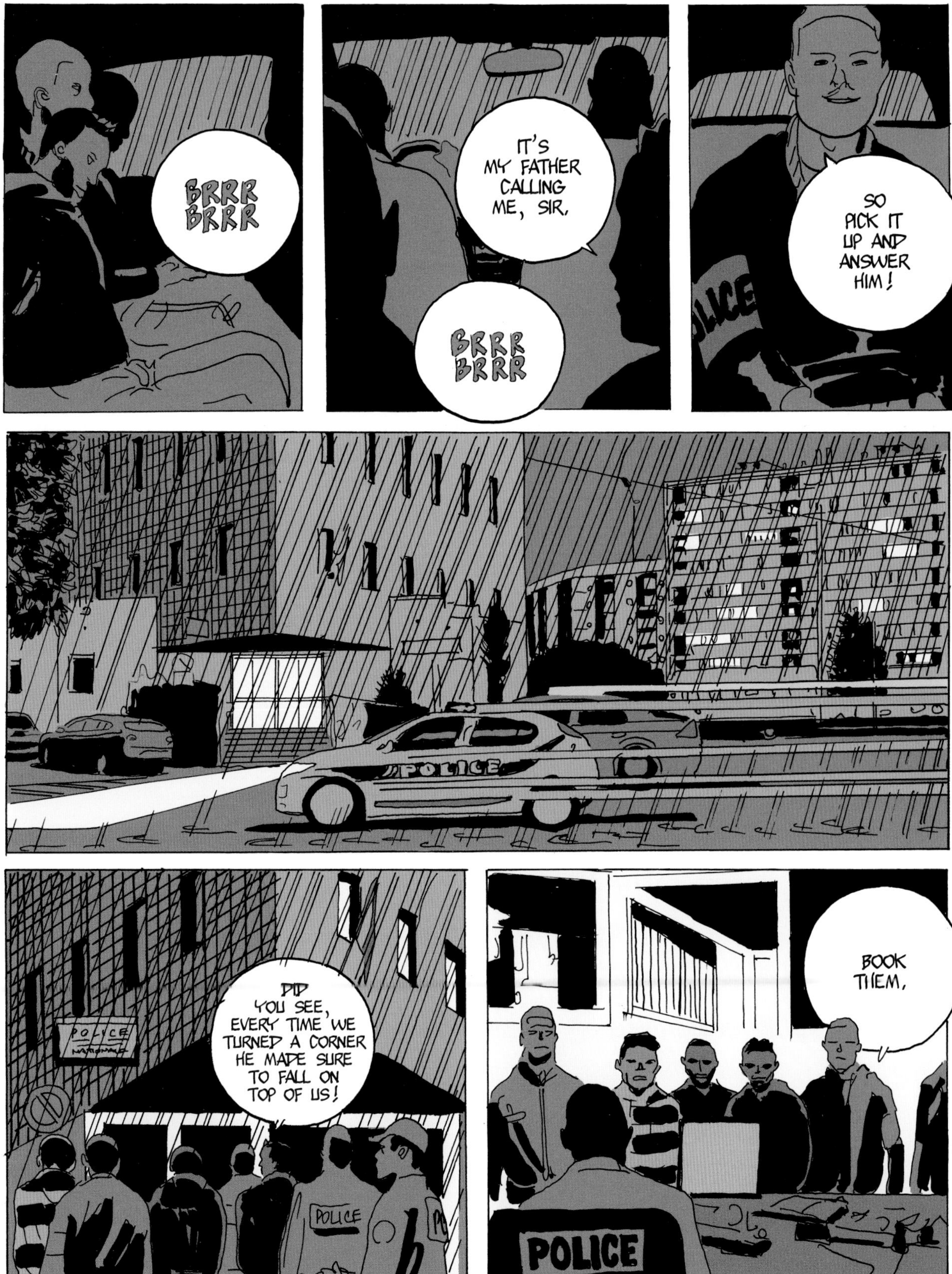
BRRR BRRR
IT'S MY FATHER CALLING ME, SIR.
BRRR BRRR
SO PICK IT UP AND ANSWER HIM!
POLICE
DID YOU SEE, EVERY TIME WE TURNED A CORNER HE MADE SURE TO FALL ON TOP OF US!
POLICE
BOOK THEM.
POLICE

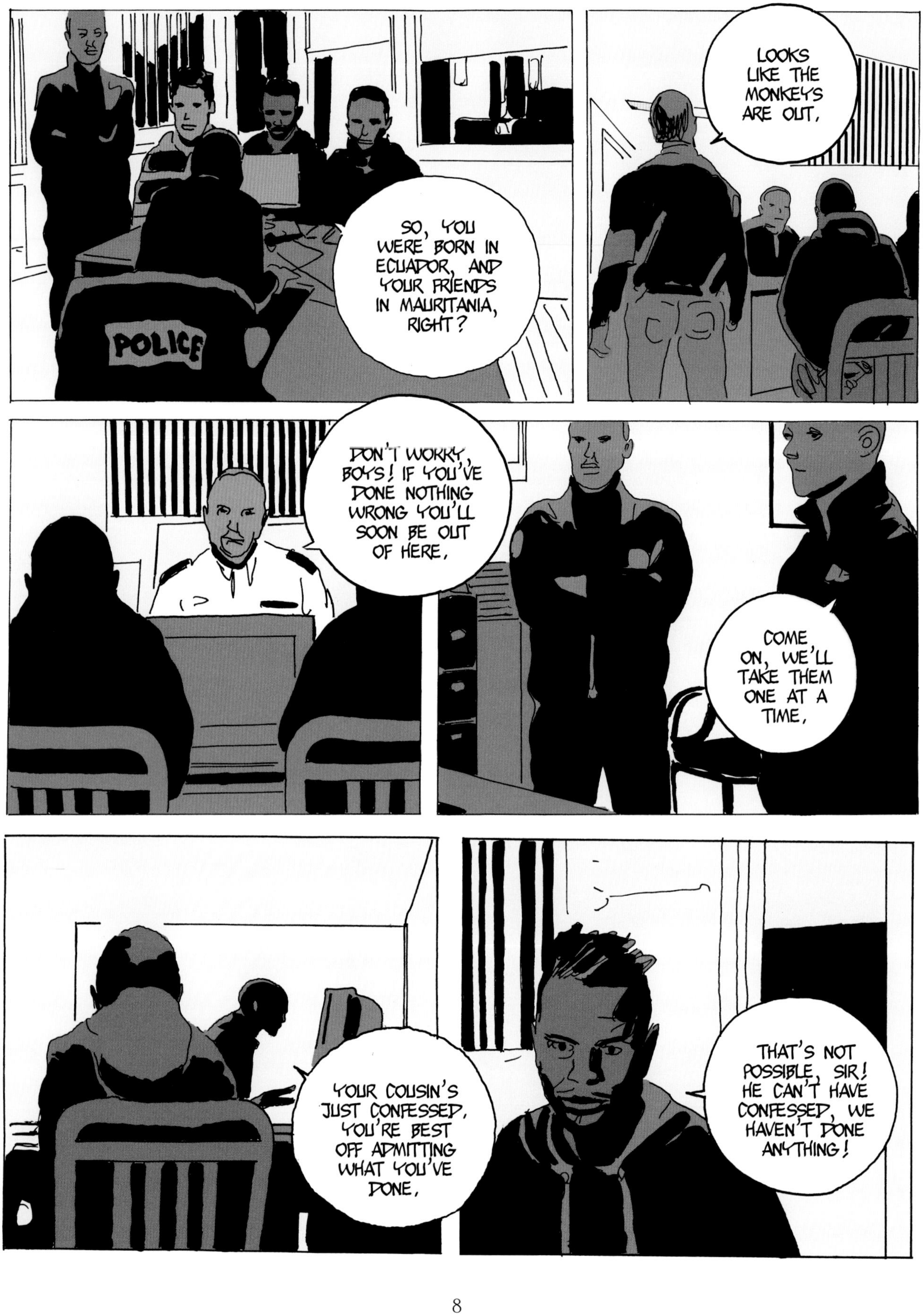
SO, YOU WERE BORN IN ECUADOR, AND YOUR FRIENDS IN MAURITANIA, RIGHT?
POLICE
LOOKS LIKE THE MONKEYS ARE OUT.
DON'T WORRY, BOYS! IF YOU'VE DONE NOTHING WRONG YOU'LL SOON BE OUT OF HERE.
COME ON, WE'LL TAKE THEM ONE AT A TIME.
YOUR COUSIN'S JUST CONFESSED. YOU'RE BEST OFF ADMITTING WHAT YOU'VE DONE.
THAT'S NOT POSSIBLE, SIR! HE CAN'T HAVE CONFESSED, WE HAVEN'T DONE ANYTHING!

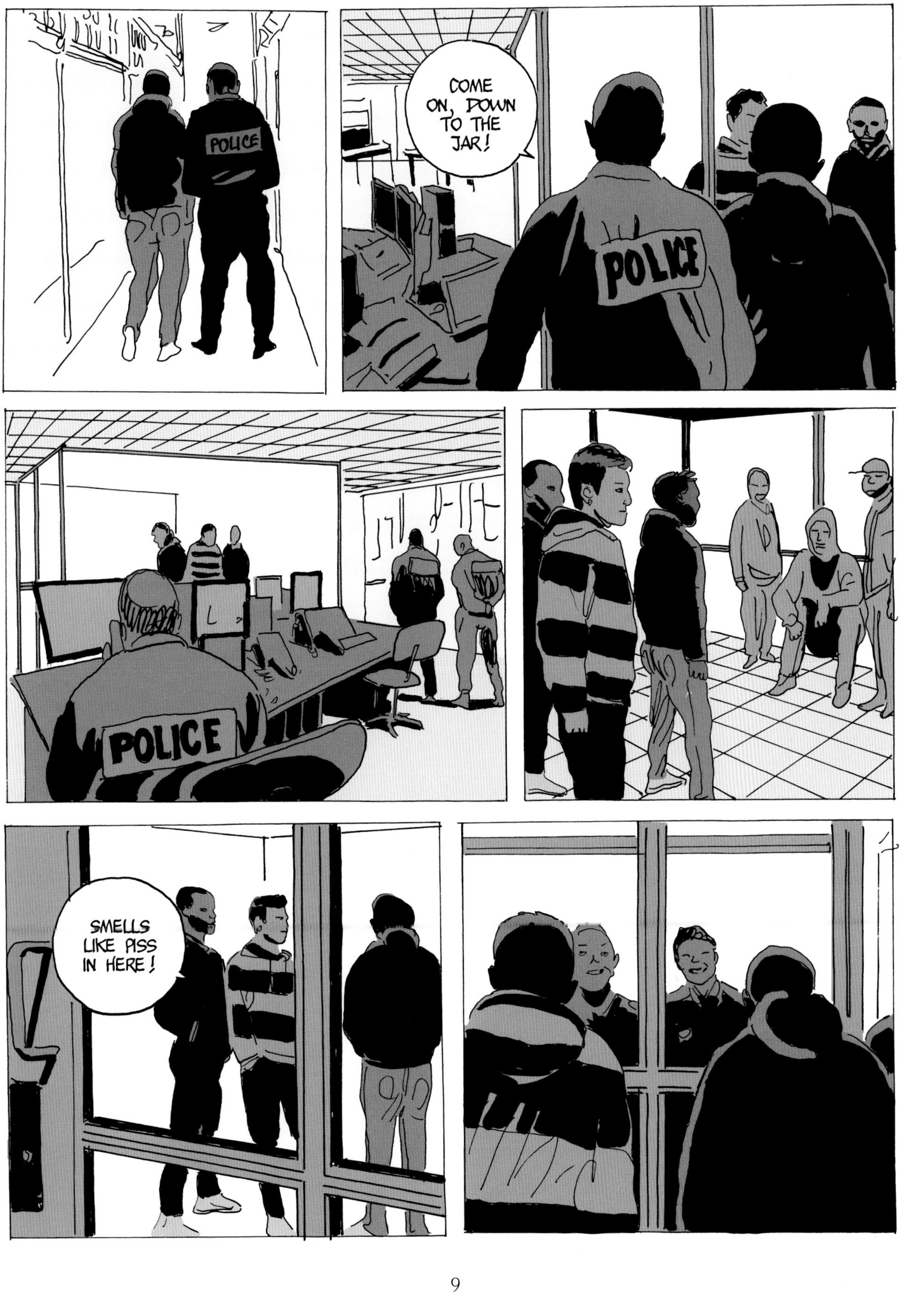
POLICE
COME ON, DOWN TO THE JAR!
POLICE
POLICE
SMELLS LIKE PISS IN HERE!

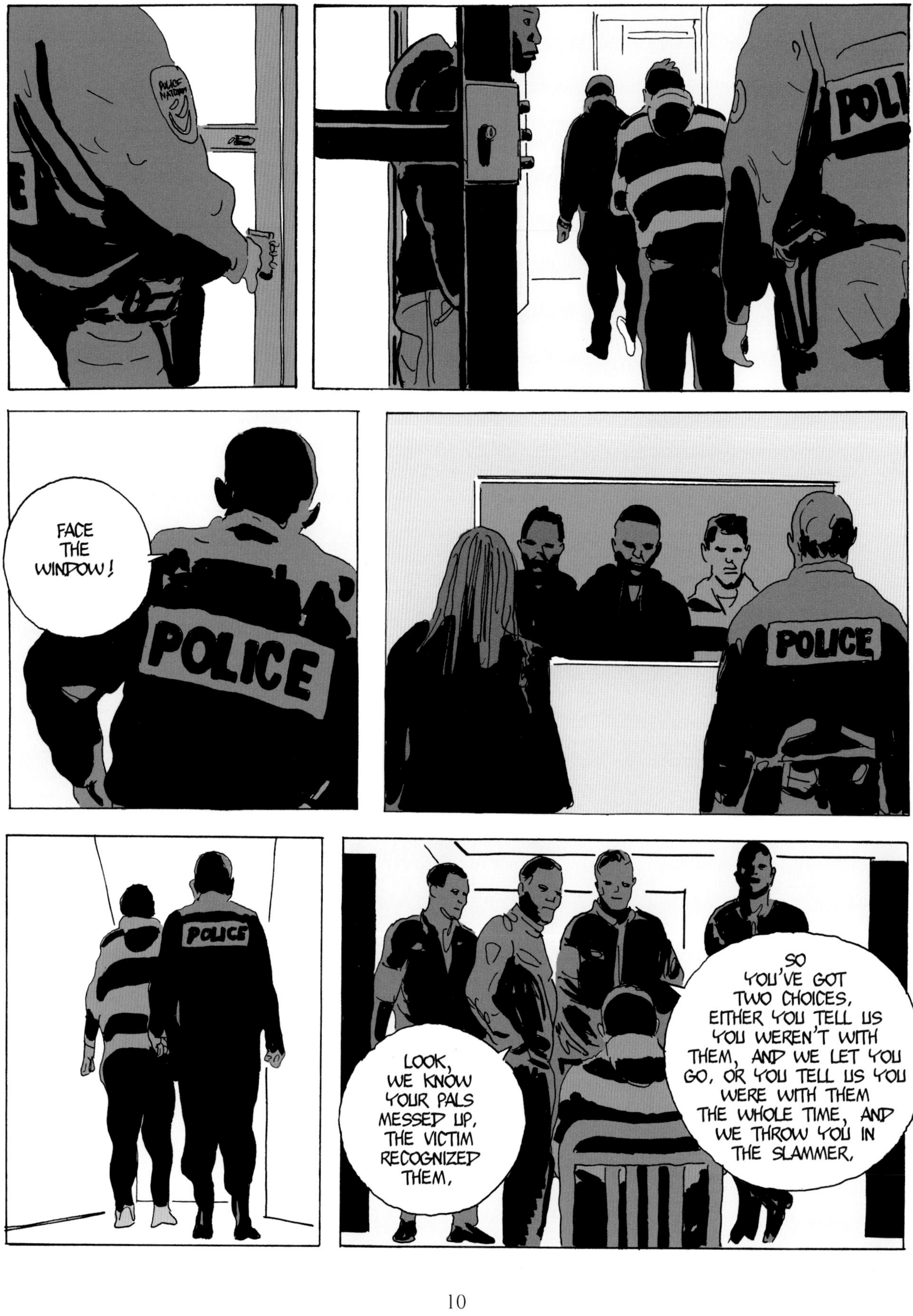
POLICE NATIONALE
POLI
FACE THE WINDOW!
POLICE
POLICE
POLICE
LOOK, WE KNOW YOUR PALS MESSED UP, THE VICTIM RECOGNIZED THEM,
SO YOU'VE GOT TWO CHOICES, EITHER YOU TELL US YOU WEREN'T WITH THEM, AND WE LET YOU GO, OR YOU TELL US YOU WERE WITH THEM THE WHOLE TIME, AND WE THROW YOU IN THE SLAMMER,

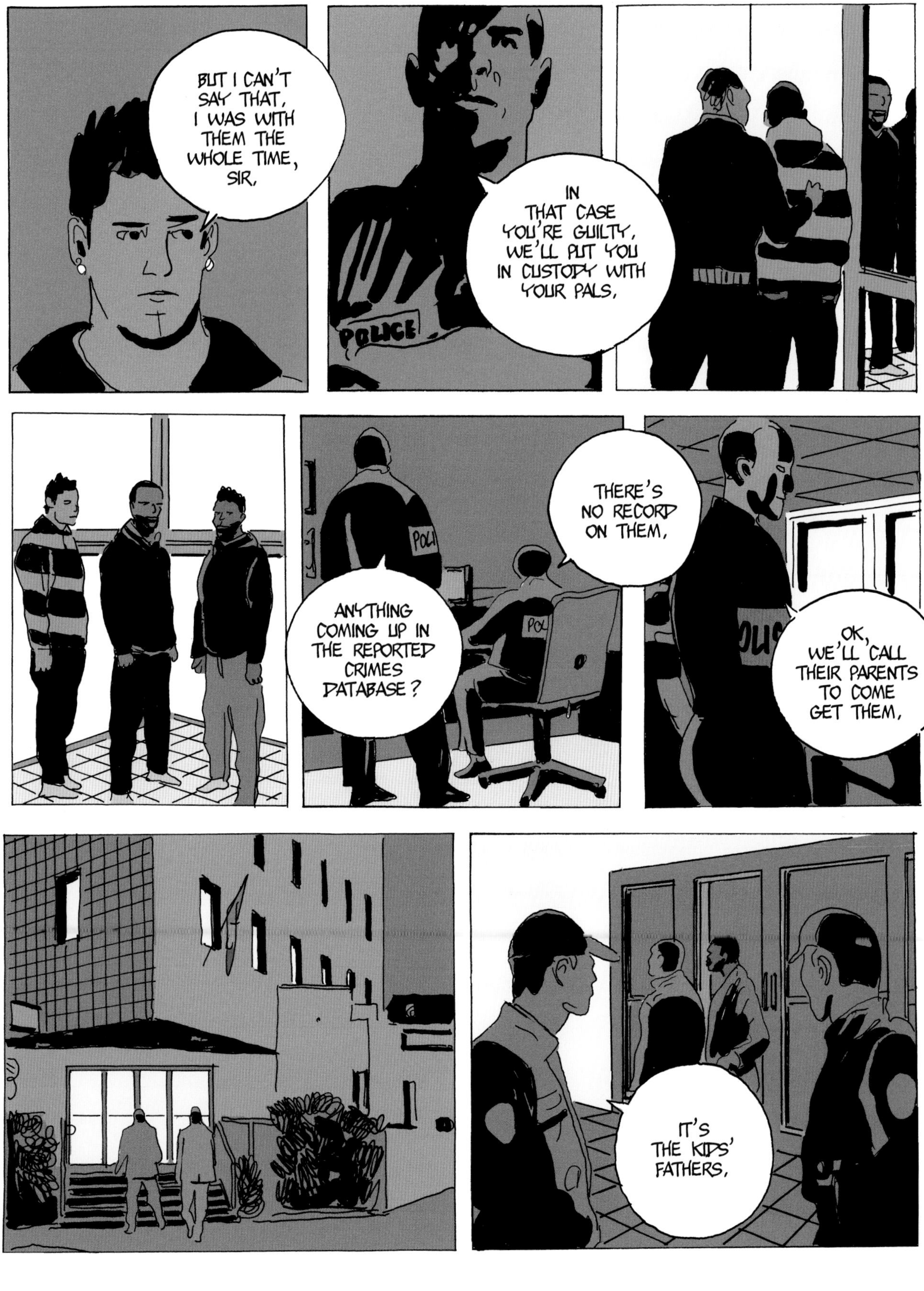
BUT I CAN'T SAY THAT, I WAS WITH THEM THE WHOLE TIME, SIR.
POLICE
IN THAT CASE YOU'RE GUILTY, WE'LL PUT YOU IN CUSTODY WITH YOUR PALS.
ANYTHING COMING UP IN THE REPORTED CRIMES DATABASE?
THERE'S NO RECORD ON THEM.
OK, WE'LL CALL THEIR PARENTS TO COME GET THEM.
IT'S THE KIDS' FATHERS.

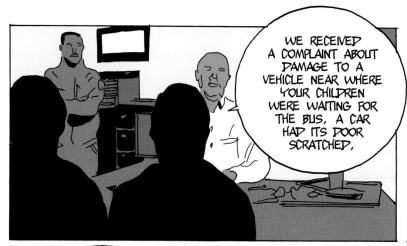

WE RECEIVED A COMPLAINT ABOUT DAMAGE TO A VEHICLE NEAR WHERE YOUR CHILDREN WERE WAITING FOR THE BUS, A CAR HAD ITS DOOR SCRATCHED,

BUT THE VICTIM SAID THEY WERE ALL WEARING DARK CLOTHES, SHE DIDN'T RECOGNIZE THE ONE IN THE STRIPED SWEATSHIRT,

THEY'RE LUCKY HE WASN'T WEARING GRAY!

POLICE

THIS SCENE RESEMBLES MANY OTHERS I WITNESSED DURING THE COURSE OF MY STUDY OF THE POLICE IN THE LOW-INCOME OUTER CITIES OF PARIS, CONDUCTED BETWEEN MAY 2005 AND JUNE 2007,

IT WOULD HAVE BEEN JUST ANOTHER OBSERVATION IN MY FIELD NOTEBOOK, HAD ONE OF THE THREE BOYS NOT BEEN MY SON,

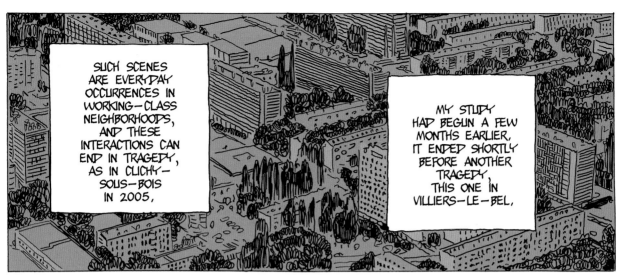

SUCH SCENES ARE EVERYDAY OCCURRENCES IN WORKING-CLASS NEIGHBORHOODS, AND THESE INTERACTIONS CAN END IN TRAGEDY, AS IN CLICHY-SOUS-BOIS IN 2005,

MY STUDY HAD BEGUN A FEW MONTHS EARLIER, IT ENDED SHORTLY BEFORE ANOTHER TRAGEDY, THIS ONE IN VILLIERS-LE-BEL,

CLICHY-SOUS-BOIS, OCTOBER 27, 2005, 5:00 P,M,

ZYED, BOUNA, AND THEIR FRIENDS ARE HEADING HOME; THERE IS NO WAY THEY CAN BE LATE FOR THE MEAL THAT BREAKS THEIR DAYLONG FAST,

LET'S GO THROUGH THE SITE,

UNBEKNOWN TO THEM A NEIGHBOR, CONCERNED AT SEEING THEM ON THE CONSTRUCTION SITE, HAS CALLED THE POLICE,

WOOOP

RUN! RUN!

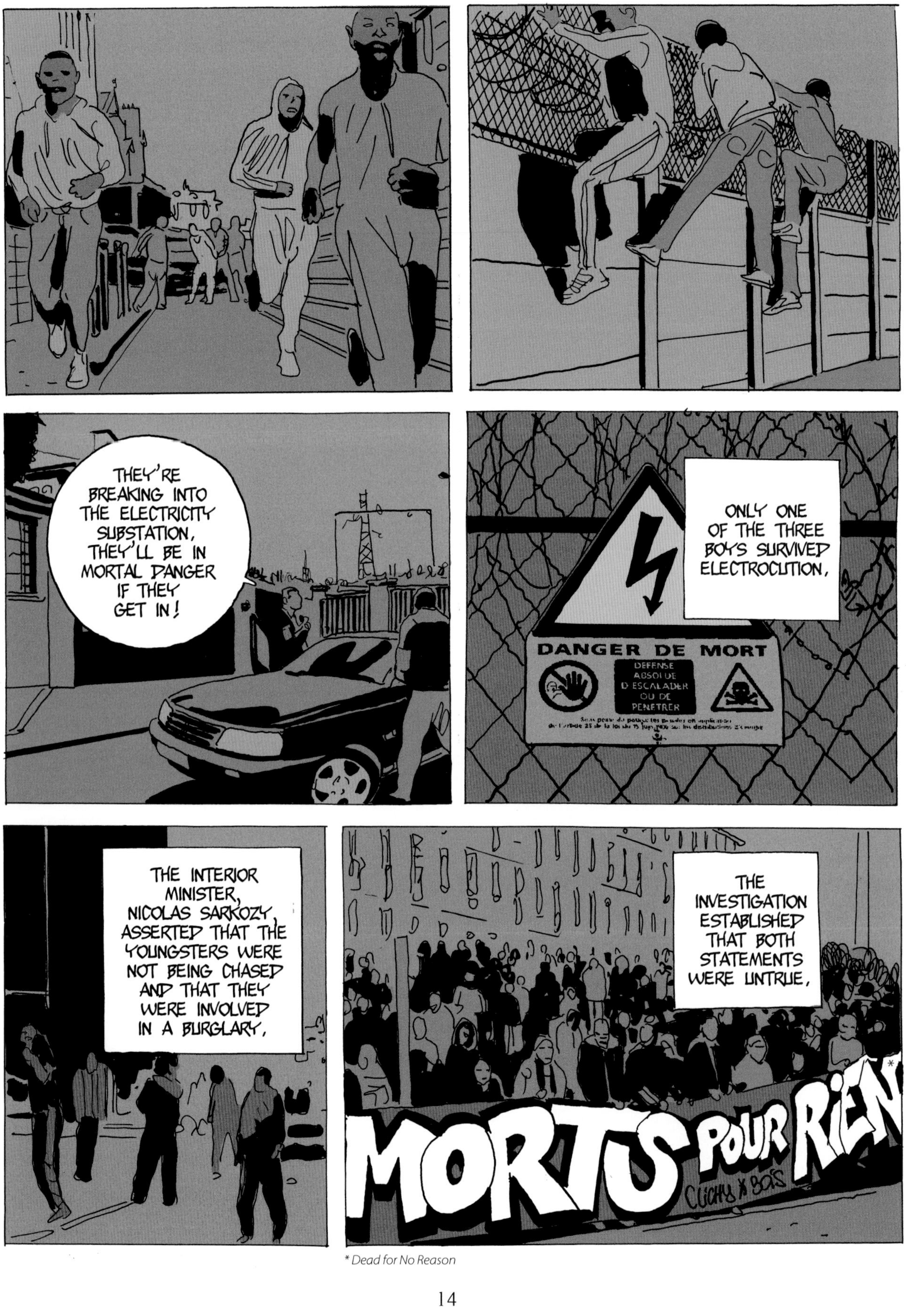
THEY'RE BREAKING INTO THE ELECTRICITY SUBSTATION, THEY'LL BE IN MORTAL DANGER IF THEY GET IN!
ONLY ONE OF THE THREE BOYS SURVIVED ELECTROCUTION.
DANGER DE MORT
DEFENSE ABSOLUE D'ESCALADER OU DE PENETRER
THE INTERIOR MINISTER, NICOLAS SARKOZY, ASSERTED THAT THE YOUNGSTERS WERE NOT BEING CHASED AND THAT THEY WERE INVOLVED IN A BURGLARY.
THE INVESTIGATION ESTABLISHED THAT BOTH STATEMENTS WERE UNTRUE.
MORTS POUR RIEN*
CLICHY X BOIS

* *Dead for No Reason*

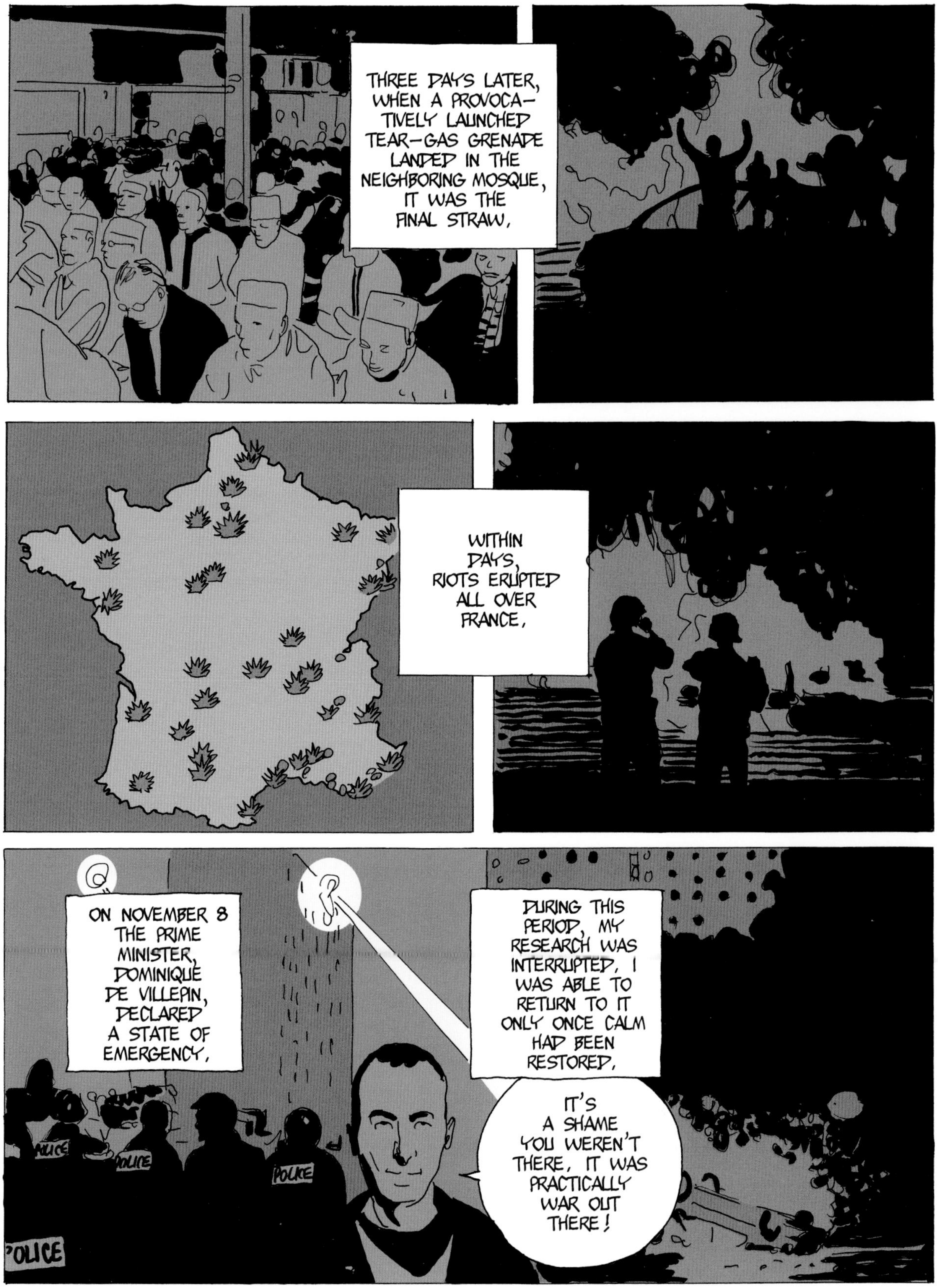
THREE DAYS LATER, WHEN A PROVOCATIVELY LAUNCHED TEAR-GAS GRENADE LANDED IN THE NEIGHBORING MOSQUE, IT WAS THE FINAL STRAW.
WITHIN DAYS, RIOTS ERUPTED ALL OVER FRANCE.
ON NOVEMBER 8 THE PRIME MINISTER, DOMINIQUE DE VILLEPIN, DECLARED A STATE OF EMERGENCY.
DURING THIS PERIOD, MY RESEARCH WAS INTERRUPTED. I WAS ABLE TO RETURN TO IT ONLY ONCE CALM HAD BEEN RESTORED.
IT'S A SHAME YOU WEREN'T THERE. IT WAS PRACTICALLY WAR OUT THERE!
POLICE
POLICE
POLICE
POLICE

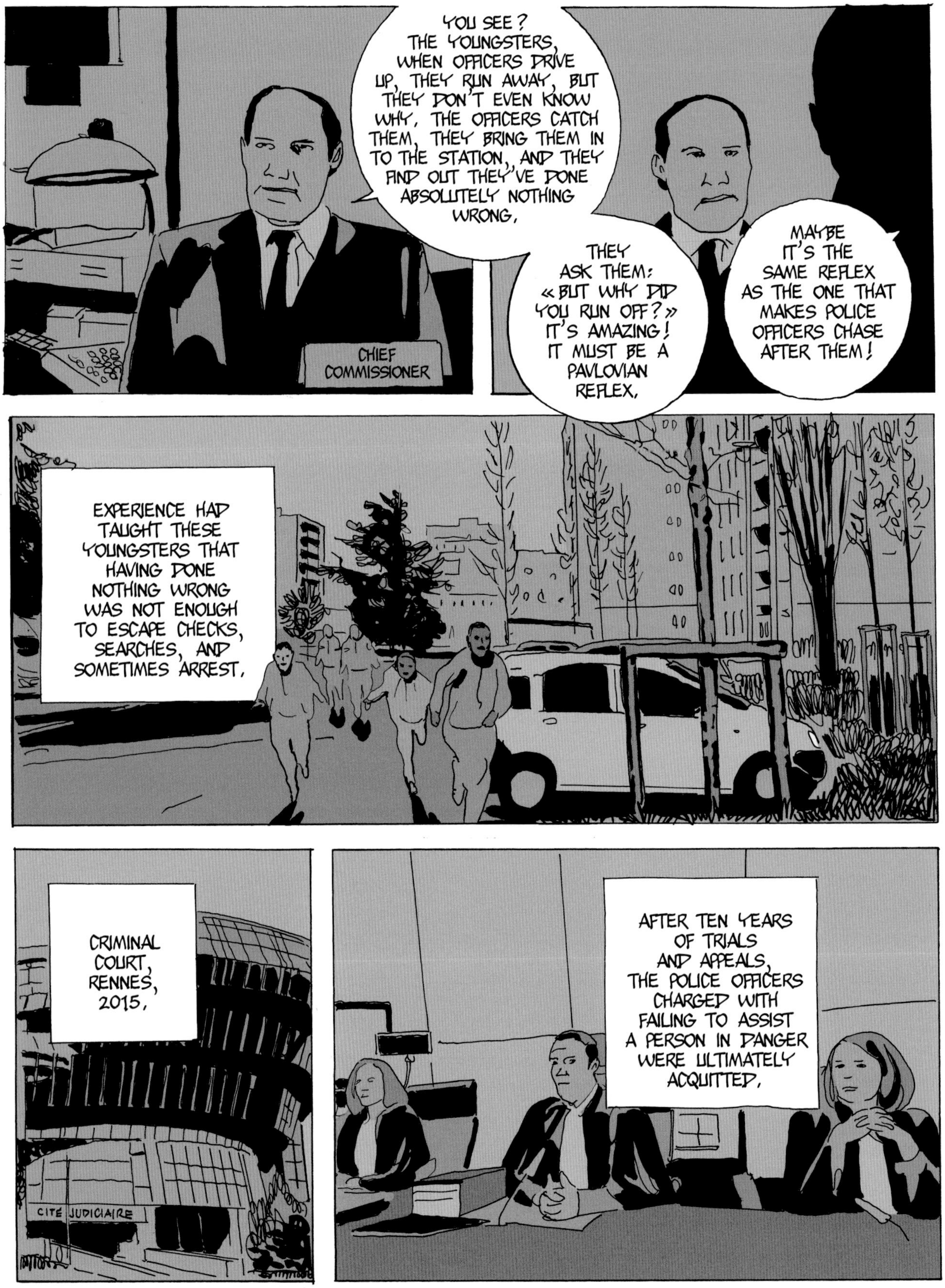
YOU SEE? THE YOUNGSTERS, WHEN OFFICERS DRIVE UP, THEY RUN AWAY, BUT THEY DON'T EVEN KNOW WHY, THE OFFICERS CATCH THEM, THEY BRING THEM IN TO THE STATION, AND THEY FIND OUT THEY'VE DONE ABSOLUTELY NOTHING WRONG.
CHIEF COMMISSIONER
THEY ASK THEM: « BUT WHY DID YOU RUN OFF? » IT'S AMAZING! IT MUST BE A PAVLOVIAN REFLEX.
MAYBE IT'S THE SAME REFLEX AS THE ONE THAT MAKES POLICE OFFICERS CHASE AFTER THEM!
EXPERIENCE HAD TAUGHT THESE YOUNGSTERS THAT HAVING DONE NOTHING WRONG WAS NOT ENOUGH TO ESCAPE CHECKS, SEARCHES, AND SOMETIMES ARREST.
CRIMINAL COURT, RENNES, 2015.
CITE JUDICIAIRE
AFTER TEN YEARS OF TRIALS AND APPEALS, THE POLICE OFFICERS CHARGED WITH FAILING TO ASSIST A PERSON IN DANGER WERE ULTIMATELY ACQUITTED.

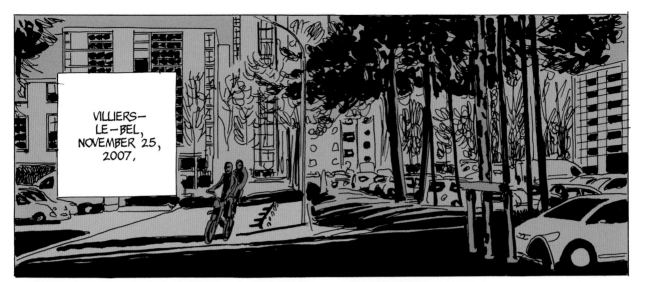

VILLIERS-LE-BEL, NOVEMBER 25, 2007.
POLICE
THE FORCE OF THE IMPACT WAS SUCH THAT, WHEN THEY SAW THE STATE OF THE VEHICLE, THE POLICE CLAIMED IT HAD BEEN VANDALIZED AFTER THE ACCIDENT,
A CLAIM THAT WAS LATER CONTRADICTED BY EXPERT ASSESSMENT,
JUSTICE ET VÉRITÉ
LARAMI ET MOUSHIN *

* *Justice and Truth for Larami and Moushin*

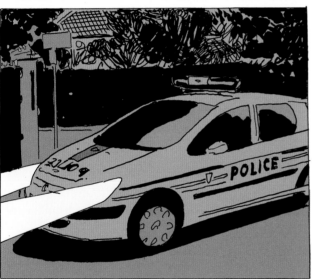

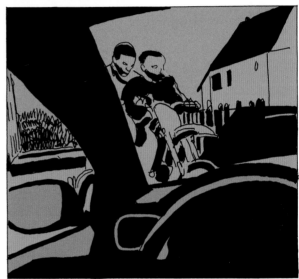

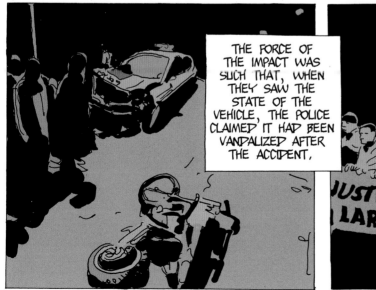

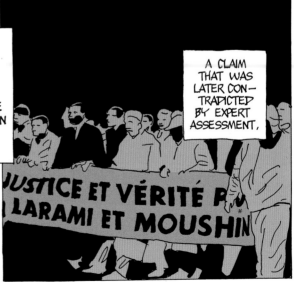

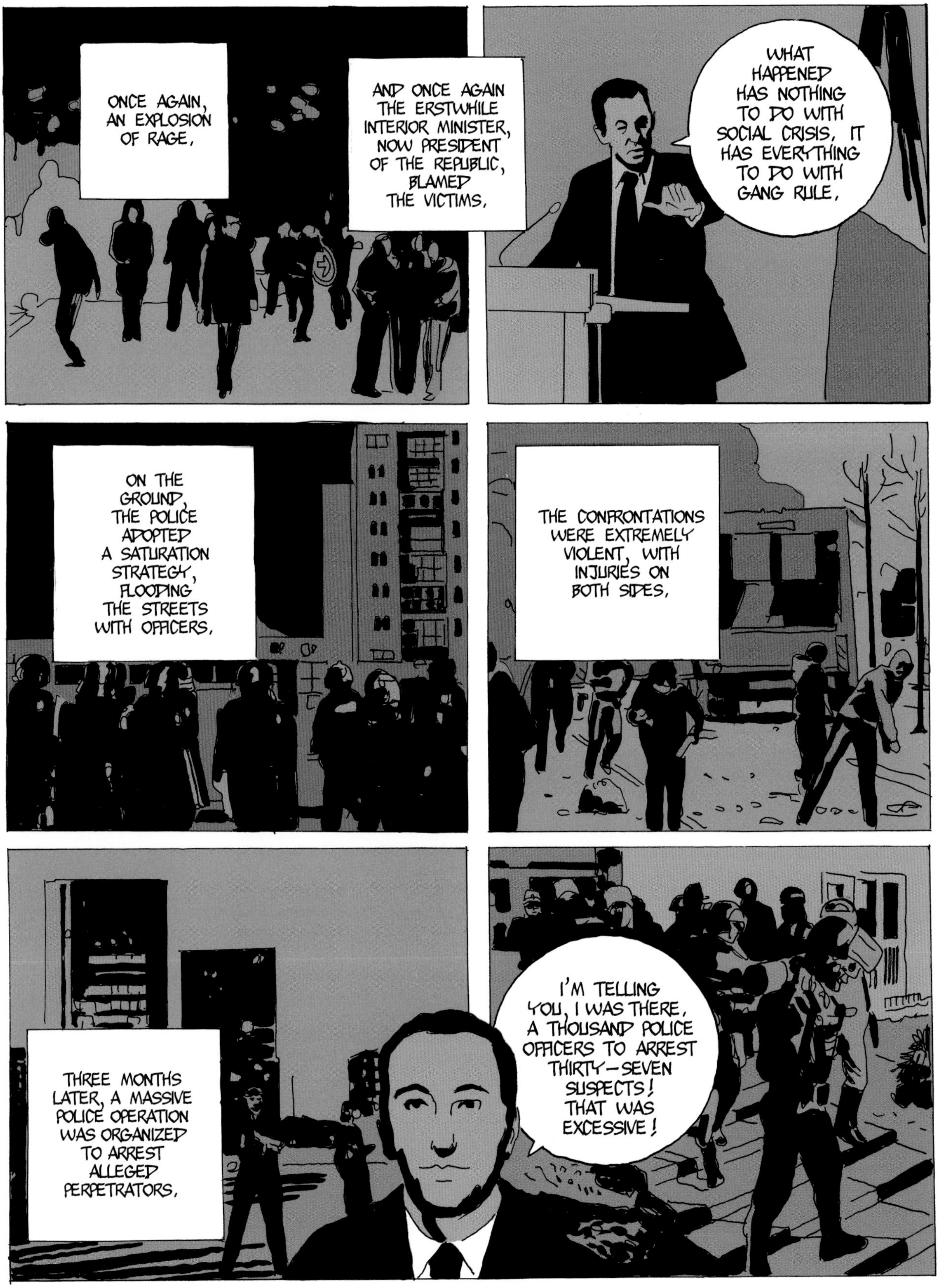
ONCE AGAIN, AN EXPLOSION OF RAGE.
AND ONCE AGAIN THE ERSTWHILE INTERIOR MINISTER, NOW PRESIDENT OF THE REPUBLIC, BLAMED THE VICTIMS.
WHAT HAPPENED HAS NOTHING TO DO WITH SOCIAL CRISIS. IT HAS EVERYTHING TO DO WITH GANG RULE.
ON THE GROUND, THE POLICE ADOPTED A SATURATION STRATEGY, FLOODING THE STREETS WITH OFFICERS.
THE CONFRONTATIONS WERE EXTREMELY VIOLENT, WITH INJURIES ON BOTH SIDES.
THREE MONTHS LATER, A MASSIVE POLICE OPERATION WAS ORGANIZED TO ARREST ALLEGED PERPETRATORS.
I'M TELLING YOU, I WAS THERE, A THOUSAND POLICE OFFICERS TO ARREST THIRTY-SEVEN SUSPECTS! THAT WAS EXCESSIVE!

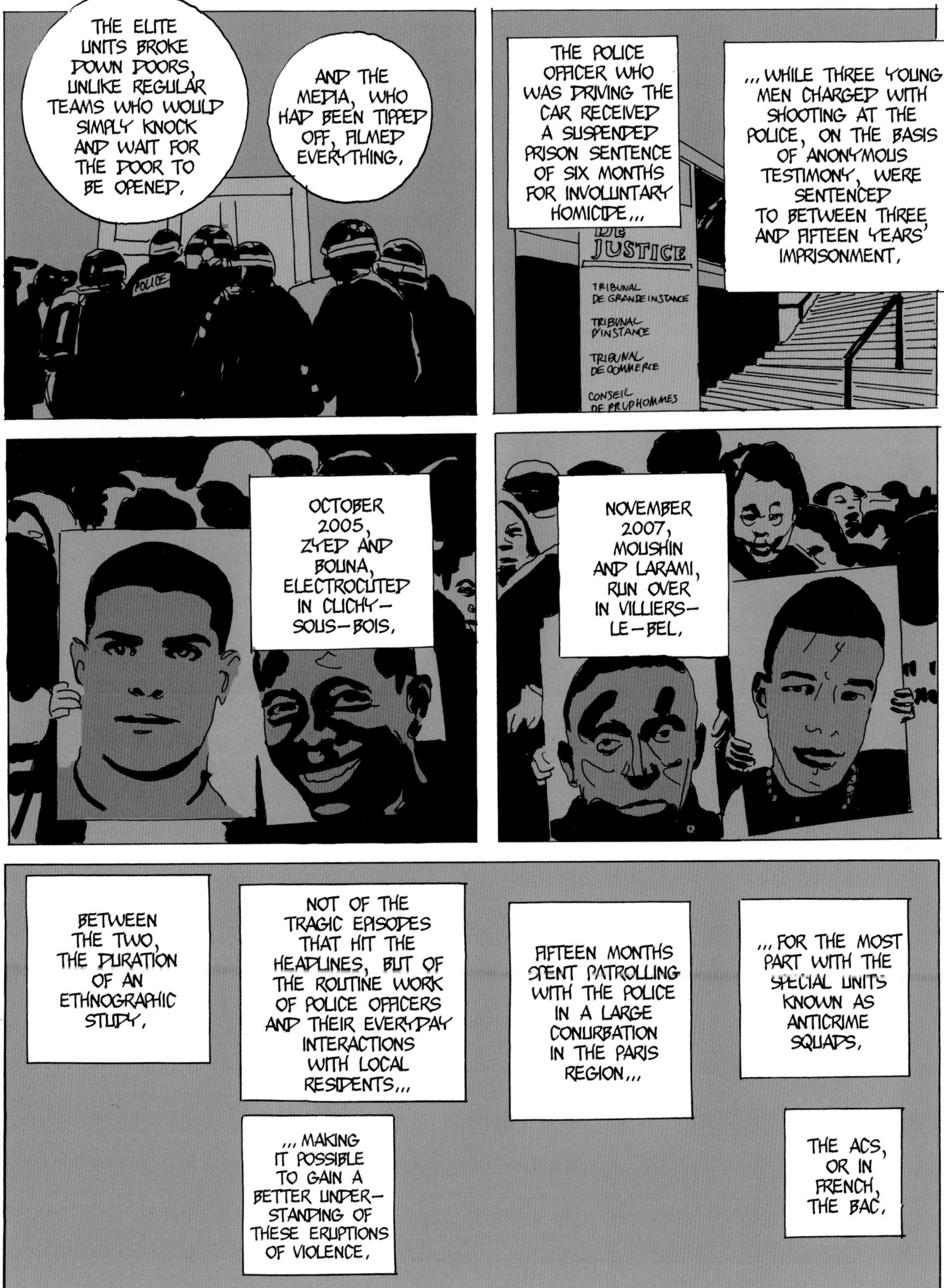

THE ELITE UNITS BROKE DOWN DOORS, UNLIKE REGULAR TEAMS WHO WOULD SIMPLY KNOCK AND WAIT FOR THE DOOR TO BE OPENED.
AND THE MEDIA, WHO HAD BEEN TIPPED OFF, FILMED EVERYTHING.
POLICE
THE POLICE OFFICER WHO WAS DRIVING THE CAR RECEIVED A SUSPENDED PRISON SENTENCE OF SIX MONTHS FOR INVOLUNTARY HOMICIDE...
...WHILE THREE YOUNG MEN CHARGED WITH SHOOTING AT THE POLICE, ON THE BASIS OF ANONYMOUS TESTIMONY, WERE SENTENCED TO BETWEEN THREE AND FIFTEEN YEARS' IMPRISONMENT.
DE JUSTICE
TRIBUNAL DE GRANDE INSTANCE
TRIBUNAL D'INSTANCE
TRIBUNAL DE COMMERCE
CONSEIL DE PRUD'HOMMES
OCTOBER 2005, ZYED AND BOUNA, ELECTROCUTED IN CLICHY-SOUS-BOIS.
NOVEMBER 2007, MOUSHIN AND LARAMI, RUN OVER IN VILLIERS-LE-BEL.
BETWEEN THE TWO, THE DURATION OF AN ETHNOGRAPHIC STUDY.
NOT OF THE TRAGIC EPISODES THAT HIT THE HEADLINES, BUT OF THE ROUTINE WORK OF POLICE OFFICERS AND THEIR EVERYDAY INTERACTIONS WITH LOCAL RESIDENTS...
...MAKING IT POSSIBLE TO GAIN A BETTER UNDER-STANDING OF THESE ERUPTIONS OF VIOLENCE.
FIFTEEN MONTHS SPENT PATROLLING WITH THE POLICE IN A LARGE CONURBATION IN THE PARIS REGION...
...FOR THE MOST PART WITH THE SPECIAL UNITS KNOWN AS ANTICRIME SQUADS.
THE ACS, OR IN FRENCH, THE BAC.

THE BAC WERE SET UP IN THE MID–1990S, AT A TIME WHEN SECURITY WAS INCREASINGLY MOVING TO THE CENTER OF POLITICAL DEBATE,

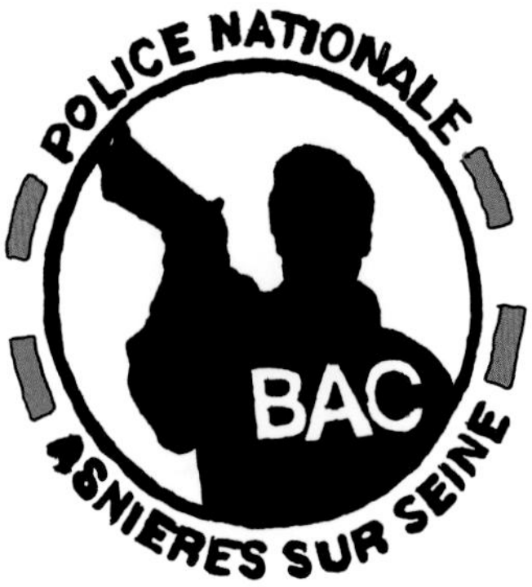
POLICE NATIONALE
BAC
ASNIERES SUR SEINE

THEY HAVE STEADILY GROWN IN NUMBER SINCE THAT TIME,

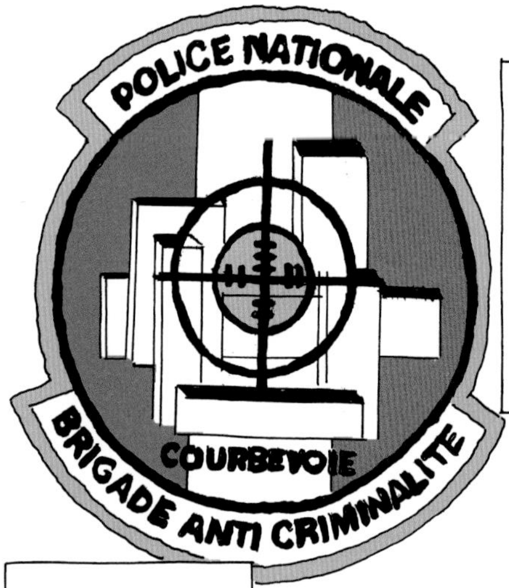
POLICE NATIONALE
COURBEVOIE
BRIGADE ANTI CRIMINALITE

THEIR ACTIVITY IS FOCUSED MAINLY ON WORKING–CLASS NEIGHBORHOODS, PARTICULARLY PUBLIC HOUSING PROJECTS,

UNLIKE THE REST OF STREET POLICE, WHO WEAR A UNIFORM, BAC OFFICERS ARE USUALLY IN PLAIN CLOTHES AND PATROL IN UNMARKED CARS,

THESE OFFICERS ARE FEARED BY RESIDENTS OF THE PROJECTS,

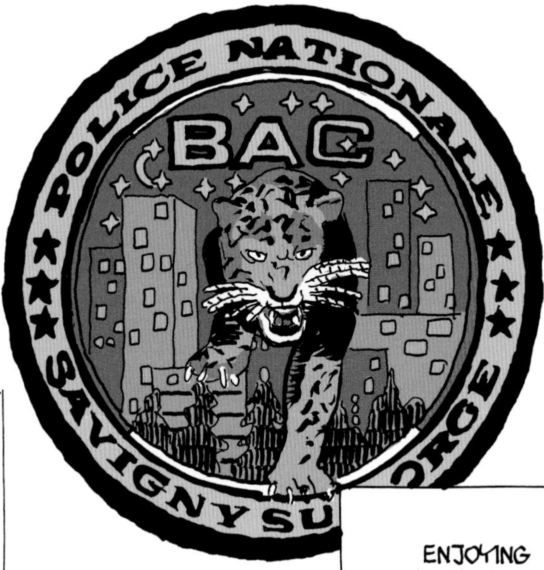
POLICE NATIONALE
BAC

«THE KIDS AREN'T SCARED OF POLICE IN A MARKED CAR, BUT THEY ARE SCARED OF THE BAC, BECAUSE THEY KNOW FULL WELL THEY'LL GO ALL THE WAY,» SAID A REPRESENTATIVE OF THE NATIONAL POLICE UNION,

ENJOYING BROAD AUTONOMY, THESE OFFICERS CAN BE ALL TOO READY TO ABUSE THEIR POWER,

IN THE WORDS OF A FORMER REGIONAL DIRECTOR OF PUBLIC SECURITY, THEY WERE OFTEN « A PACK THAT CAUSED MORE DAMAGE WHEN THEY WENT OUT ON PATROL THAN THEY SOLVED PROBLEMS. »

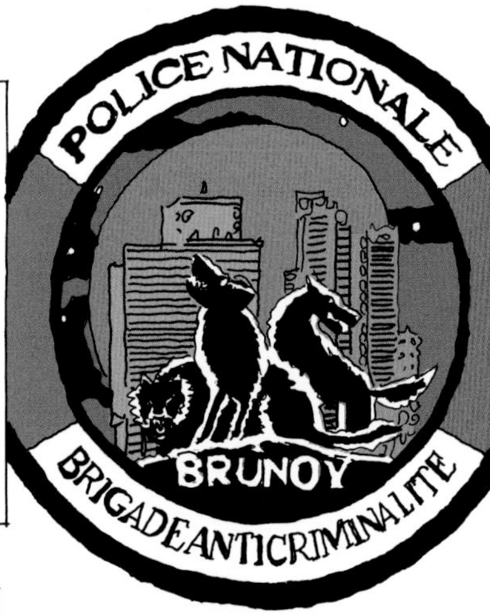
POLICE NATIONALE
BRUNOY
BRIGADE ANTICRIMINALITE

DESPITE THESE EXCESSES, THE BAC ENJOY A SPECIAL STATUS IN POLICE PRECINCTS, THANKS TO THE ARRESTS THEY MAKE.

ACCORDING TO A SENIOR OFFICIAL IN THE INTERIOR MINISTRY, «THE TOP BRASS LOVE THEM BECAUSE THEY BRING IN THE NUMBERS. »

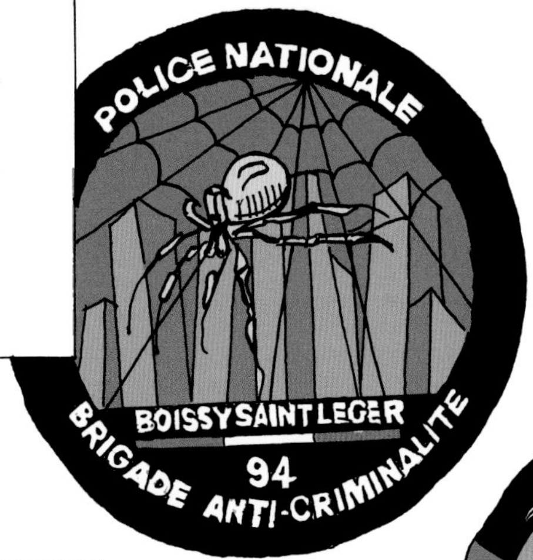
POLICE NATIONALE
BOISSY SAINT LEGER
94
BRIGADE ANTI-CRIMINALITE

IN OTHER WORDS, IT IS THEY WHO MAKE THE MOST ARRESTS.

SO ALTHOUGH THE BAC ARE RESPONSIBLE FOR MOST OF THE DEATHS LINKED TO INTERACTIONS WITH THE POLICE, THEY REMAIN AT THE HEART OF LAW ENFORCEMENT.

«THEY ARE A NECESSARY EVIL, » DECLARED THE CHIEF OF POLICE FOR ONE LARGE DISTRICT IN THE OUTER CITY.

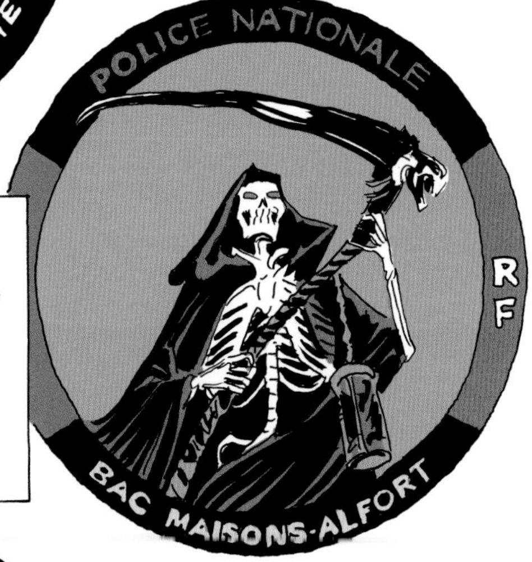
POLICE NATIONALE
RF
BAC MAISONS-ALFORT

THE BADGES DESIGNED FOR THE BAC REFLECT THEIR TENSE RELATIONSHIPS WITH WORKING-CLASS NEIGHBORHOODS.

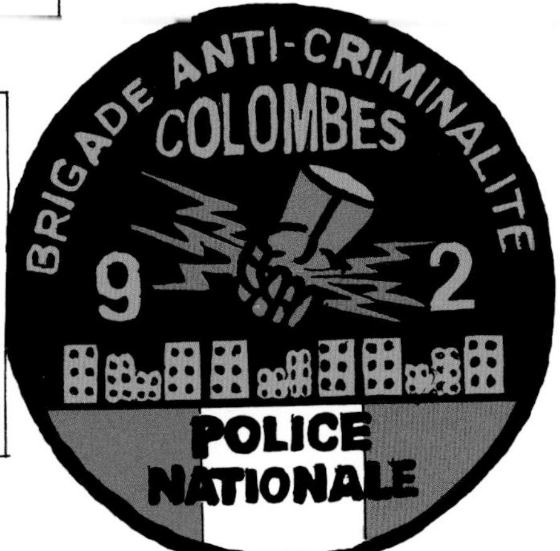
BRIGADE ANTI-CRIMINALITE
COLOMBES
9 2
POLICE NATIONALE

EVEN GOING SO FAR AS TO SHOW A FIST GRIPPING A LIGHTNING FLASH ABOVE A HOUSING PROJECT, AN IMAGE THAT INEVITABLY EVOKES THE TRAGEDY IN CLICHY-SOUS-BOIS.

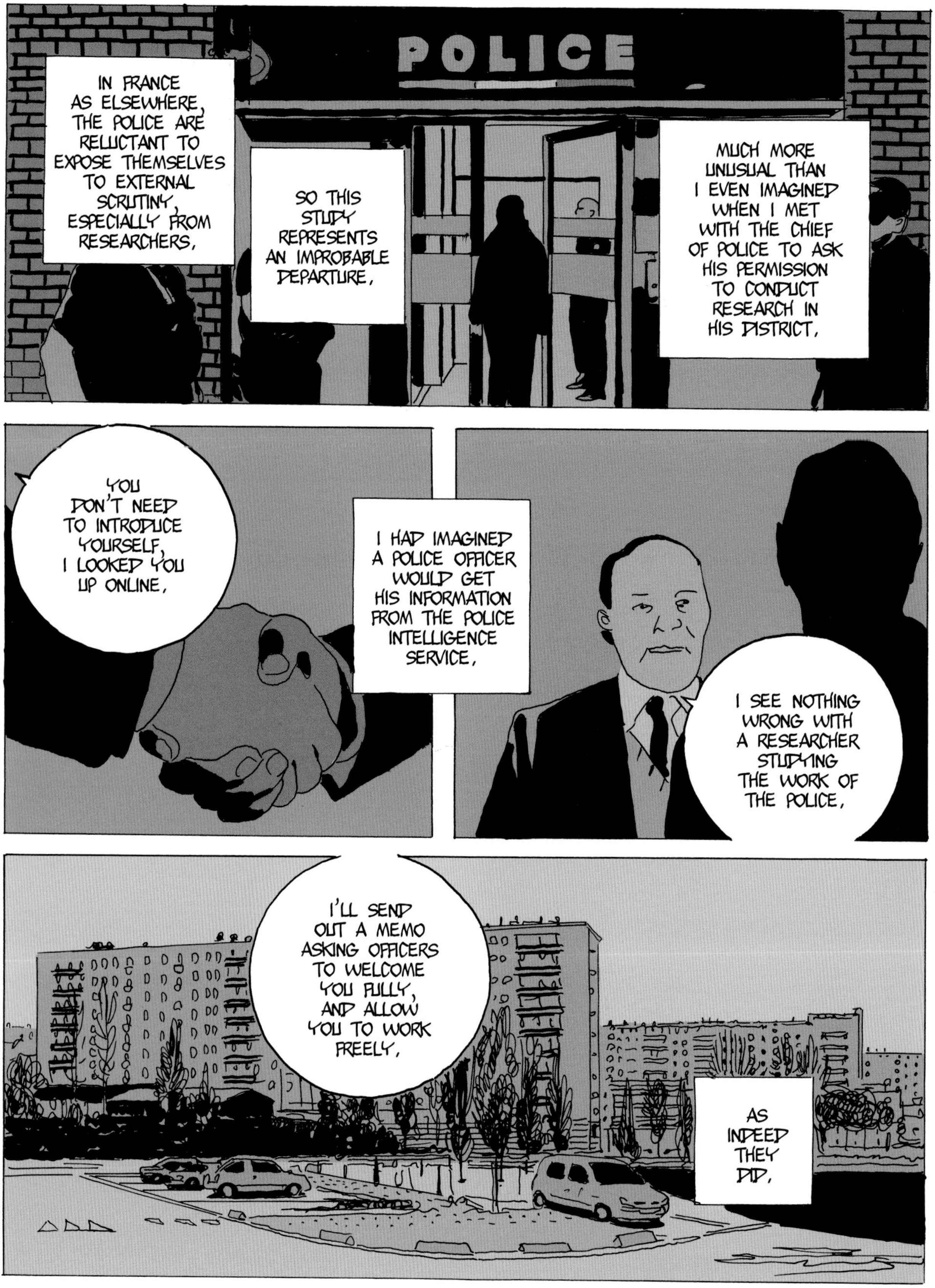
POLICE
IN FRANCE AS ELSEWHERE, THE POLICE ARE RELUCTANT TO EXPOSE THEMSELVES TO EXTERNAL SCRUTINY, ESPECIALLY FROM RESEARCHERS.
SO THIS STUDY REPRESENTS AN IMPROBABLE DEPARTURE,
MUCH MORE UNUSUAL THAN I EVEN IMAGINED WHEN I MET WITH THE CHIEF OF POLICE TO ASK HIS PERMISSION TO CONDUCT RESEARCH IN HIS DISTRICT.
YOU DON'T NEED TO INTRODUCE YOURSELF. I LOOKED YOU UP ONLINE.
I HAD IMAGINED A POLICE OFFICER WOULD GET HIS INFORMATION FROM THE POLICE INTELLIGENCE SERVICE.
I SEE NOTHING WRONG WITH A RESEARCHER STUDYING THE WORK OF THE POLICE.
I'LL SEND OUT A MEMO ASKING OFFICERS TO WELCOME YOU FULLY, AND ALLOW YOU TO WORK FREELY.
AS INDEED THEY DID.

REMARKABLY, I THUS HAD ALMOST COMPLETE FREEDOM TO CONDUCT MY RESEARCH FOR FIFTEEN MONTHS,

THE BAC OFFICE, TURNOVER BETWEEN THE DAY AND NIGHT SHIFT TEAMS,

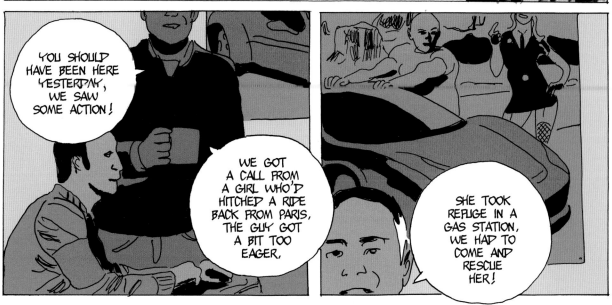

YOU SHOULD HAVE BEEN HERE YESTERDAY, WE SAW SOME ACTION!

WE GOT A CALL FROM A GIRL WHO'D HITCHED A RIDE BACK FROM PARIS, THE GUY GOT A BIT TOO EAGER,

SHE TOOK REFUGE IN A GAS STATION, WE HAD TO COME AND RESCUE HER!

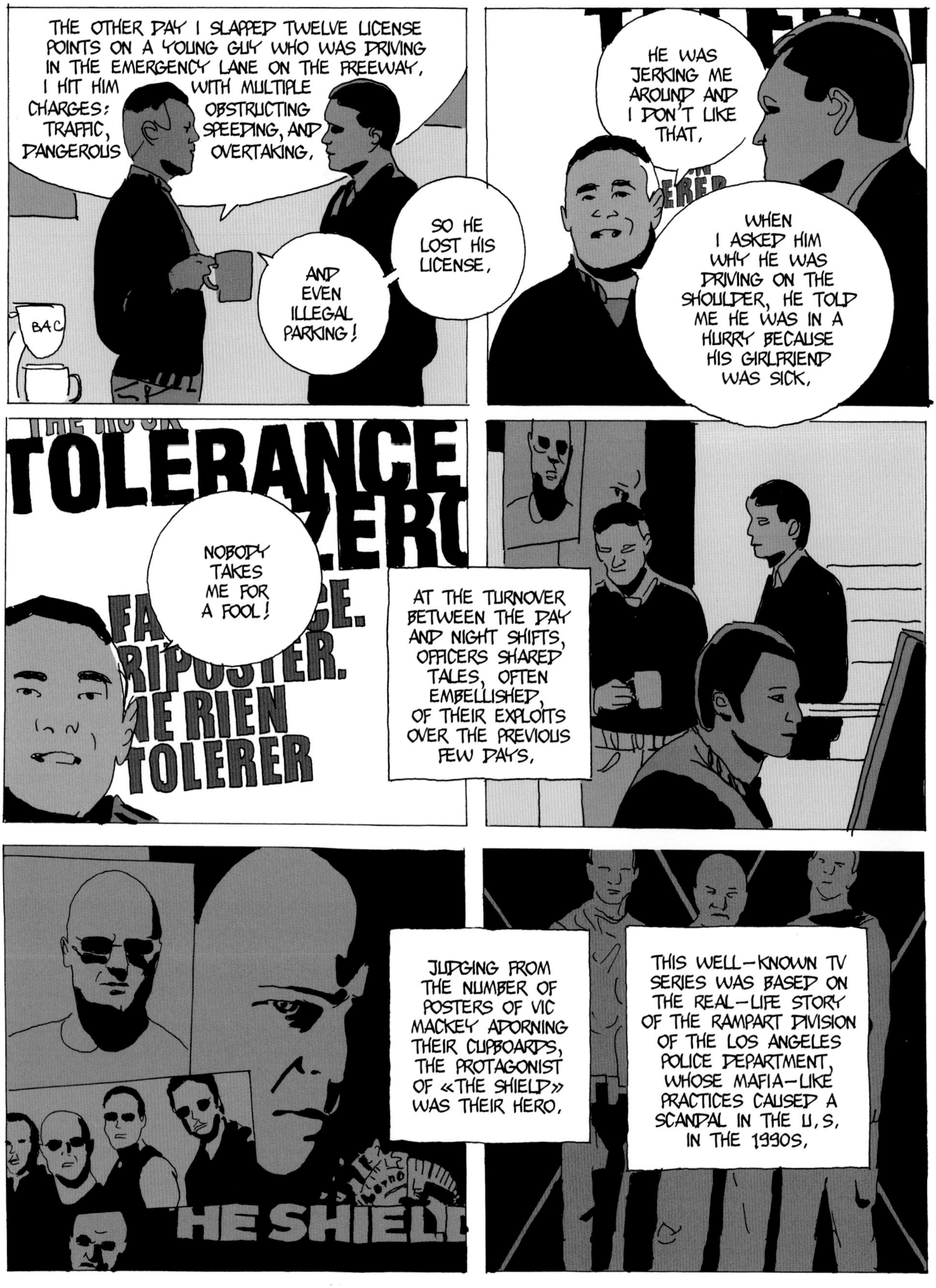
THE OTHER DAY I SLAPPED TWELVE LICENSE POINTS ON A YOUNG GUY WHO WAS DRIVING IN THE EMERGENCY LANE ON THE FREEWAY.
I HIT HIM WITH MULTIPLE CHARGES: OBSTRUCTING TRAFFIC, SPEEDING, AND DANGEROUS OVERTAKING.
SO HE LOST HIS LICENSE.
AND EVEN ILLEGAL PARKING!
BAC
HE WAS JERKING ME AROUND AND I DON'T LIKE THAT.
WHEN I ASKED HIM WHY HE WAS DRIVING ON THE SHOULDER, HE TOLD ME HE WAS IN A HURRY BECAUSE HIS GIRLFRIEND WAS SICK.
TOLERANCE ZERO
RIPOSTER.
NE RIEN TOLERER
NOBODY TAKES ME FOR A FOOL!
AT THE TURNOVER BETWEEN THE DAY AND NIGHT SHIFTS, OFFICERS SHARED TALES, OFTEN EMBELLISHED, OF THEIR EXPLOITS OVER THE PREVIOUS FEW DAYS.
JUDGING FROM THE NUMBER OF POSTERS OF VIC MACKEY ADORNING THEIR CUPBOARDS, THE PROTAGONIST OF «THE SHIELD» WAS THEIR HERO.
HE SHIELD
THIS WELL-KNOWN TV SERIES WAS BASED ON THE REAL-LIFE STORY OF THE RAMPART DIVISION OF THE LOS ANGELES POLICE DEPARTMENT, WHOSE MAFIA-LIKE PRACTICES CAUSED A SCANDAL IN THE U.S. IN THE 1990S.

IN THEIR FIGHT AGAINST CRIMINAL NETWORKS, MACKEY AND HIS CREW HAVE NO QUALMS ABOUT BREAKING THE LAW,,,

,,, TORTURING SUSPECTS, KILLING GANG MEMBERS, HELPING THEMSELVES TO THE DRUGS THEY SEIZE,,,

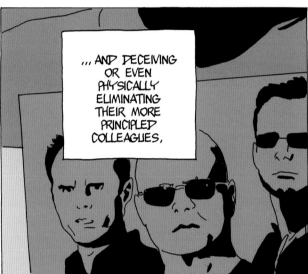

,,, AND DECEIVING OR EVEN PHYSICALLY ELIMINATING THEIR MORE PRINCIPLED COLLEAGUES,

MY PATROL COMPANIONS IDENTIFIED WITH THESE OFFICERS' SPIRIT OF FREEDOM AND THEIR SHOW OF POWER,

FASCINATED BY THESE FICTIONAL CHARACTERS, THE BAC OFFICERS DID NOT ASPIRE TO IMITATE THEIR CORRUPT PRACTICES AND BRUTAL METHODS, BUT DREAMED OF A LIFE OF SIMILAR INTENSITY,

IN FACT THEIR MONOTONOUS DAILY ROUTINE BORE LITTLE RELATION TO THE ACTION—FILLED ACCOUNTS THEY SHARED WITH THEIR COLLEAGUES,

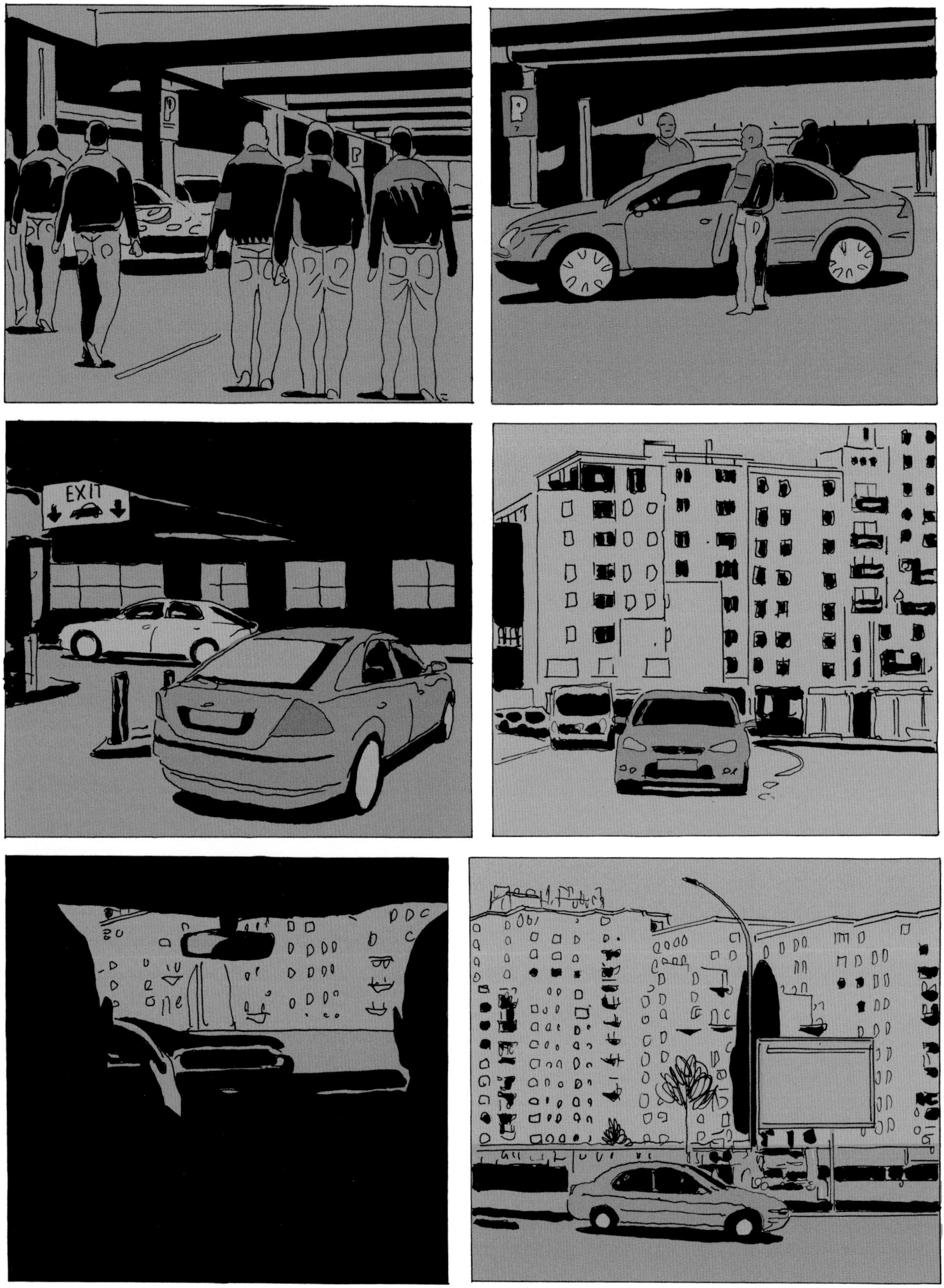
P
P
P
EXIT

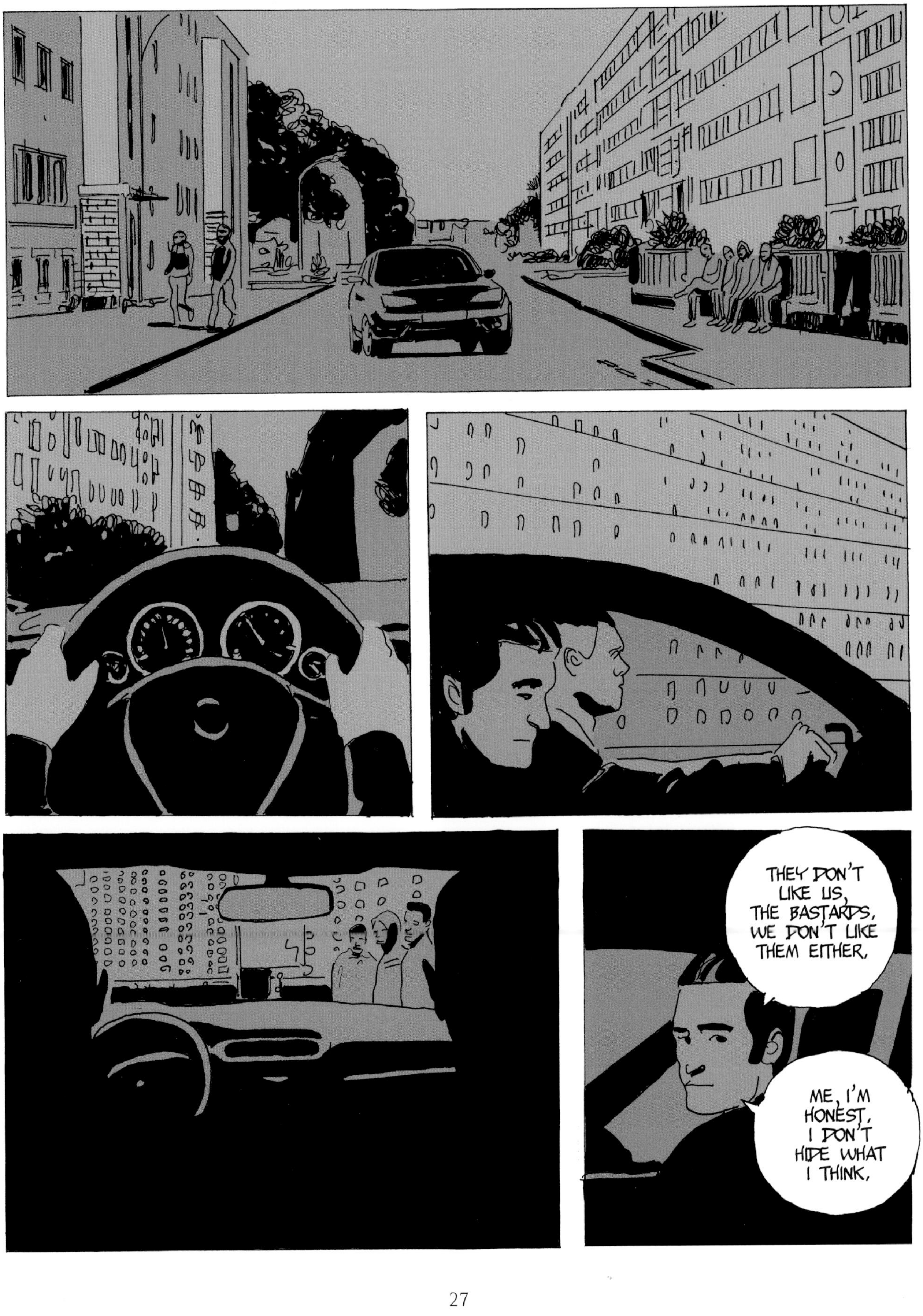
THEY DON'T LIKE US, THE BASTARDS, WE DON'T LIKE THEM EITHER,
ME, I'M HONEST, I DON'T HIDE WHAT I THINK,

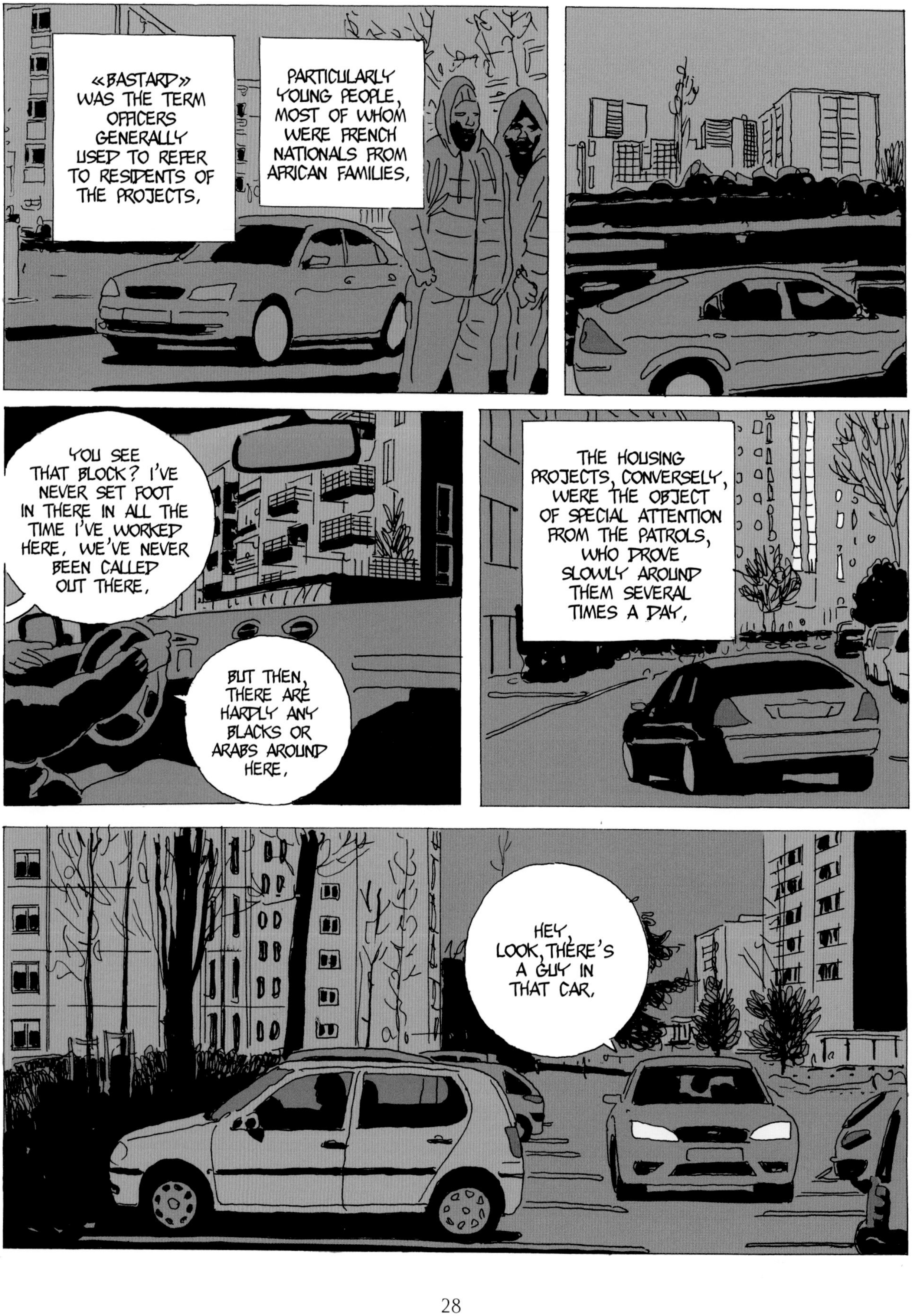

«BASTARD» WAS THE TERM OFFICERS GENERALLY USED TO REFER TO RESIDENTS OF THE PROJECTS,
PARTICULARLY YOUNG PEOPLE, MOST OF WHOM WERE FRENCH NATIONALS FROM AFRICAN FAMILIES,
YOU SEE THAT BLOCK? I'VE NEVER SET FOOT IN THERE IN ALL THE TIME I'VE WORKED HERE, WE'VE NEVER BEEN CALLED OUT THERE,
BUT THEN, THERE ARE HARDLY ANY BLACKS OR ARABS AROUND HERE,
THE HOUSING PROJECTS, CONVERSELY, WERE THE OBJECT OF SPECIAL ATTENTION FROM THE PATROLS, WHO DROVE SLOWLY AROUND THEM SEVERAL TIMES A DAY,
HEY, LOOK, THERE'S A GUY IN THAT CAR,

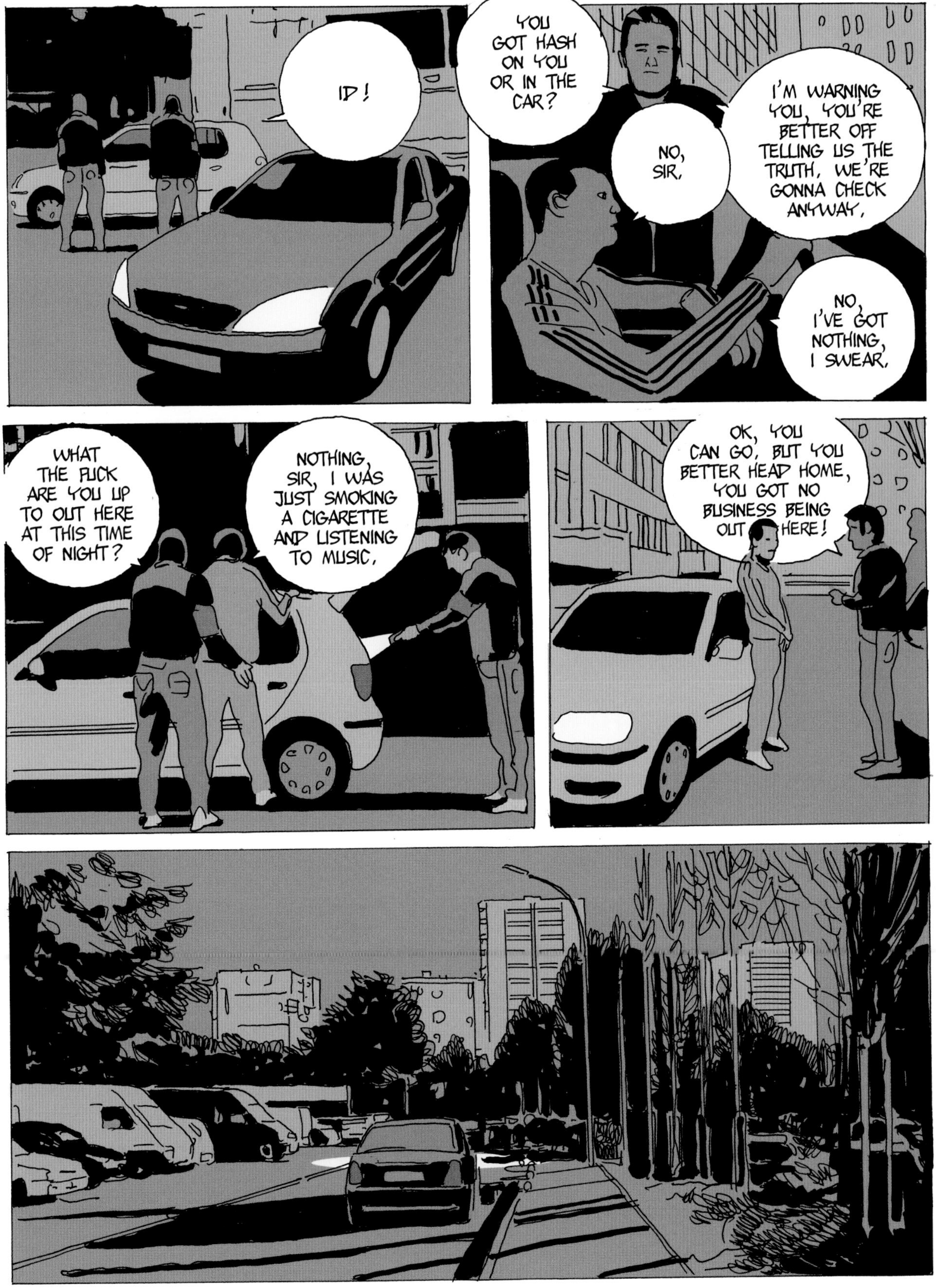
ID!
YOU GOT HASH ON YOU OR IN THE CAR?
NO, SIR.
I'M WARNING YOU, YOU'RE BETTER OFF TELLING US THE TRUTH, WE'RE GONNA CHECK ANYWAY.
NO, I'VE GOT NOTHING, I SWEAR.
WHAT THE FUCK ARE YOU UP TO OUT HERE AT THIS TIME OF NIGHT?
NOTHING, SIR, I WAS JUST SMOKING A CIGARETTE AND LISTENING TO MUSIC.
OK, YOU CAN GO, BUT YOU BETTER HEAD HOME, YOU GOT NO BUSINESS BEING OUT HERE!

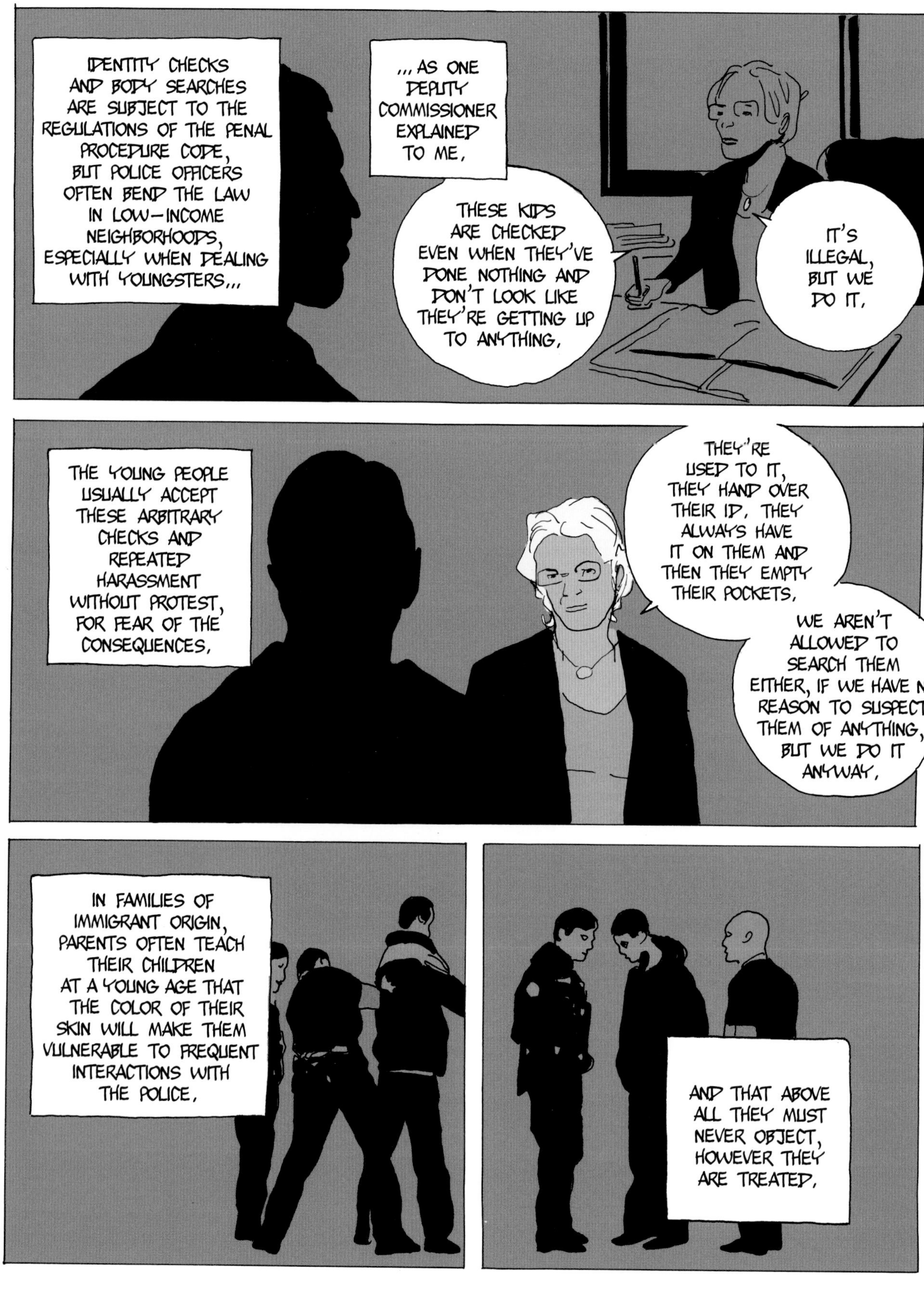
IDENTITY CHECKS AND BODY SEARCHES ARE SUBJECT TO THE REGULATIONS OF THE PENAL PROCEDURE CODE, BUT POLICE OFFICERS OFTEN BEND THE LAW IN LOW-INCOME NEIGHBORHOODS, ESPECIALLY WHEN DEALING WITH YOUNGSTERS...
...AS ONE DEPUTY COMMISSIONER EXPLAINED TO ME.
THESE KIDS ARE CHECKED EVEN WHEN THEY'VE DONE NOTHING AND DON'T LOOK LIKE THEY'RE GETTING UP TO ANYTHING.
IT'S ILLEGAL, BUT WE DO IT.
THE YOUNG PEOPLE USUALLY ACCEPT THESE ARBITRARY CHECKS AND REPEATED HARASSMENT WITHOUT PROTEST, FOR FEAR OF THE CONSEQUENCES.
THEY'RE USED TO IT. THEY HAND OVER THEIR ID. THEY ALWAYS HAVE IT ON THEM AND THEN THEY EMPTY THEIR POCKETS.
WE AREN'T ALLOWED TO SEARCH THEM EITHER, IF WE HAVE NO REASON TO SUSPECT THEM OF ANYTHING, BUT WE DO IT ANYWAY.
IN FAMILIES OF IMMIGRANT ORIGIN, PARENTS OFTEN TEACH THEIR CHILDREN AT A YOUNG AGE THAT THE COLOR OF THEIR SKIN WILL MAKE THEM VULNERABLE TO FREQUENT INTERACTIONS WITH THE POLICE.
AND THAT ABOVE ALL THEY MUST NEVER OBJECT, HOWEVER THEY ARE TREATED.

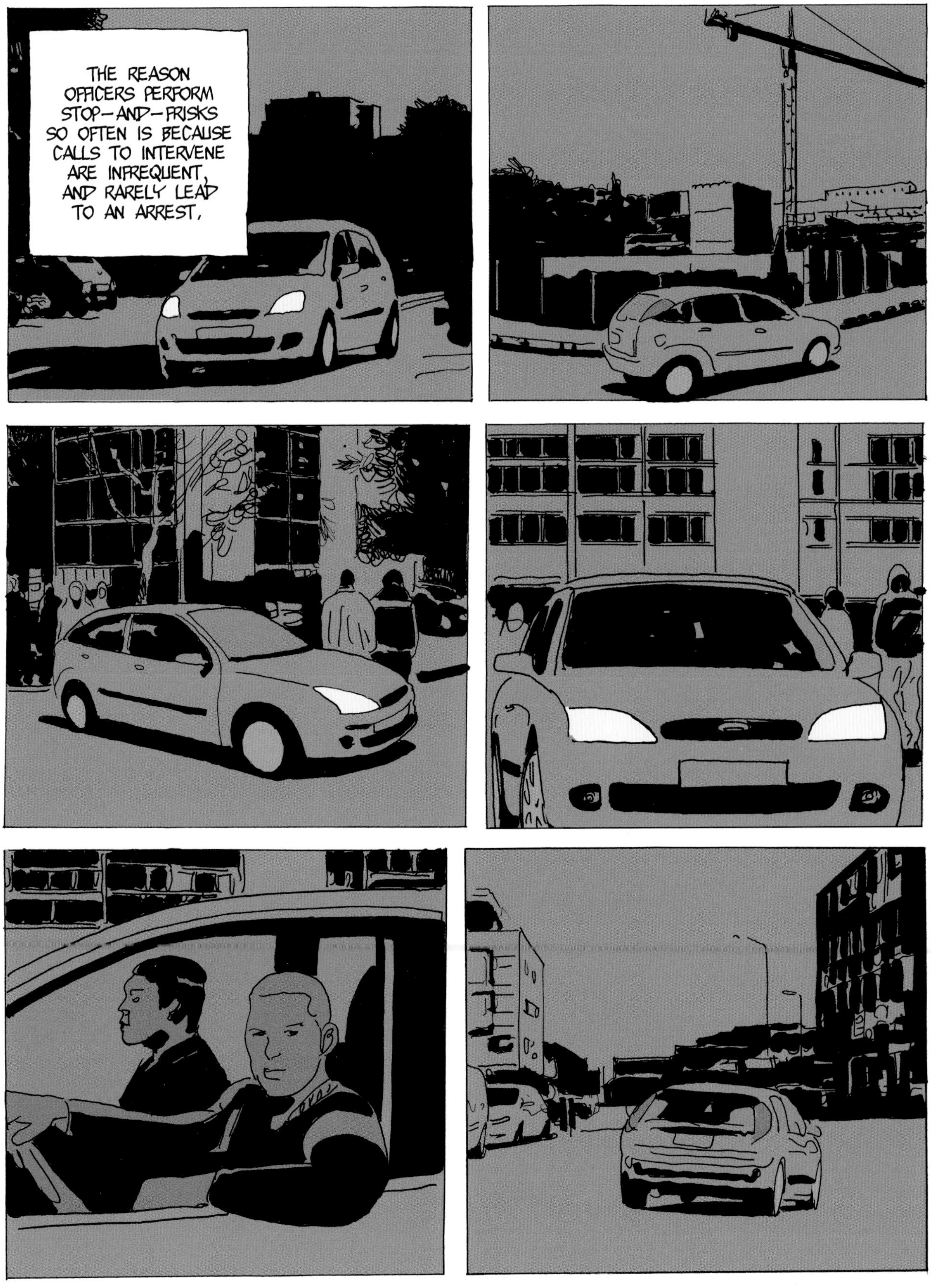
THE REASON OFFICERS PERFORM STOP-AND-FRISKS SO OFTEN IS BECAUSE CALLS TO INTERVENE ARE INFREQUENT, AND RARELY LEAD TO AN ARREST,

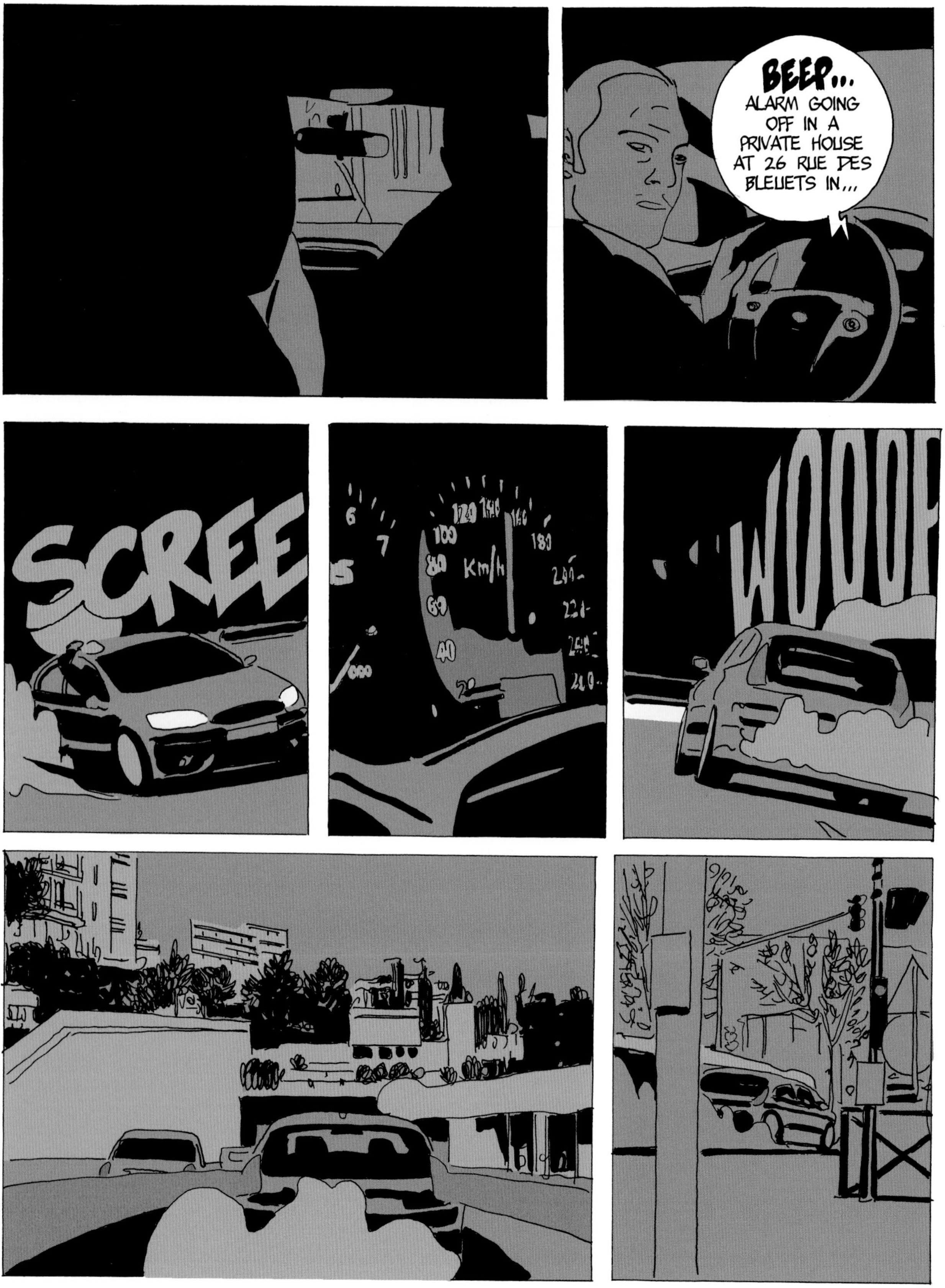
BEEP...
ALARM GOING OFF IN A PRIVATE HOUSE AT 26 RUE DES BLEUETS IN...
SCREE
WOOOP

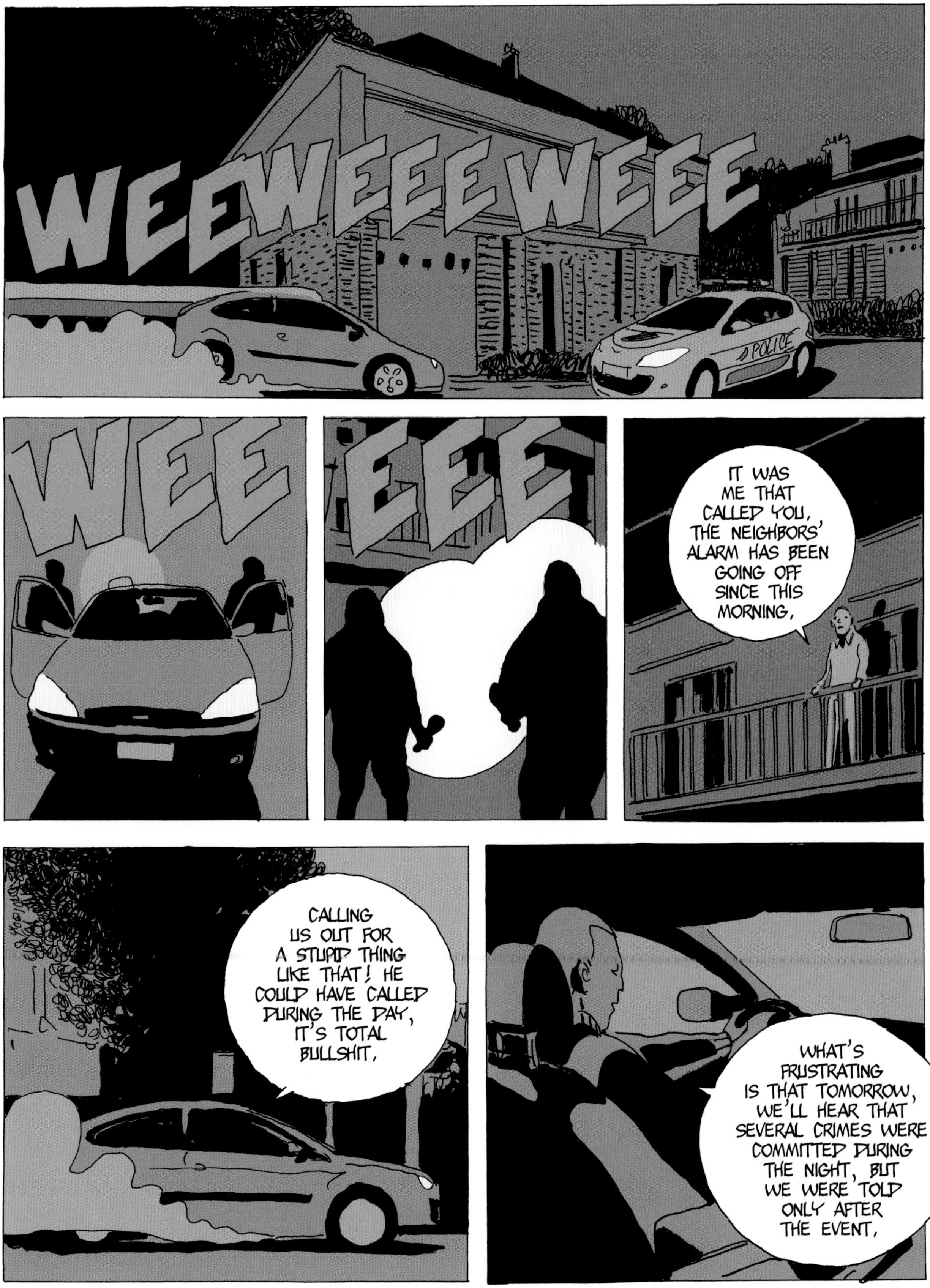
WEEWEEEWEEE
WEE EEE
IT WAS ME THAT CALLED YOU, THE NEIGHBORS' ALARM HAS BEEN GOING OFF SINCE THIS MORNING.
CALLING US OUT FOR A STUPID THING LIKE THAT! HE COULD HAVE CALLED DURING THE DAY, IT'S TOTAL BULLSHIT.
WHAT'S FRUSTRATING IS THAT TOMORROW, WE'LL HEAR THAT SEVERAL CRIMES WERE COMMITTED DURING THE NIGHT, BUT WE WERE TOLD ONLY AFTER THE EVENT.

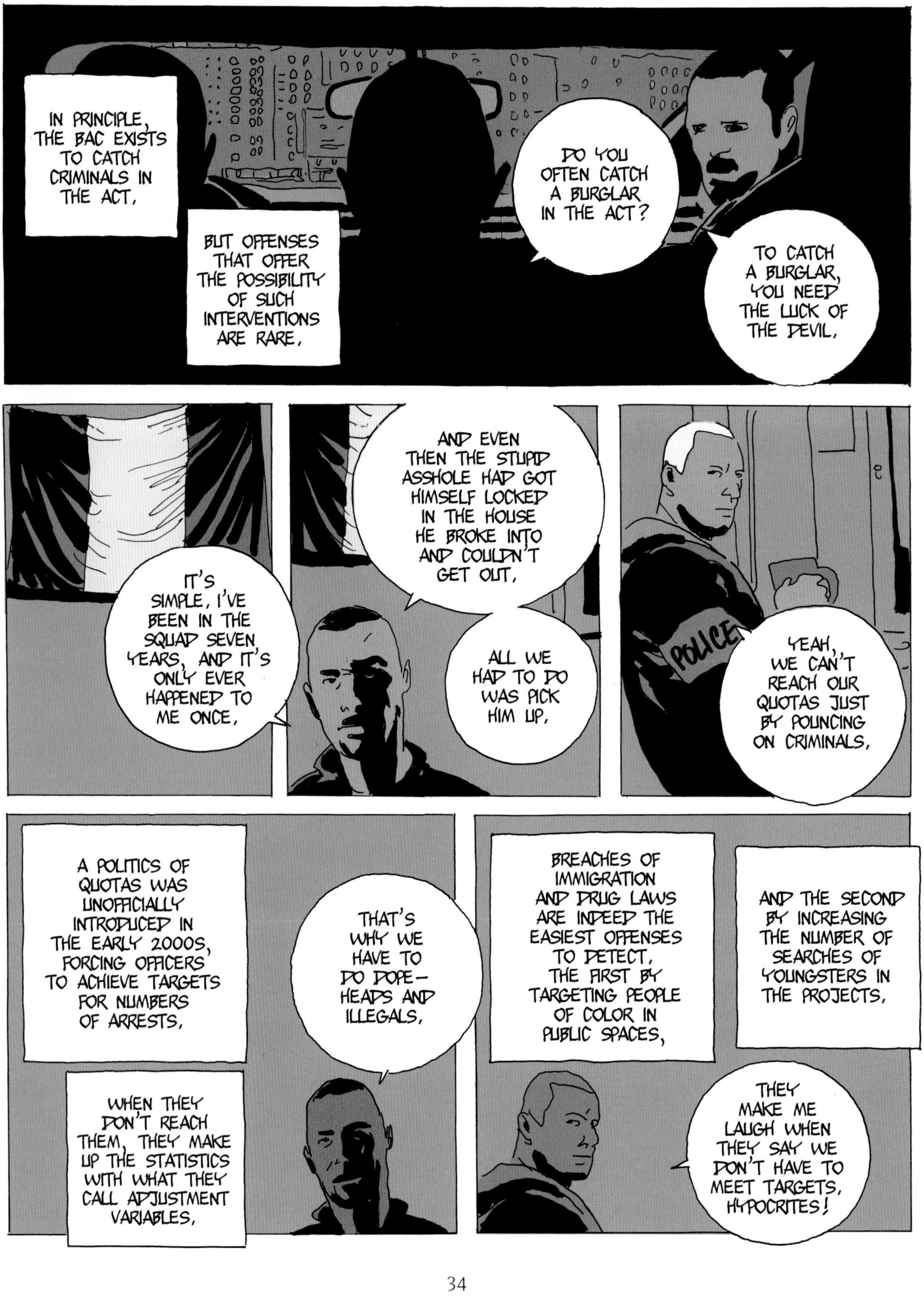
IN PRINCIPLE, THE BAC EXISTS TO CATCH CRIMINALS IN THE ACT,
BUT OFFENSES THAT OFFER THE POSSIBILITY OF SUCH INTERVENTIONS ARE RARE,
DO YOU OFTEN CATCH A BURGLAR IN THE ACT?
TO CATCH A BURGLAR, YOU NEED THE LUCK OF THE DEVIL,
IT'S SIMPLE, I'VE BEEN IN THE SQUAD SEVEN YEARS, AND IT'S ONLY EVER HAPPENED TO ME ONCE,
AND EVEN THEN THE STUPID ASSHOLE HAD GOT HIMSELF LOCKED IN THE HOUSE HE BROKE INTO AND COULDN'T GET OUT,
ALL WE HAD TO DO WAS PICK HIM UP,
POLICE
YEAH, WE CAN'T REACH OUR QUOTAS JUST BY POUNCING ON CRIMINALS,
A POLITICS OF QUOTAS WAS UNOFFICIALLY INTRODUCED IN THE EARLY 2000S, FORCING OFFICERS TO ACHIEVE TARGETS FOR NUMBERS OF ARRESTS,
THAT'S WHY WE HAVE TO DO DOPE-HEADS AND ILLEGALS,
WHEN THEY DON'T REACH THEM, THEY MAKE UP THE STATISTICS WITH WHAT THEY CALL ADJUSTMENT VARIABLES,
BREACHES OF IMMIGRATION AND DRUG LAWS ARE INDEED THE EASIEST OFFENSES TO DETECT, THE FIRST BY TARGETING PEOPLE OF COLOR IN PUBLIC SPACES,
AND THE SECOND BY INCREASING THE NUMBER OF SEARCHES OF YOUNGSTERS IN THE PROJECTS,
THEY MAKE ME LAUGH WHEN THEY SAY WE DON'T HAVE TO MEET TARGETS, HYPOCRITES!

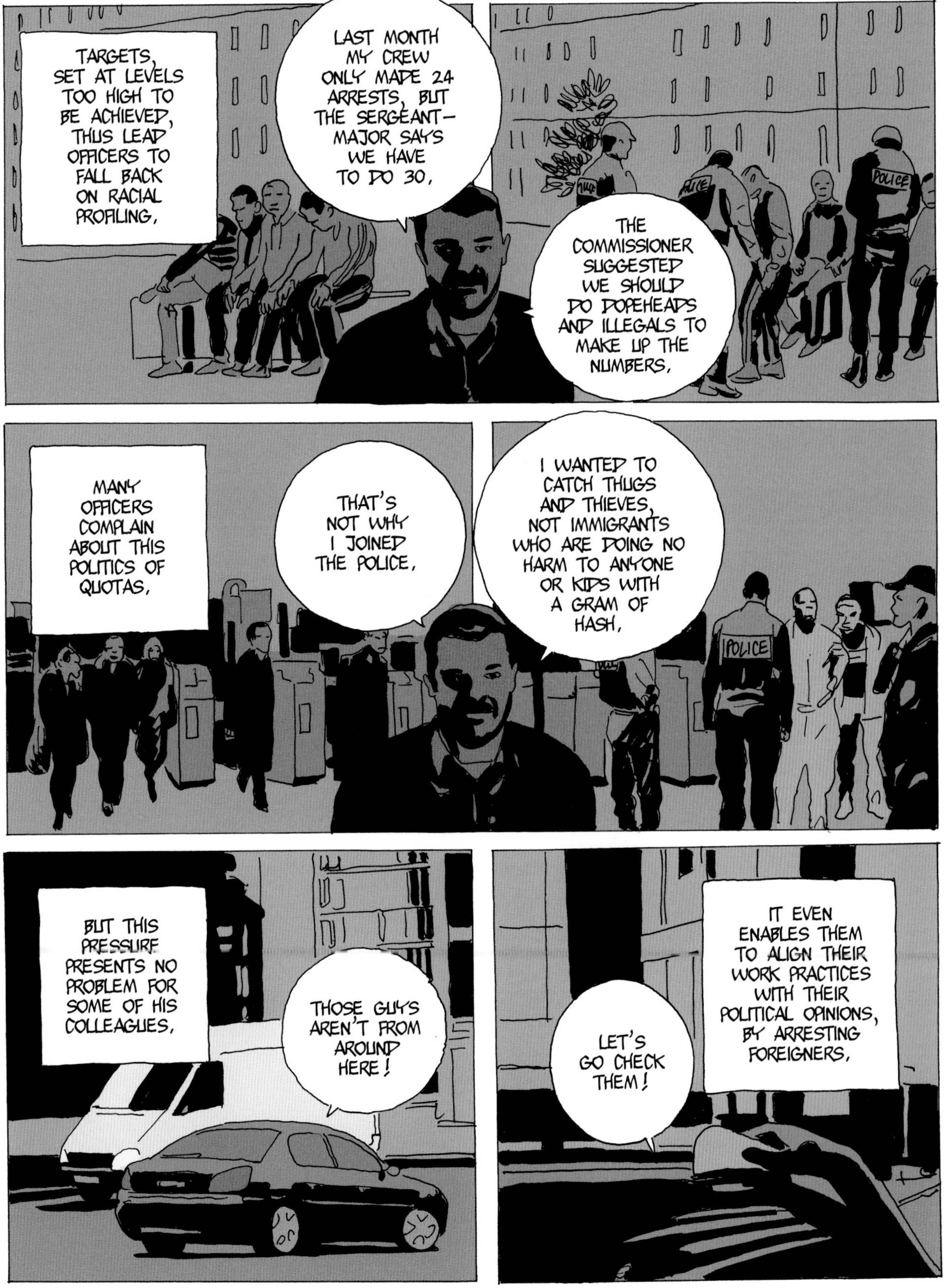
TARGETS, SET AT LEVELS TOO HIGH TO BE ACHIEVED, THUS LEAD OFFICERS TO FALL BACK ON RACIAL PROFILING.
LAST MONTH MY CREW ONLY MADE 24 ARRESTS, BUT THE SERGEANT-MAJOR SAYS WE HAVE TO DO 30.
THE COMMISSIONER SUGGESTED WE SHOULD DO DOPEHEADS AND ILLEGALS TO MAKE UP THE NUMBERS.
MANY OFFICERS COMPLAIN ABOUT THIS POLITICS OF QUOTAS.
THAT'S NOT WHY I JOINED THE POLICE.
I WANTED TO CATCH THUGS AND THIEVES, NOT IMMIGRANTS WHO ARE DOING NO HARM TO ANYONE OR KIDS WITH A GRAM OF HASH.
POLICE
BUT THIS PRESSURE PRESENTS NO PROBLEM FOR SOME OF HIS COLLEAGUES.
THOSE GUYS AREN'T FROM AROUND HERE!
IT EVEN ENABLES THEM TO ALIGN THEIR WORK PRACTICES WITH THEIR POLITICAL OPINIONS, BY ARRESTING FOREIGNERS.
LET'S GO CHECK THEM!

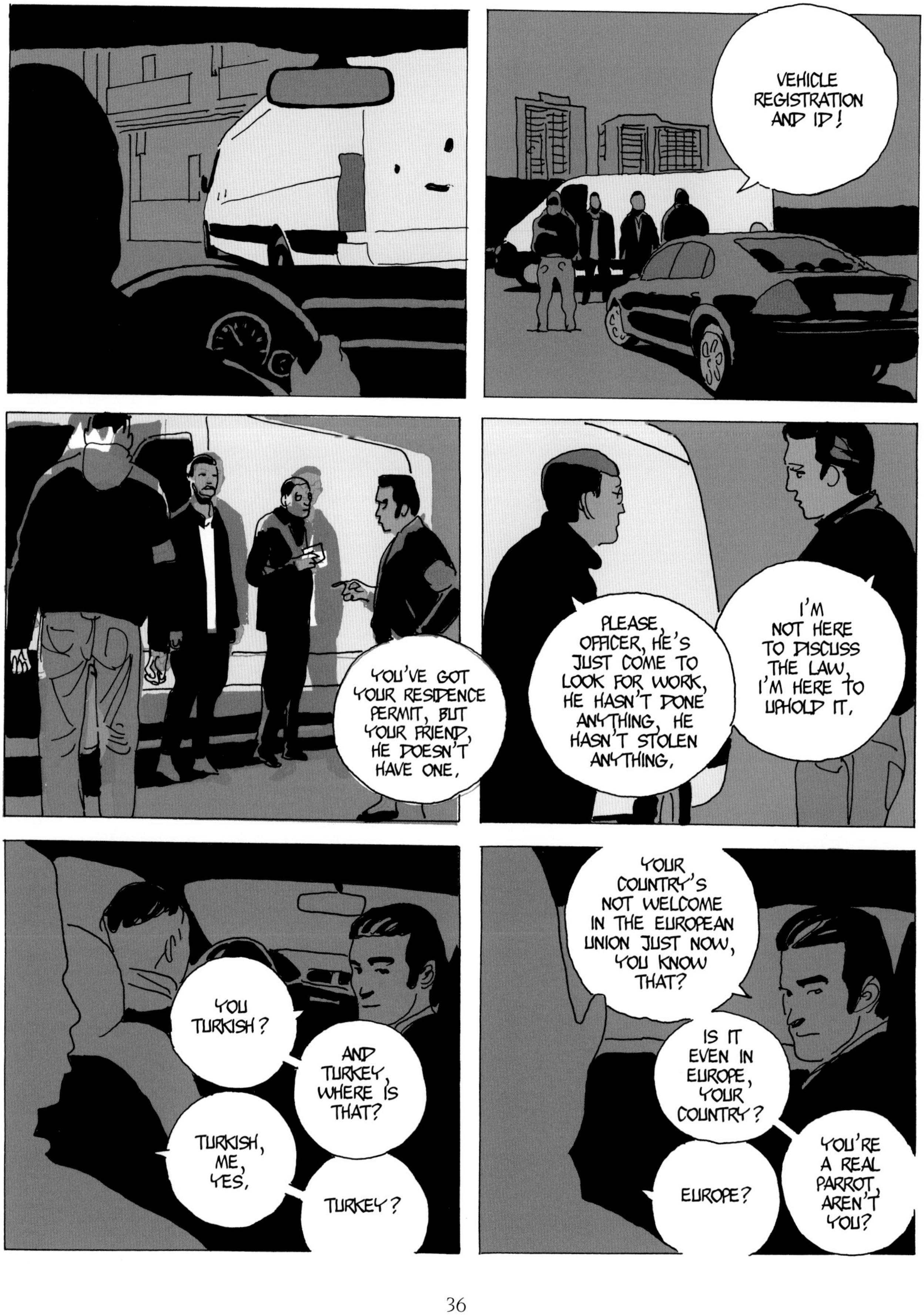

VEHICLE REGISTRATION AND ID!
YOU'VE GOT YOUR RESIDENCE PERMIT, BUT YOUR FRIEND, HE DOESN'T HAVE ONE.
PLEASE, OFFICER, HE'S JUST COME TO LOOK FOR WORK, HE HASN'T DONE ANYTHING, HE HASN'T STOLEN ANYTHING.
I'M NOT HERE TO DISCUSS THE LAW, I'M HERE TO UPHOLD IT.
YOU TURKISH?
TURKISH, ME, YES.
AND TURKEY, WHERE IS THAT?
TURKEY?
YOUR COUNTRY'S NOT WELCOME IN THE EUROPEAN UNION JUST NOW, YOU KNOW THAT?
IS IT EVEN IN EUROPE, YOUR COUNTRY?
EUROPE?
YOU'RE A REAL PARROT, AREN'T YOU?

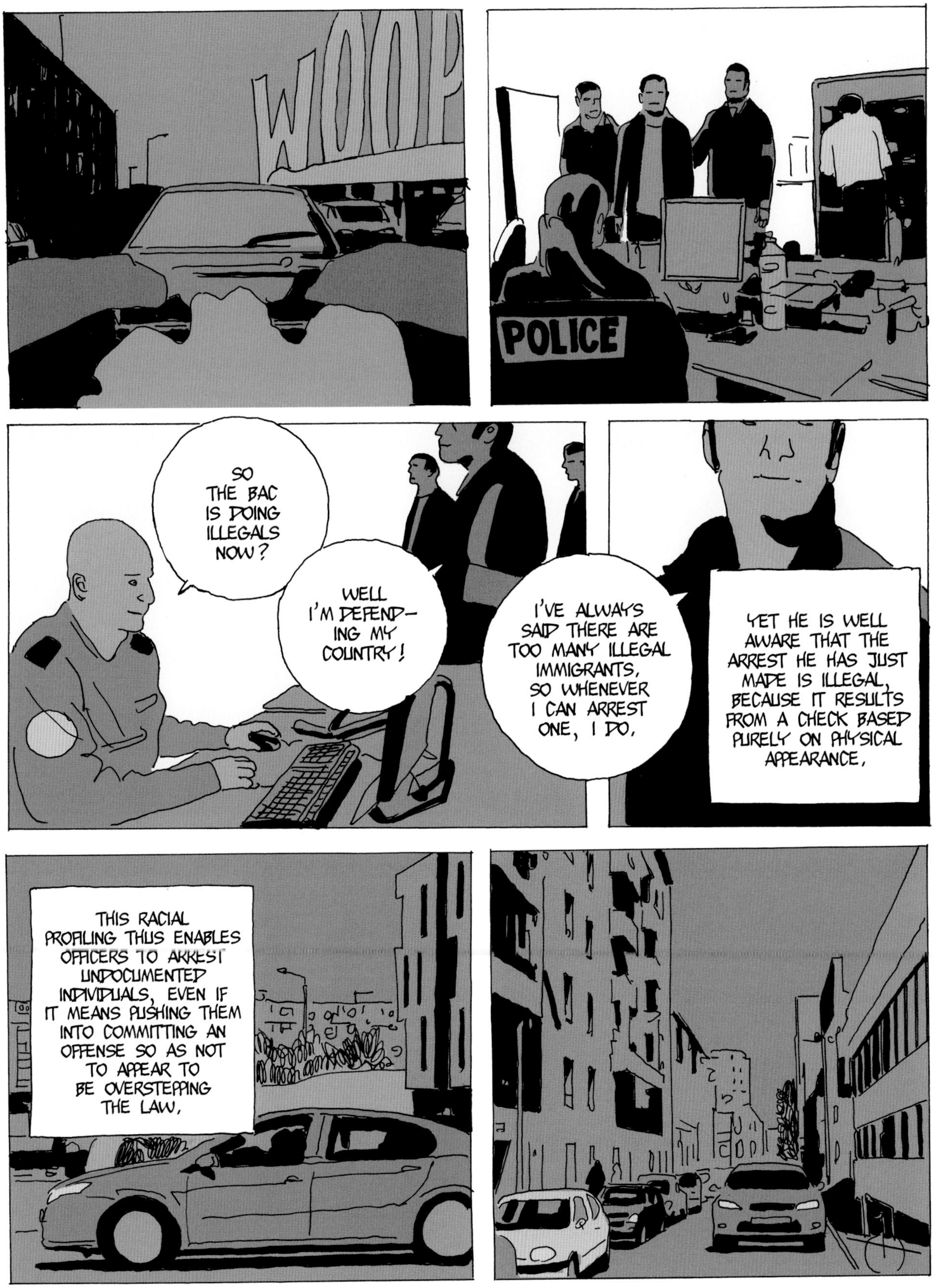
WOOP
POLICE
SO THE BAC IS DOING ILLEGALS NOW?
WELL I'M DEFENDING MY COUNTRY!
I'VE ALWAYS SAID THERE ARE TOO MANY ILLEGAL IMMIGRANTS, SO WHENEVER I CAN ARREST ONE, I DO.
YET HE IS WELL AWARE THAT THE ARREST HE HAS JUST MADE IS ILLEGAL, BECAUSE IT RESULTS FROM A CHECK BASED PURELY ON PHYSICAL APPEARANCE.
THIS RACIAL PROFILING THUS ENABLES OFFICERS TO ARREST UNDOCUMENTED INDIVIDUALS, EVEN IF IT MEANS PUSHING THEM INTO COMMITTING AN OFFENSE SO AS NOT TO APPEAR TO BE OVERSTEPPING THE LAW.

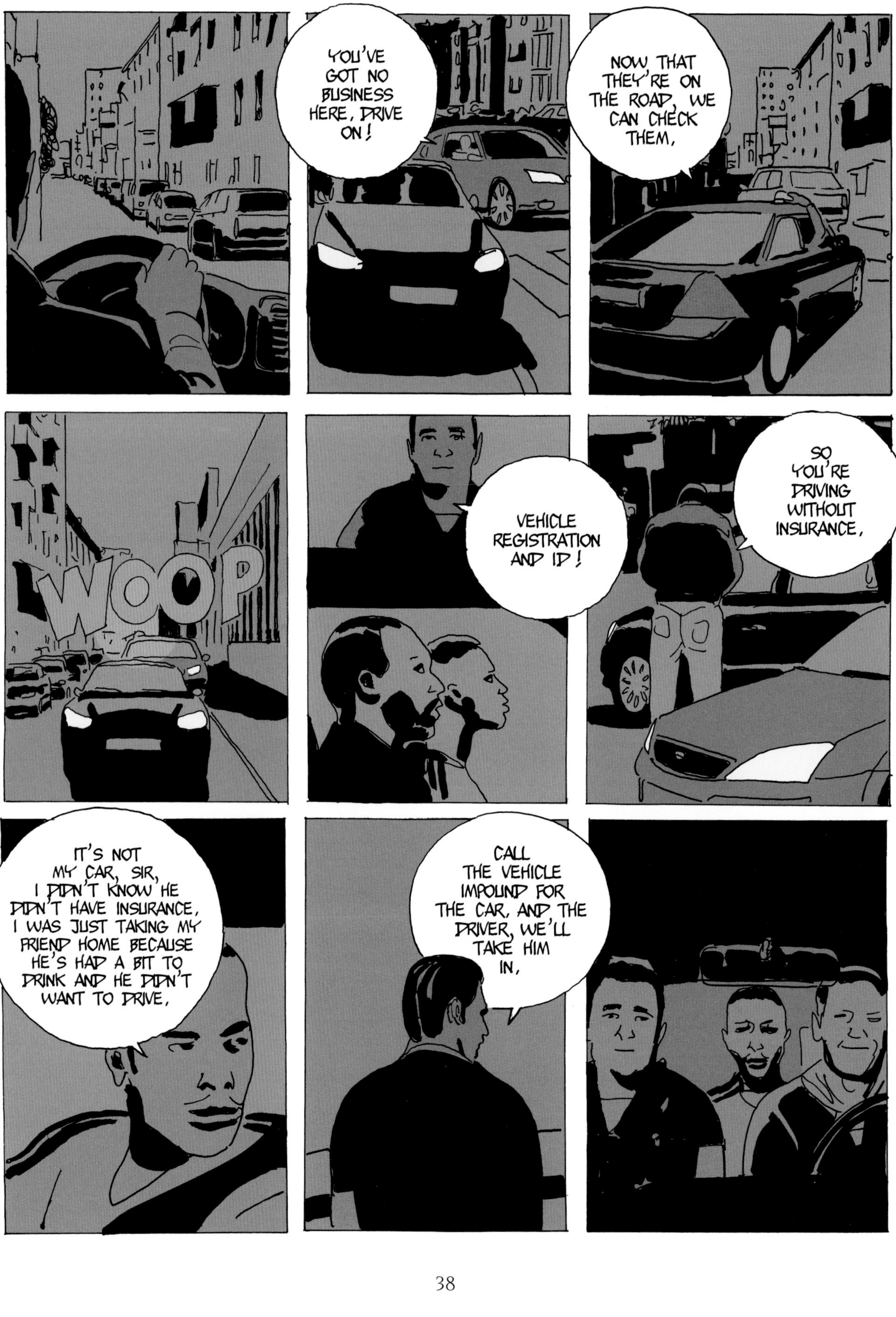
YOU'VE GOT NO BUSINESS HERE, DRIVE ON!
NOW THAT THEY'RE ON THE ROAD, WE CAN CHECK THEM.
WOOP
VEHICLE REGISTRATION AND ID!
SO YOU'RE DRIVING WITHOUT INSURANCE.
IT'S NOT MY CAR, SIR, I DIDN'T KNOW HE DIDN'T HAVE INSURANCE, I WAS JUST TAKING MY FRIEND HOME BECAUSE HE'S HAD A BIT TO DRINK AND HE DIDN'T WANT TO DRIVE.
CALL THE VEHICLE IMPOUND FOR THE CAR, AND THE DRIVER, WE'LL TAKE HIM IN.

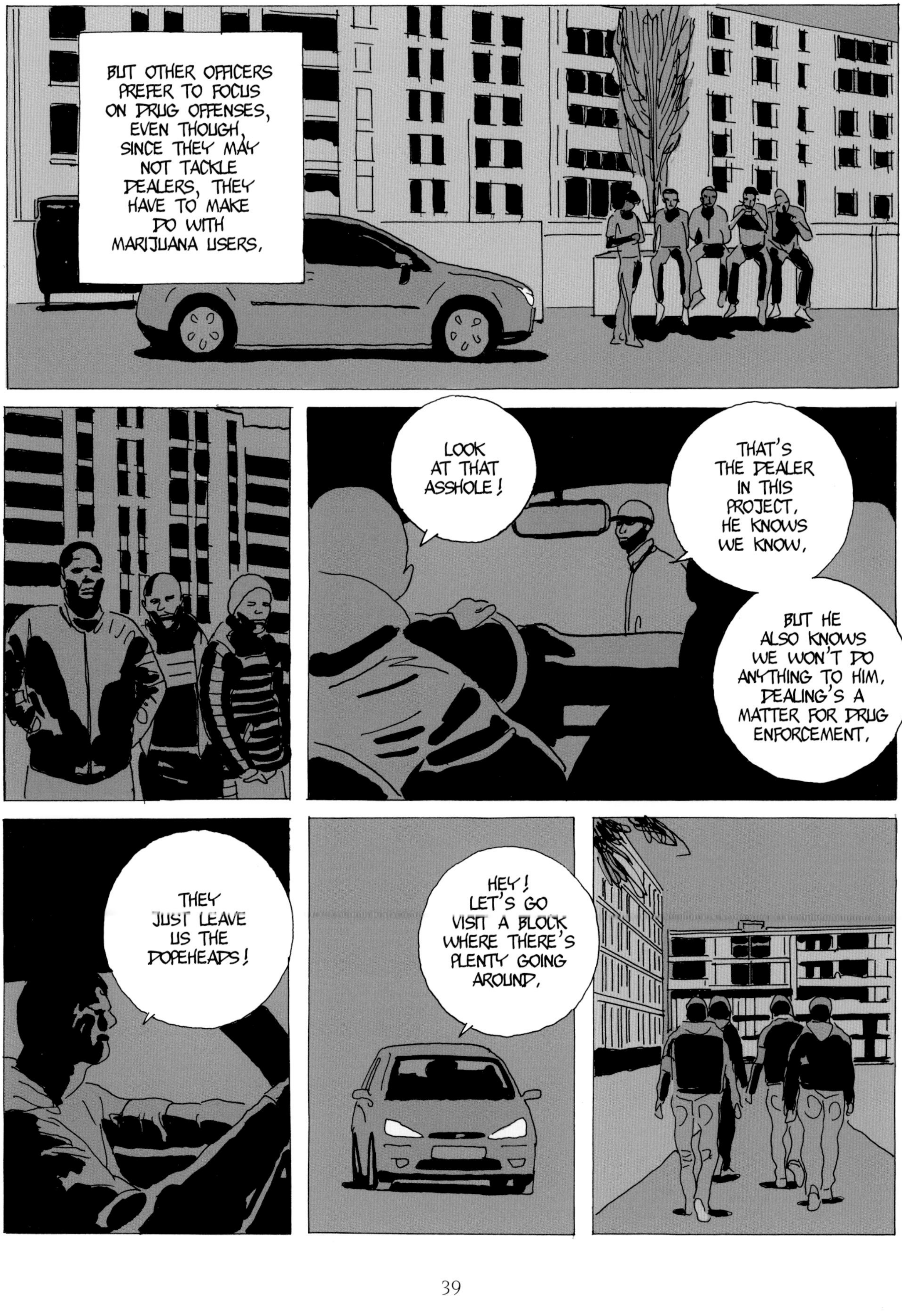
BUT OTHER OFFICERS PREFER TO FOCUS ON DRUG OFFENSES, EVEN THOUGH, SINCE THEY MAY NOT TACKLE DEALERS, THEY HAVE TO MAKE DO WITH MARIJUANA USERS.
LOOK AT THAT ASSHOLE!
THAT'S THE DEALER IN THIS PROJECT. HE KNOWS WE KNOW.
BUT HE ALSO KNOWS WE WON'T DO ANYTHING TO HIM. DEALING'S A MATTER FOR DRUG ENFORCEMENT.
THEY JUST LEAVE US THE DOPEHEADS!
HEY! LET'S GO VISIT A BLOCK WHERE THERE'S PLENTY GOING AROUND.

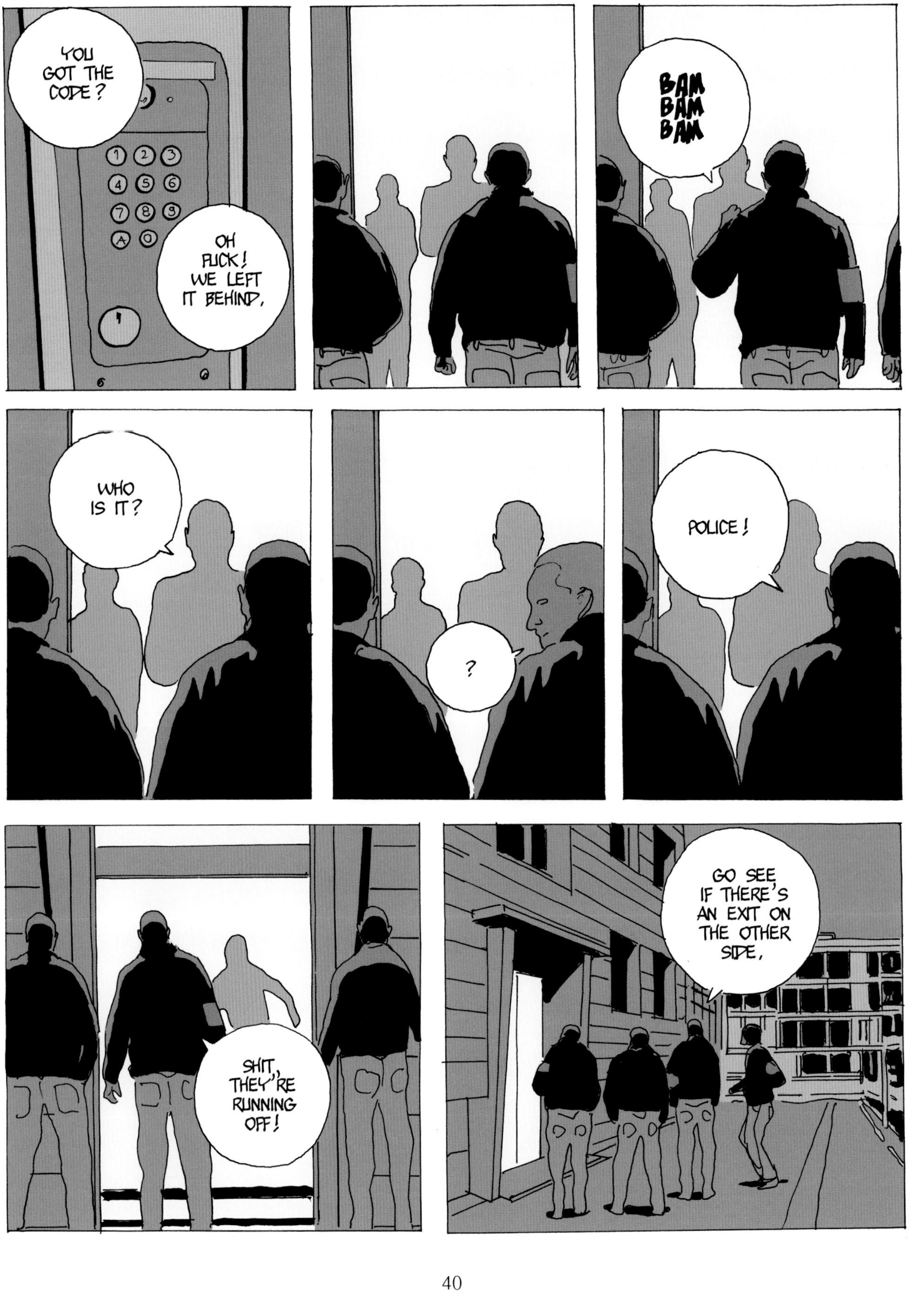
YOU GOT THE CODE?
OH FUCK! WE LEFT IT BEHIND.
BAM BAM BAM
WHO IS IT?
?
POLICE!
SHIT, THEY'RE RUNNING OFF!
GO SEE IF THERE'S AN EXIT ON THE OTHER SIDE.

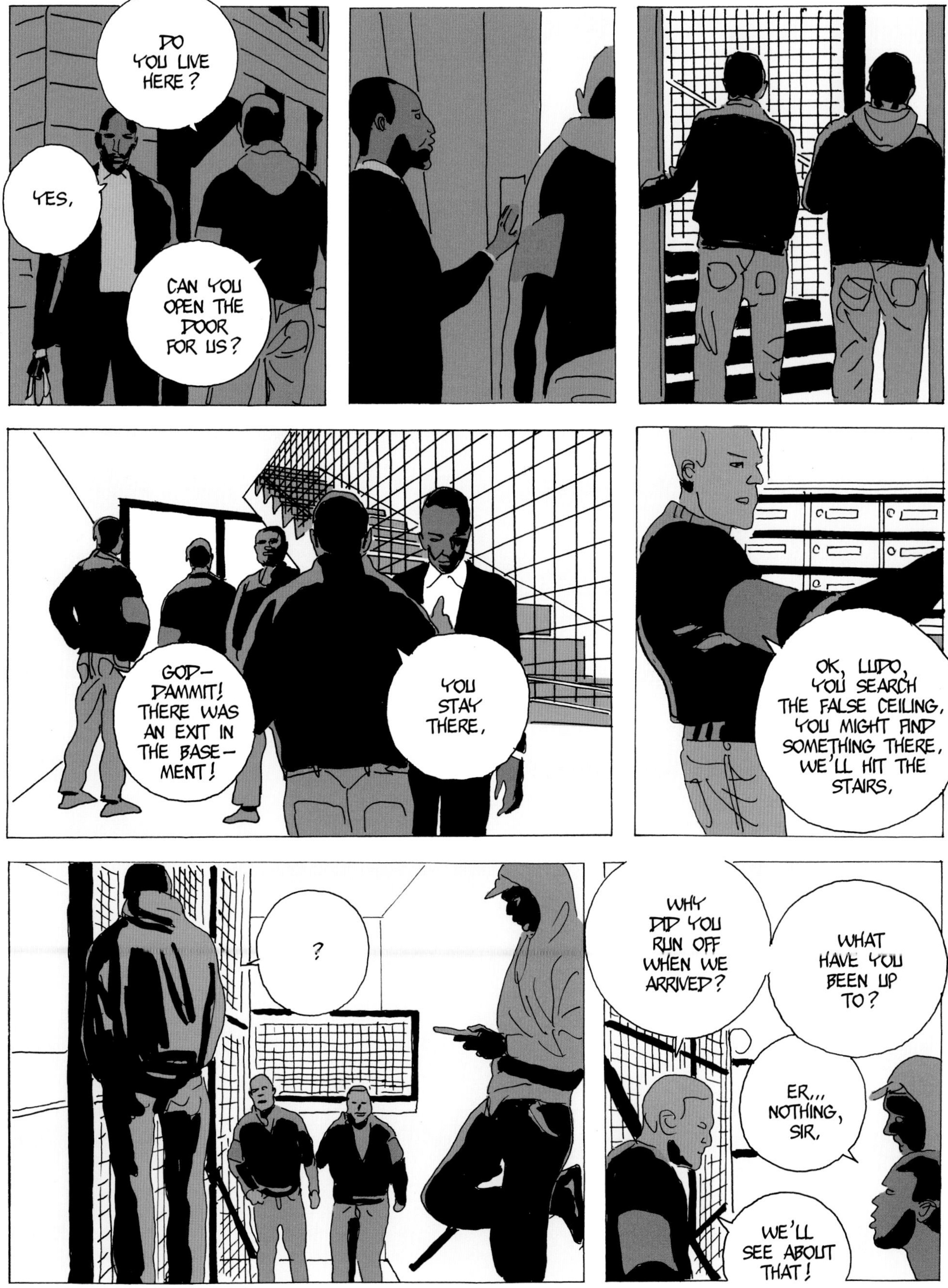
DO YOU LIVE HERE?
YES.
CAN YOU OPEN THE DOOR FOR US?
GODDAMMIT! THERE WAS AN EXIT IN THE BASEMENT!
YOU STAY THERE.
OK, LUDO, YOU SEARCH THE FALSE CEILING. YOU MIGHT FIND SOMETHING THERE. WE'LL HIT THE STAIRS.
?
WHY DID YOU RUN OFF WHEN WE ARRIVED?
WHAT HAVE YOU BEEN UP TO?
ER... NOTHING, SIR.
WE'LL SEE ABOUT THAT!

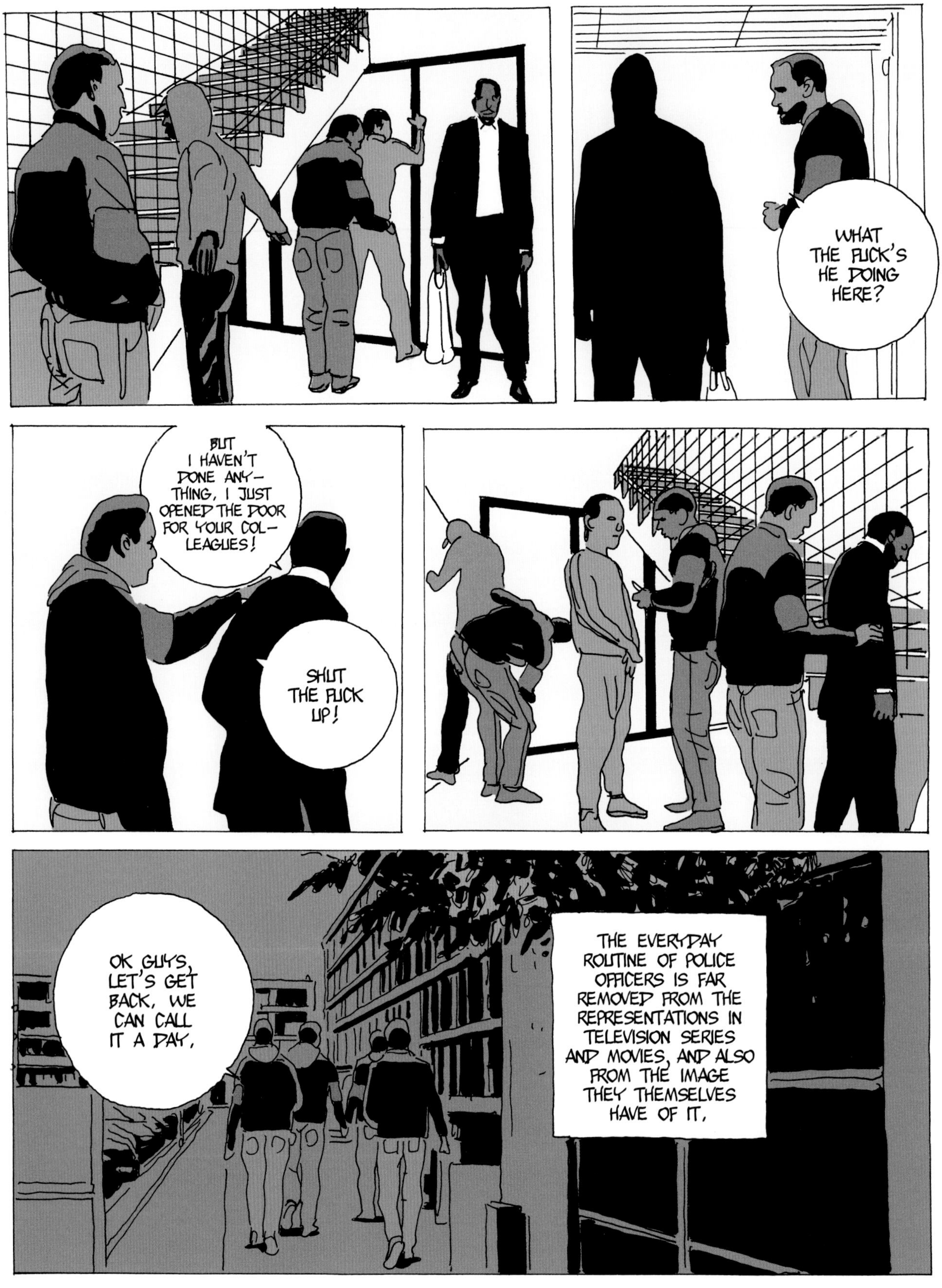
WHAT THE FUCK'S HE DOING HERE?
BUT I HAVEN'T DONE ANY-THING, I JUST OPENED THE DOOR FOR YOUR COL-LEAGUES!
SHUT THE FUCK UP!
OK GUYS, LET'S GET BACK, WE CAN CALL IT A DAY.
THE EVERYDAY ROUTINE OF POLICE OFFICERS IS FAR REMOVED FROM THE REPRESENTATIONS IN TELEVISION SERIES AND MOVIES, AND ALSO FROM THE IMAGE THEY THEMSELVES HAVE OF IT.

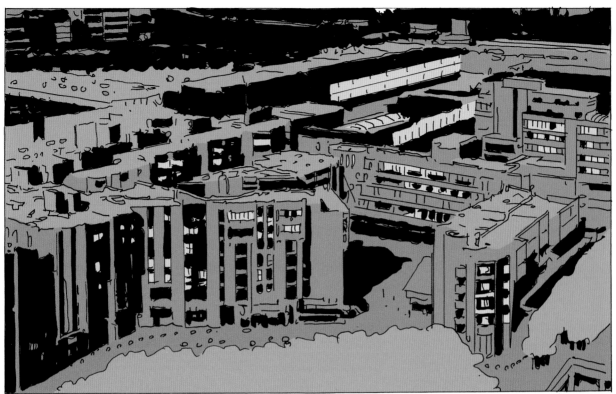

PATROLS CONSIST OF DRIVING AROUND FROM PROJECTS TO CITY CENTER, FROM STATIONS TO INDUSTRIAL ZONES, IN SEARCH OF AN UNLIKELY CRIME IN PROGRESS,

9:30 P,M,

WHAT DID YOU DO THIS WEEKEND?

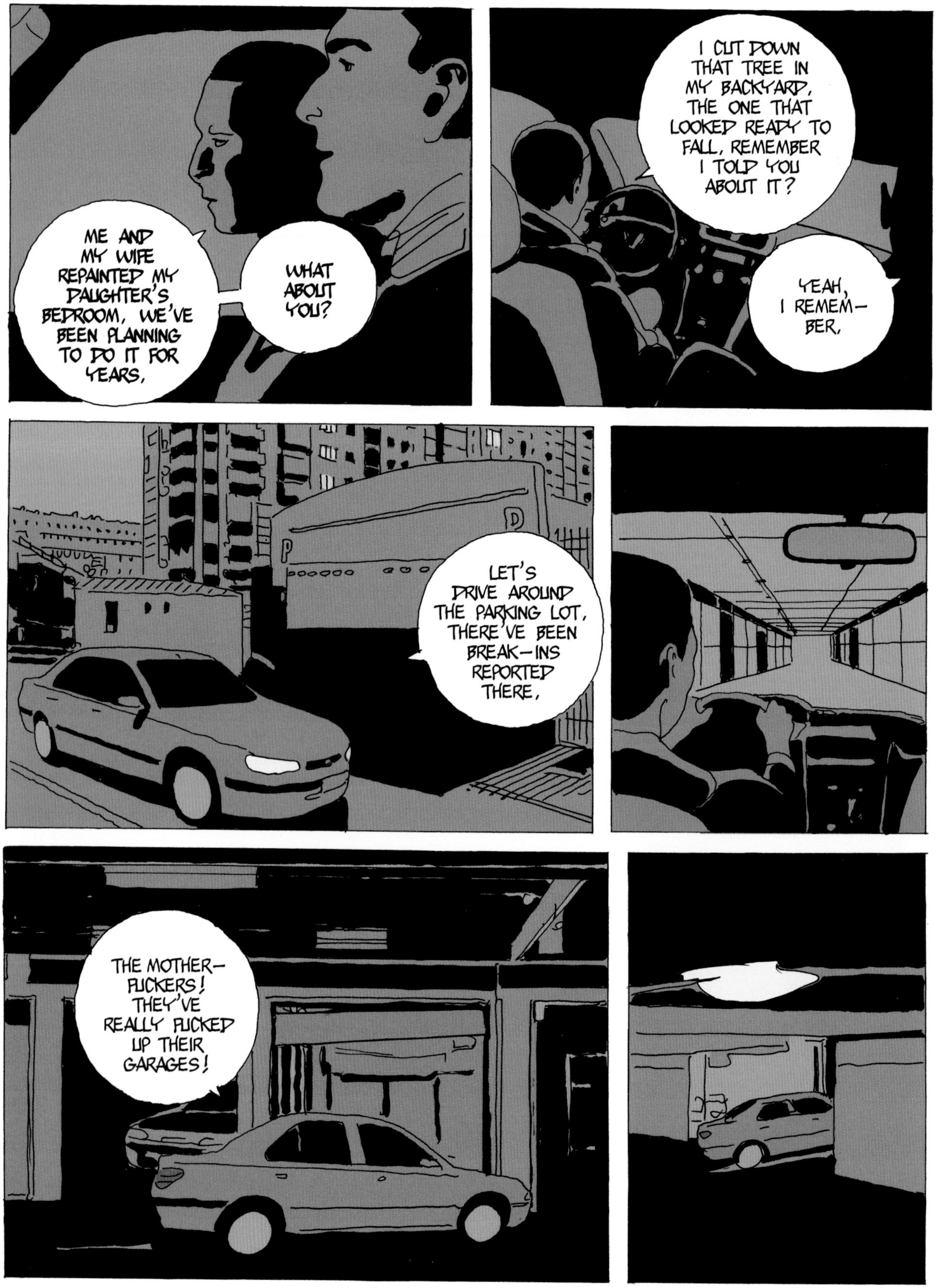
ME AND MY WIFE REPAINTED MY DAUGHTER'S BEDROOM, WE'VE BEEN PLANNING TO DO IT FOR YEARS.
WHAT ABOUT YOU?
I CUT DOWN THAT TREE IN MY BACKYARD, THE ONE THAT LOOKED READY TO FALL, REMEMBER I TOLD YOU ABOUT IT?
YEAH, I REMEM-BER.
LET'S DRIVE AROUND THE PARKING LOT, THERE'VE BEEN BREAK-INS REPORTED THERE.
THE MOTHER-FUCKERS! THEY'VE REALLY FUCKED UP THEIR GARAGES!

10:30 P,M,

DID YOU SEE THE VIDEO OF WHEN THEY STOPPED THAT KID IN ROUEN?

AT FIRST IT'S ALL GOING FINE, YOU EVEN HEAR A COP CALLING THE GUY «SIR», I THOUGHT, NO WAY, THE COP MUST HAVE SEEN THE CAMERA,,,

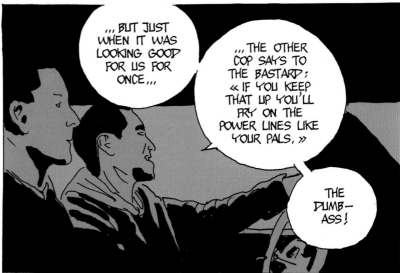

,,, BUT JUST WHEN IT WAS LOOKING GOOD FOR US FOR ONCE,,,

,,, THE OTHER COP SAYS TO THE BASTARD: «IF YOU KEEP THAT UP YOU'LL FRY ON THE POWER LINES LIKE YOUR PALS,»

THE DUMB-ASS!

11:30 P,M,

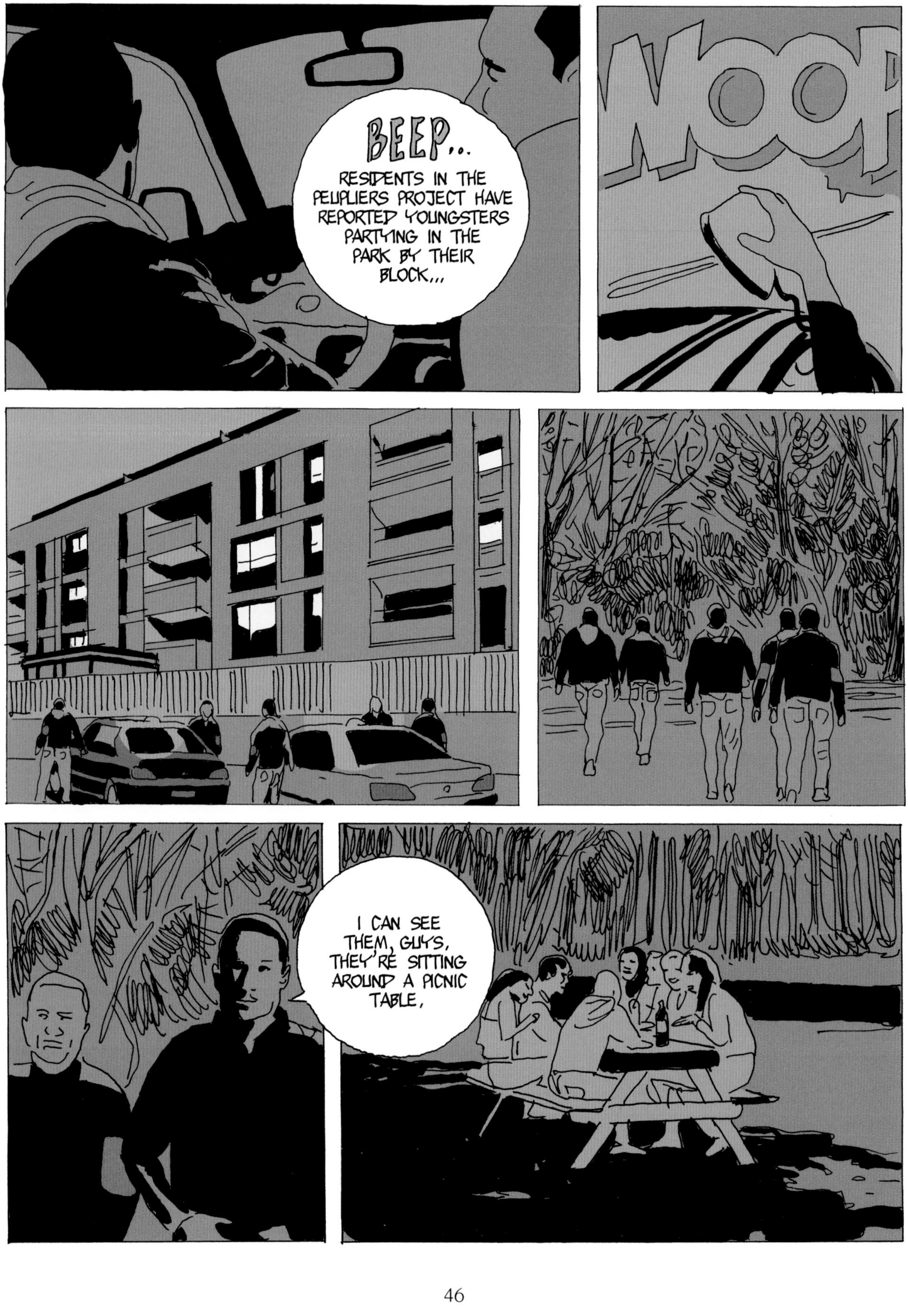
BEEP...
RESIDENTS IN THE PEUPLIERS PROJECT HAVE REPORTED YOUNGSTERS PARTYING IN THE PARK BY THEIR BLOCK...
WOOP
I CAN SEE THEM, GUYS, THEY'RE SITTING AROUND A PICNIC TABLE.

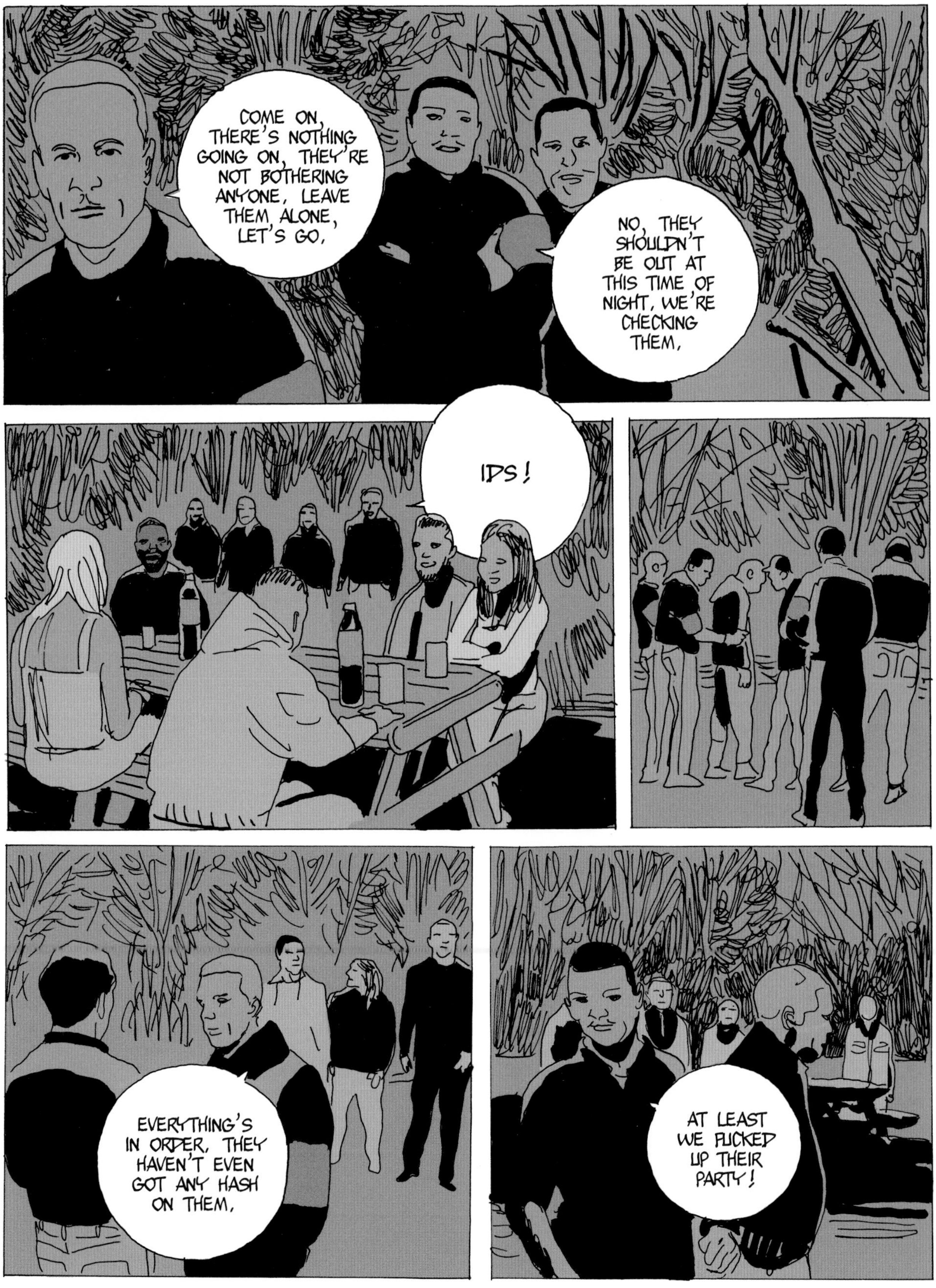
COME ON, THERE'S NOTHING GOING ON, THEY'RE NOT BOTHERING ANYONE, LEAVE THEM ALONE, LET'S GO.
NO, THEY SHOULDN'T BE OUT AT THIS TIME OF NIGHT, WE'RE CHECKING THEM.
IDS!
EVERYTHING'S IN ORDER, THEY HAVEN'T EVEN GOT ANY HASH ON THEM.
AT LEAST WE FUCKED UP THEIR PARTY!

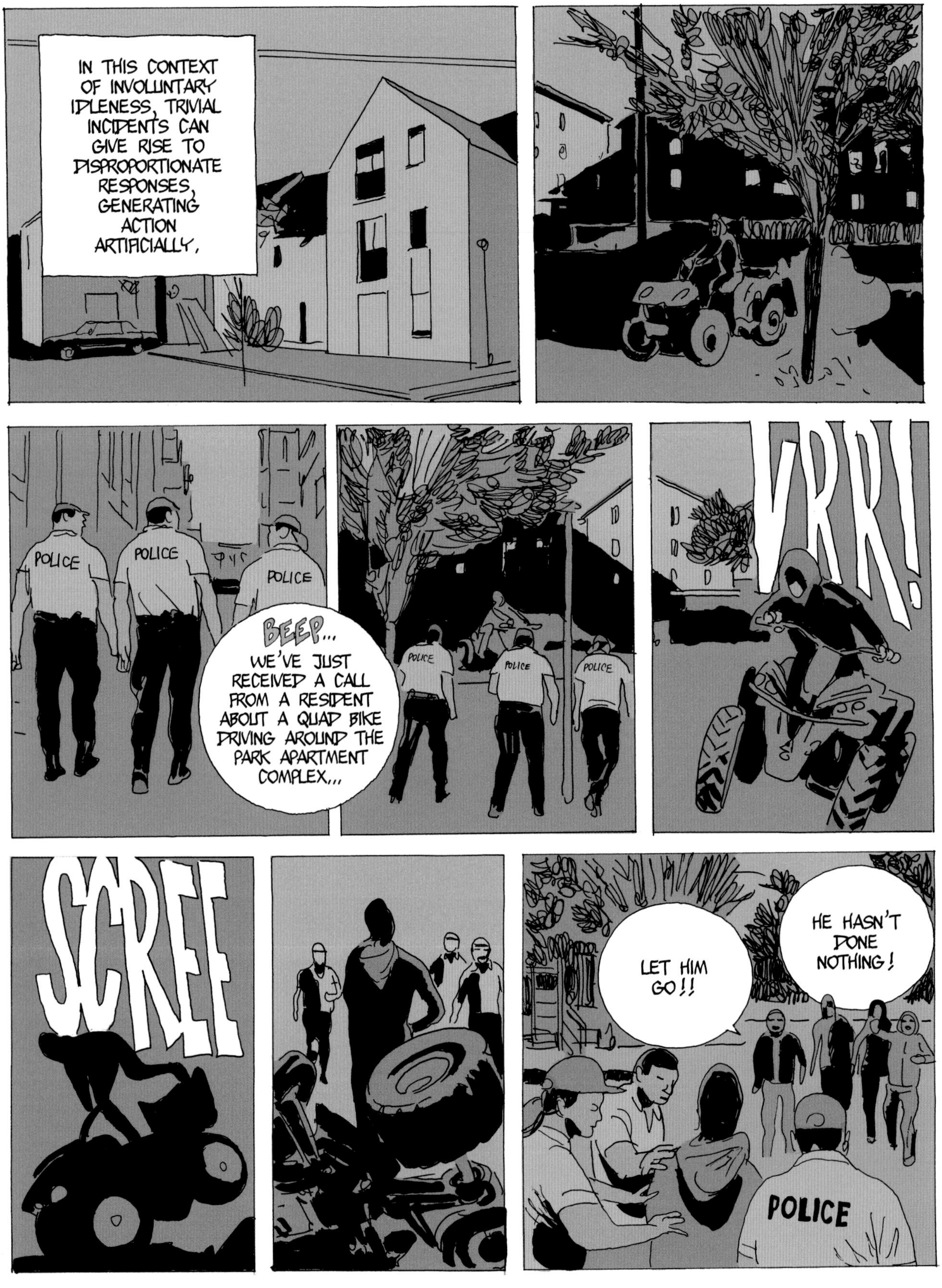
IN THIS CONTEXT OF INVOLUNTARY IDLENESS, TRIVIAL INCIDENTS CAN GIVE RISE TO DISPROPORTIONATE RESPONSES, GENERATING ACTION ARTIFICIALLY.
POLICE
POLICE
POLICE
BEEP... WE'VE JUST RECEIVED A CALL FROM A RESIDENT ABOUT A QUAD BIKE DRIVING AROUND THE PARK APARTMENT COMPLEX...
POLICE
POLICE
POLICE
VRRR!
SCREE
LET HIM GO!!
HE HASN'T DONE NOTHING!
POLICE

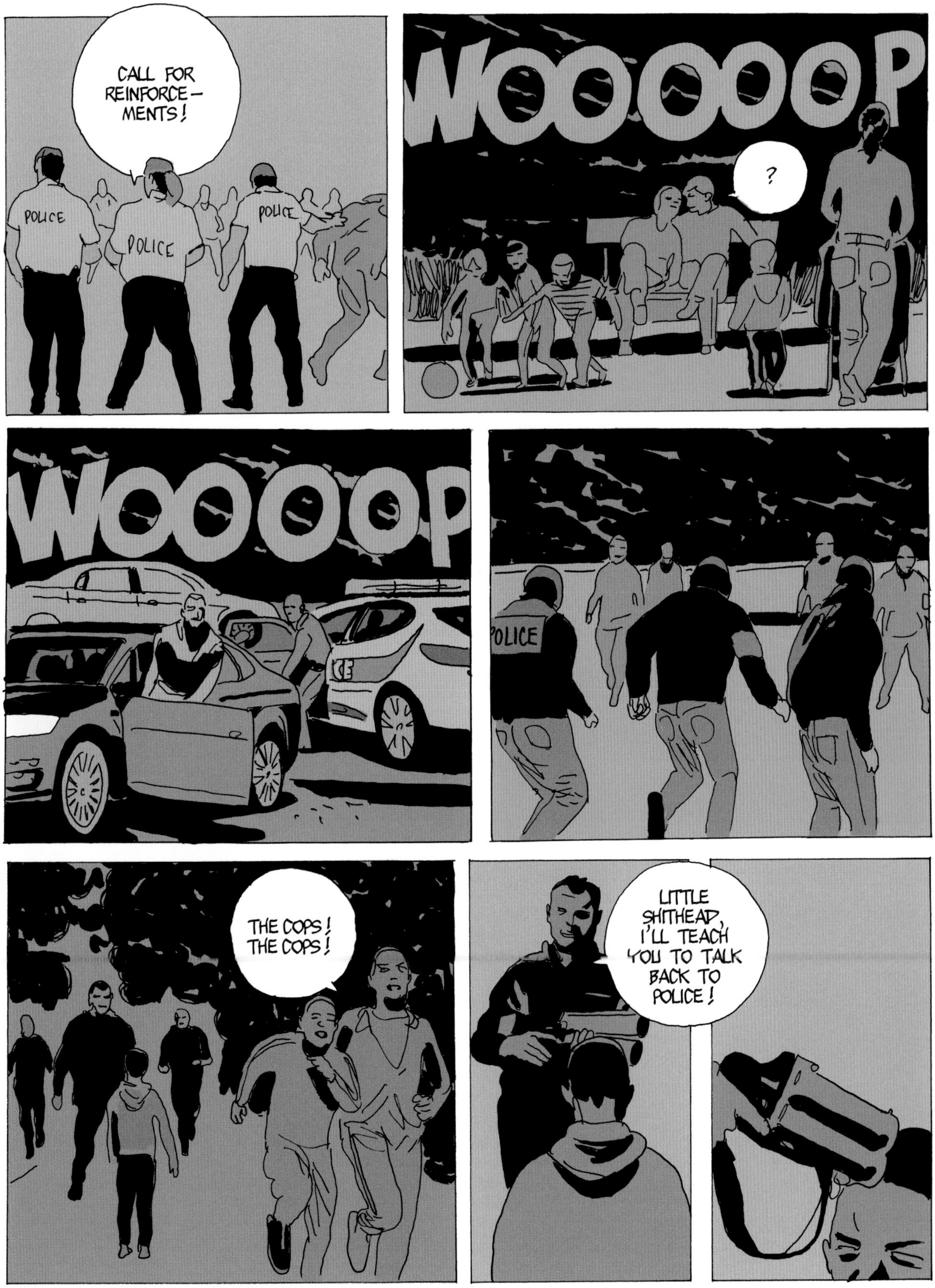
CALL FOR REINFORCE-MENTS!
POLICE
POLICE
POLICE
WOOOOOP
?
WOOOOP
POLICE
THE COPS! THE COPS!
LITTLE SHITHEAD, I'LL TEACH YOU TO TALK BACK TO POLICE!

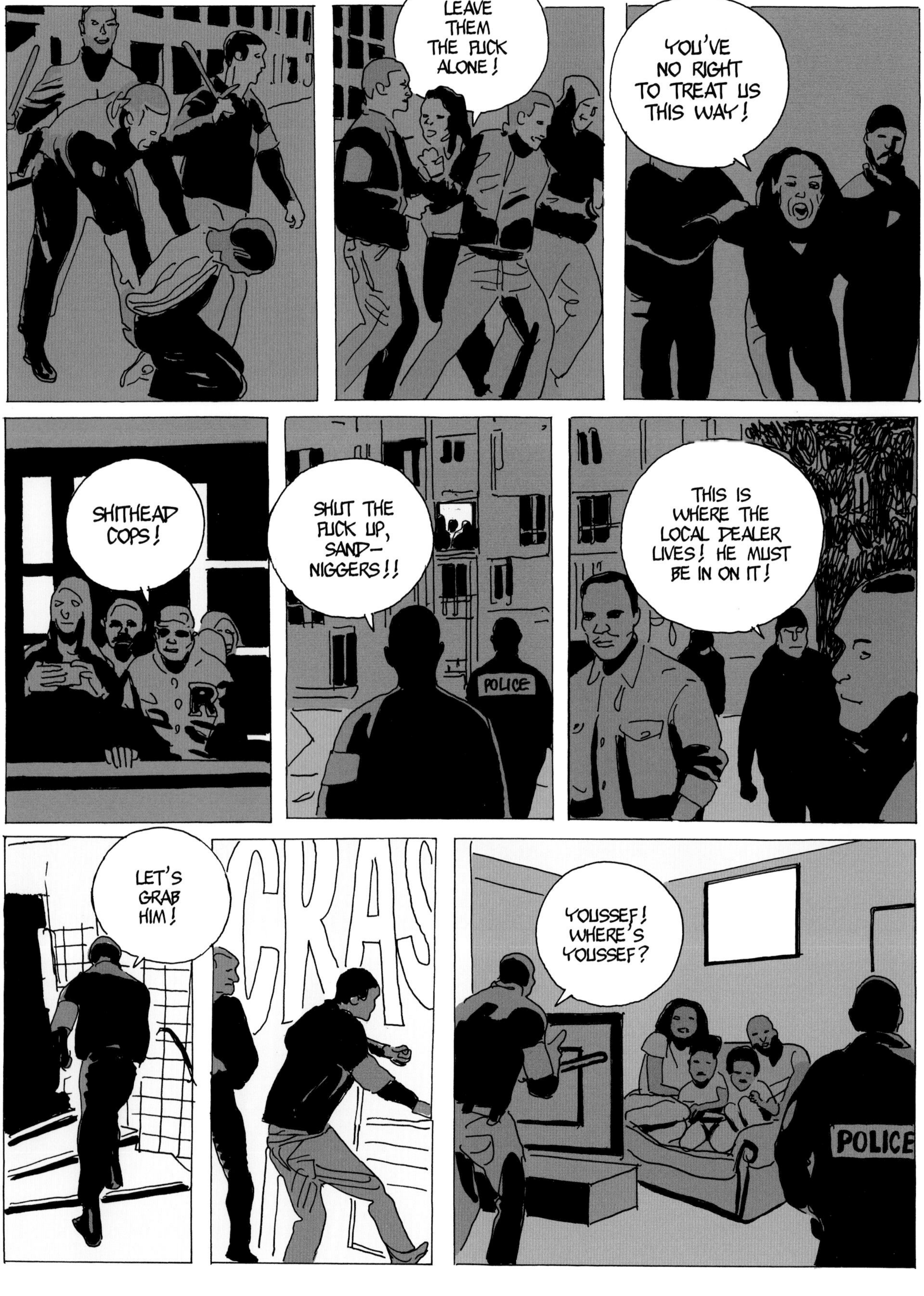
LEAVE THEM THE FUCK ALONE!
YOU'VE NO RIGHT TO TREAT US THIS WAY!
SHITHEAD COPS!
SHUT THE FUCK UP, SAND-NIGGERS!!
THIS IS WHERE THE LOCAL DEALER LIVES! HE MUST BE IN ON IT!
LET'S GRAB HIM!
CRAS
YOUSSEF! WHERE'S YOUSSEF?
POLICE

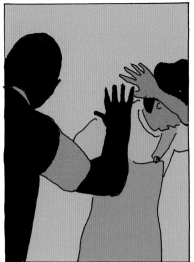

??!

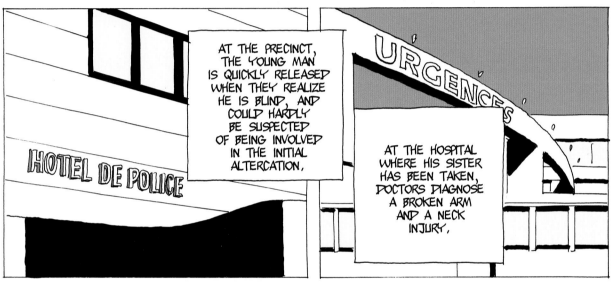

HOTEL DE POLICE

AT THE PRECINCT, THE YOUNG MAN IS QUICKLY RELEASED WHEN THEY REALIZE HE IS BLIND, AND COULD HARDLY BE SUSPECTED OF BEING INVOLVED IN THE INITIAL ALTERCATION,

URGENCES

AT THE HOSPITAL WHERE HIS SISTER HAS BEEN TAKEN, DOCTORS DIAGNOSE A BROKEN ARM AND A NECK INJURY,

THE FOUR YOUTHS INJURED DURING THE INTERVENTION ARE ARRESTED AND CHARGED WITH INSULT AND OBSTRUCTION,,, SO AS TO COUNTER ANY COMPLAINT THEY MIGHT MAKE AGAINST THE OFFICERS,

THE OTHER SIX ARE RELEASED WITHOUT THEIR SHOES, IN THE MIDDLE OF THE NIGHT, AND HAVE TO WALK THE TWO MILES BACK HOME,

Code of Ethics of the National Police. Article 1. The National Police works nationwide to guarantee the right to freedom and to defend the institutions of the French Republic, to maintain peace and public order, and to protect persons and property.

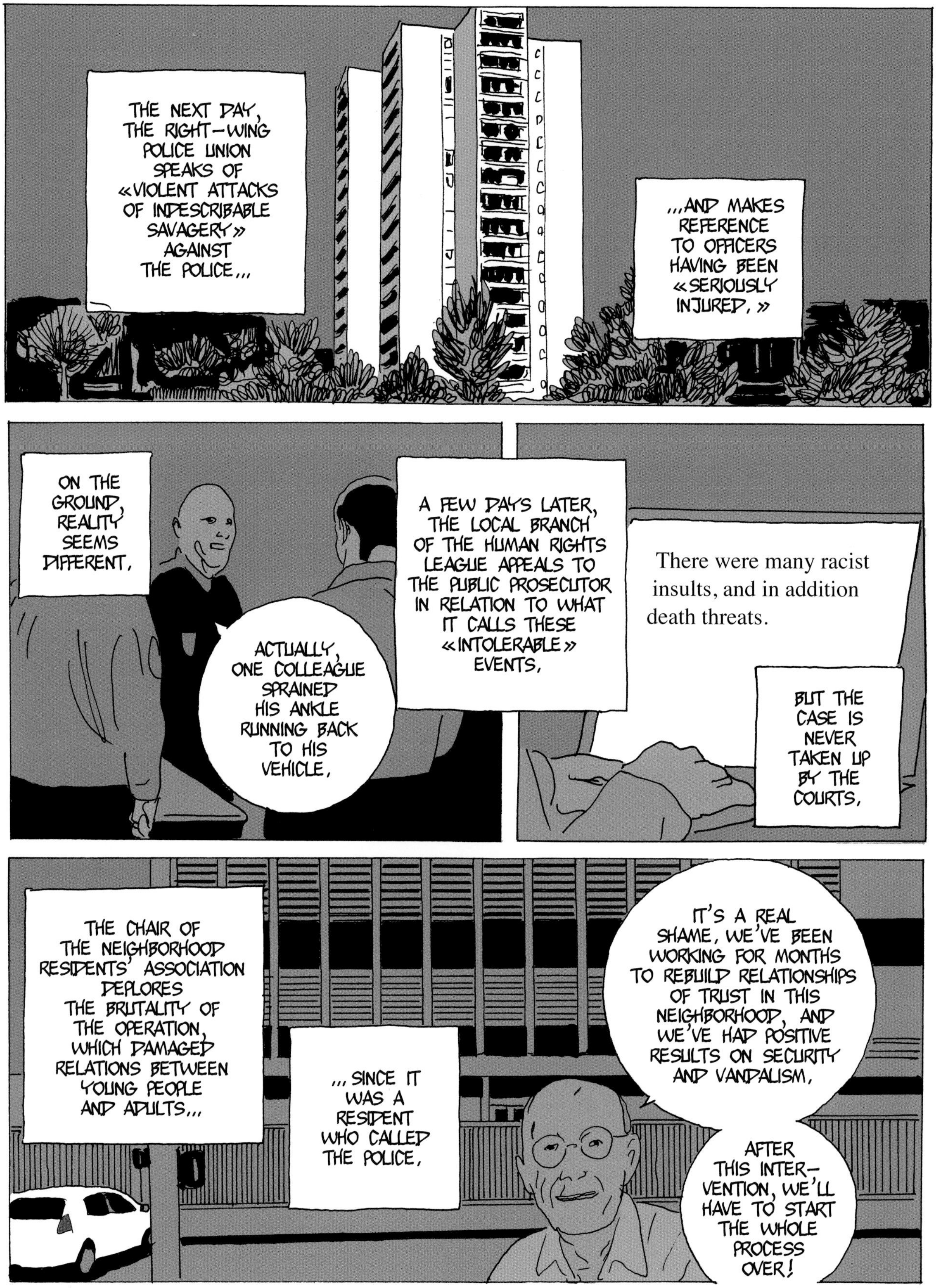

THE NEXT DAY, THE RIGHT-WING POLICE UNION SPEAKS OF «VIOLENT ATTACKS OF INDESCRIBABLE SAVAGERY» AGAINST THE POLICE...
...AND MAKES REFERENCE TO OFFICERS HAVING BEEN «SERIOUSLY INJURED.»
ON THE GROUND, REALITY SEEMS DIFFERENT.
ACTUALLY, ONE COLLEAGUE SPRAINED HIS ANKLE RUNNING BACK TO HIS VEHICLE.
A FEW DAYS LATER, THE LOCAL BRANCH OF THE HUMAN RIGHTS LEAGUE APPEALS TO THE PUBLIC PROSECUTOR IN RELATION TO WHAT IT CALLS THESE «INTOLERABLE» EVENTS.
There were many racist insults, and in addition death threats.
BUT THE CASE IS NEVER TAKEN UP BY THE COURTS.
THE CHAIR OF THE NEIGHBORHOOD RESIDENTS' ASSOCIATION DEPLORES THE BRUTALITY OF THE OPERATION, WHICH DAMAGED RELATIONS BETWEEN YOUNG PEOPLE AND ADULTS...
...SINCE IT WAS A RESIDENT WHO CALLED THE POLICE.
IT'S A REAL SHAME, WE'VE BEEN WORKING FOR MONTHS TO REBUILD RELATIONSHIPS OF TRUST IN THIS NEIGHBORHOOD, AND WE'VE HAD POSITIVE RESULTS ON SECURITY AND VANDALISM.
AFTER THIS INTER-VENTION, WE'LL HAVE TO START THE WHOLE PROCESS OVER!

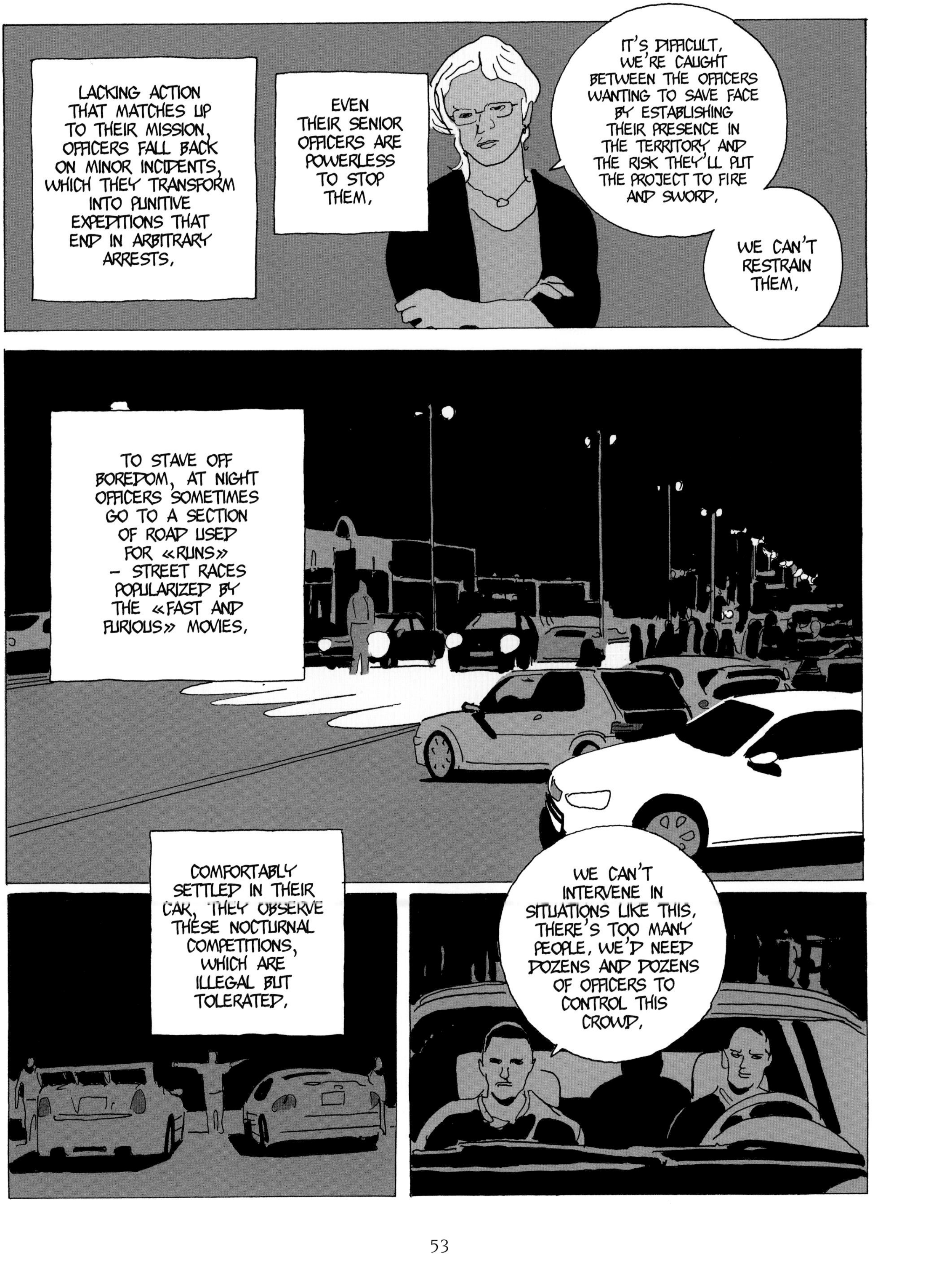

LACKING ACTION THAT MATCHES UP TO THEIR MISSION, OFFICERS FALL BACK ON MINOR INCIDENTS, WHICH THEY TRANSFORM INTO PUNITIVE EXPEDITIONS THAT END IN ARBITRARY ARRESTS.
EVEN THEIR SENIOR OFFICERS ARE POWERLESS TO STOP THEM.
IT'S DIFFICULT. WE'RE CAUGHT BETWEEN THE OFFICERS WANTING TO SAVE FACE BY ESTABLISHING THEIR PRESENCE IN THE TERRITORY AND THE RISK THEY'LL PUT THE PROJECT TO FIRE AND SWORD.
WE CAN'T RESTRAIN THEM.
TO STAVE OFF BOREDOM, AT NIGHT OFFICERS SOMETIMES GO TO A SECTION OF ROAD USED FOR «RUNS» – STREET RACES POPULARIZED BY THE «FAST AND FURIOUS» MOVIES.
COMFORTABLY SETTLED IN THEIR CAR, THEY OBSERVE THESE NOCTURNAL COMPETITIONS, WHICH ARE ILLEGAL BUT TOLERATED.
WE CAN'T INTERVENE IN SITUATIONS LIKE THIS. THERE'S TOO MANY PEOPLE. WE'D NEED DOZENS AND DOZENS OF OFFICERS TO CONTROL THIS CROWD.

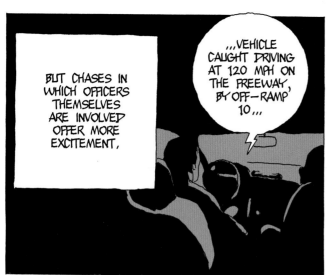

BUT CHASES IN WHICH OFFICERS THEMSELVES ARE INVOLVED OFFER MORE EXCITEMENT,

...VEHICLE CAUGHT DRIVING AT 120 MPH ON THE FREEWAY, BY OFF-RAMP 10,...

THEY ALMOST NEVER RESULT IN CATCHING UP WITH THE DRIVERS GUILTY OF TRAFFIC VIOLATIONS OR OTHER OFFENSES,

BUT THEY ALLOW OFFICERS TO FEEL THEIR JOB IS SOMETHING LIKE WHAT THEY IMAGINED WHEN THEY JOINED,

HOWEVER, THE CHASES ARE FORBIDDEN BY THEIR SUPERIORS, WHO FEAR THE RISKS TO RESIDENTS, OFFICERS,,, AND VEHICLES,

WHILE THERE ARE NO STATISTICS ON THE NUMBER OF PEOPLE KILLED IN ACCIDENTS CAUSED BY POLICE VEHICLES, IT IS KNOWN THAT TWO-THIRDS OF THE OFFICERS WHO DIE IN THE COURSE OF THEIR WORK ARE VICTIMS OF MOTOR VEHICLE ACCIDENTS,

ASIDE FROM THESE RARE MOMENTS OF INTENSITY IN THEIR WORKING LIFE, LAW ENFORCEMENT OFFICERS USUALLY HAVE TO MAKE DO WITH A FEW IDENTITY CHECKS TO LIVEN UP THEIR UNEVENTFUL PATROLS AND REACH THEIR QUOTAS,

BUT THESE CHECKS ARE CLEARLY TARGETED,

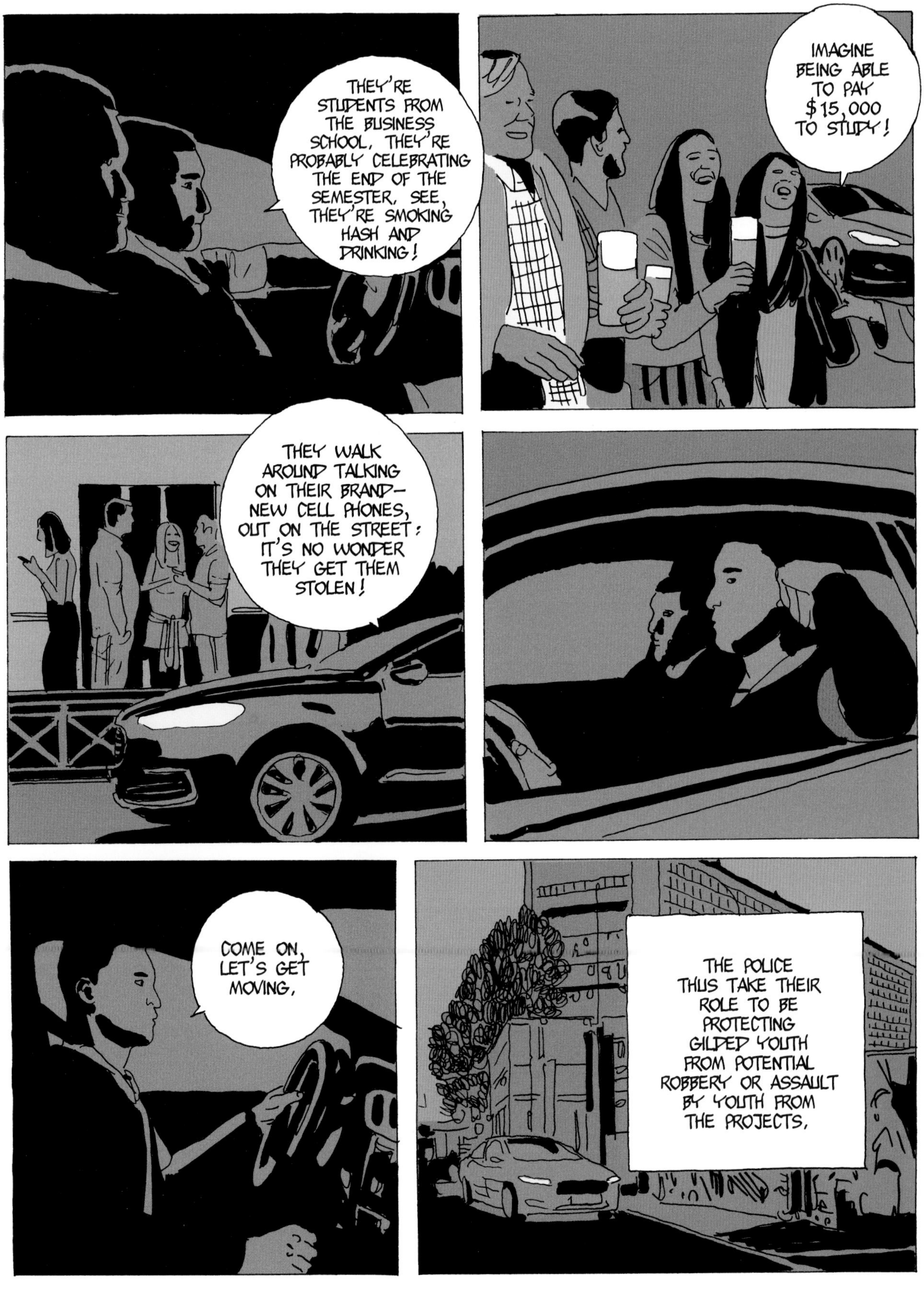
THEY'RE STUDENTS FROM THE BUSINESS SCHOOL, THEY'RE PROBABLY CELEBRATING THE END OF THE SEMESTER, SEE, THEY'RE SMOKING HASH AND DRINKING!
IMAGINE BEING ABLE TO PAY $15,000 TO STUDY!
THEY WALK AROUND TALKING ON THEIR BRAND-NEW CELL PHONES, OUT ON THE STREET: IT'S NO WONDER THEY GET THEM STOLEN!
COME ON, LET'S GET MOVING.
THE POLICE THUS TAKE THEIR ROLE TO BE PROTECTING GILDED YOUTH FROM POTENTIAL ROBBERY OR ASSAULT BY YOUTH FROM THE PROJECTS.

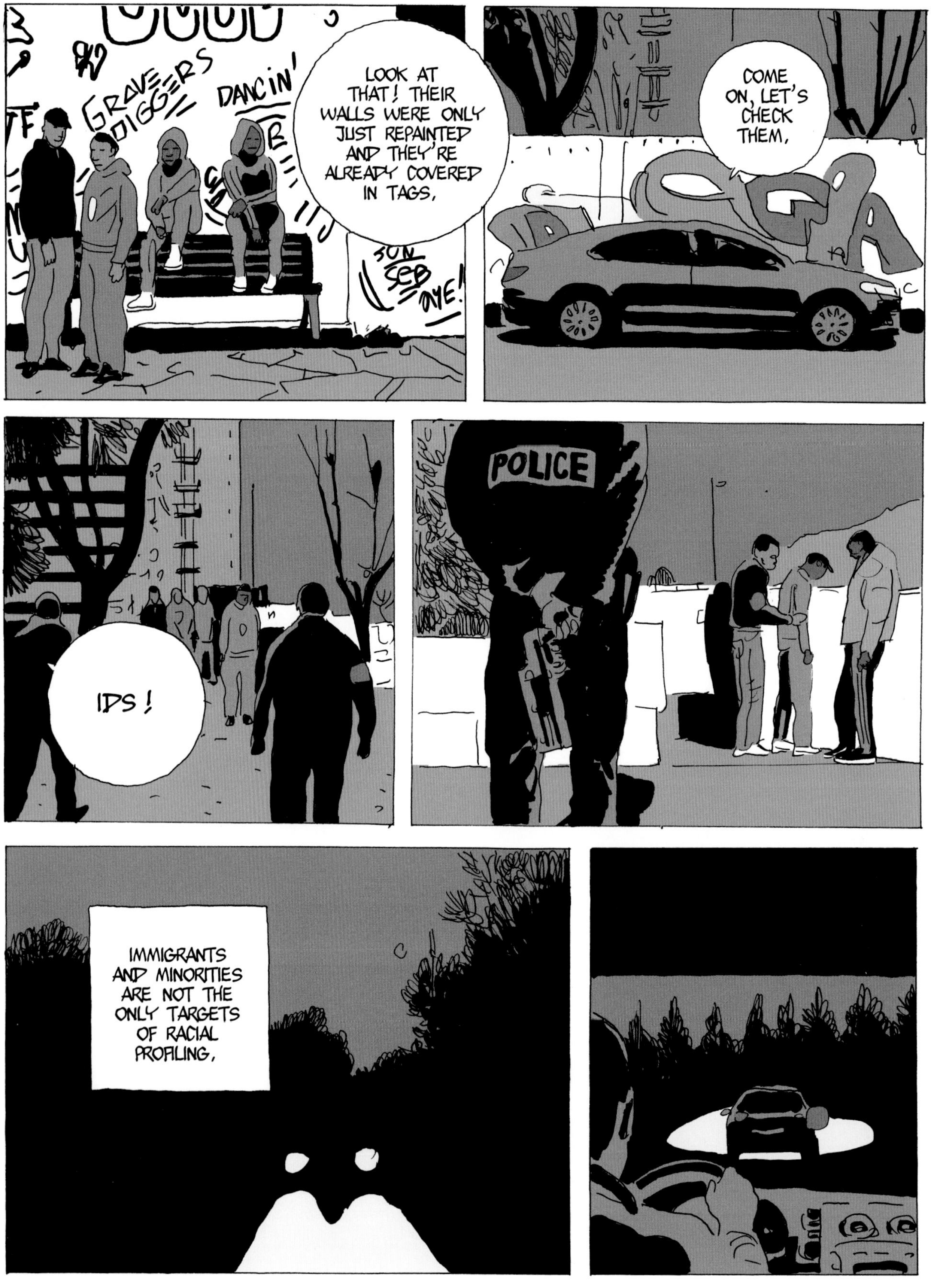
GRAVE DIGGERS
DANCIN'
LOOK AT THAT! THEIR WALLS WERE ONLY JUST REPAINTED AND THEY'RE ALREADY COVERED IN TAGS.
COME ON, LET'S CHECK THEM.
IDS!
POLICE
IMMIGRANTS AND MINORITIES ARE NOT THE ONLY TARGETS OF RACIAL PROFILING.

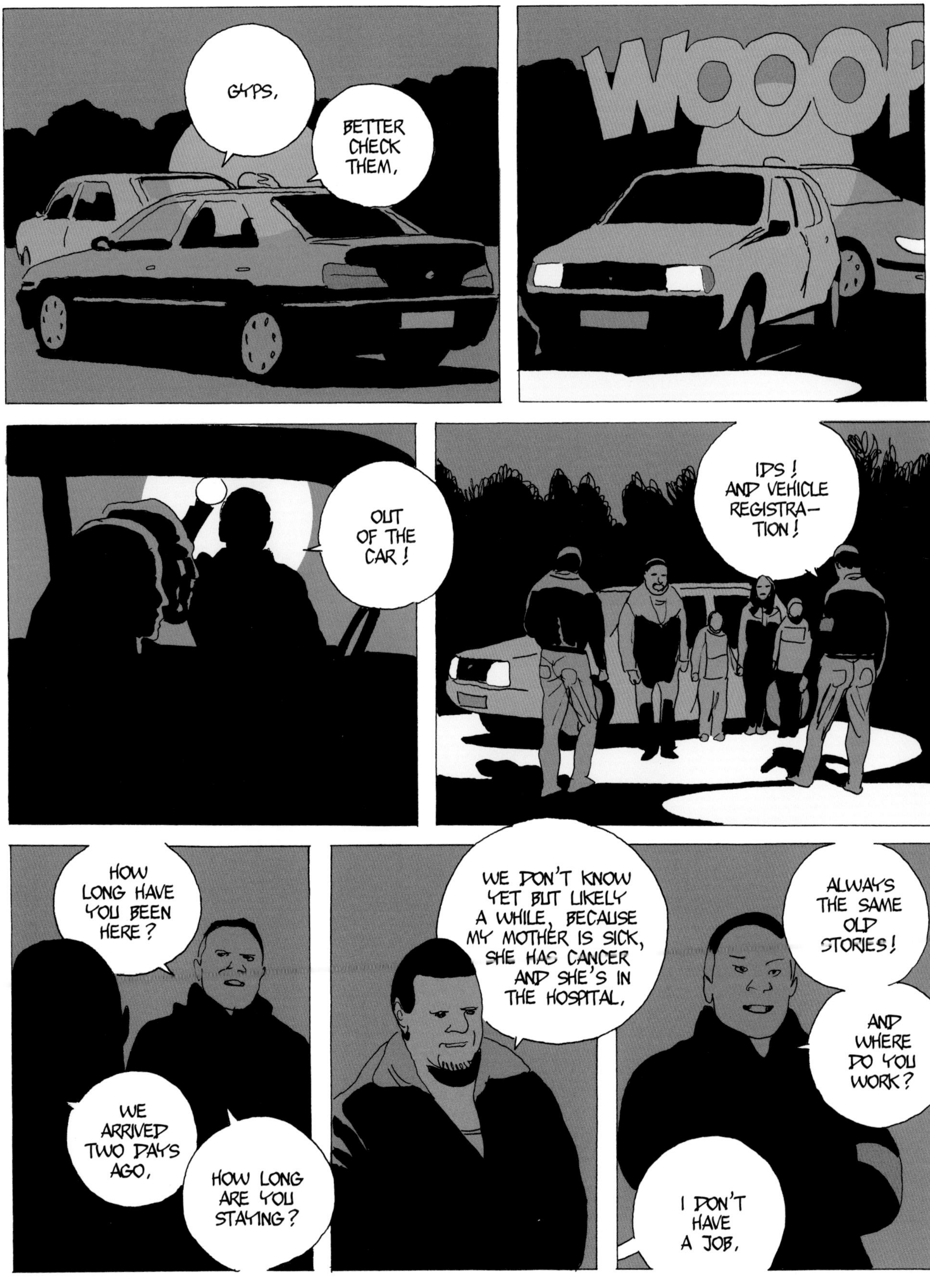
GYPS,
BETTER CHECK THEM,
WOOOP
OUT OF THE CAR!
IDS! AND VEHICLE REGISTRATION!
HOW LONG HAVE YOU BEEN HERE?
WE ARRIVED TWO DAYS AGO,
HOW LONG ARE YOU STAYING?
WE DON'T KNOW YET BUT LIKELY A WHILE, BECAUSE MY MOTHER IS SICK, SHE HAS CANCER AND SHE'S IN THE HOSPITAL,
ALWAYS THE SAME OLD STORIES!
AND WHERE DO YOU WORK?
I DON'T HAVE A JOB,

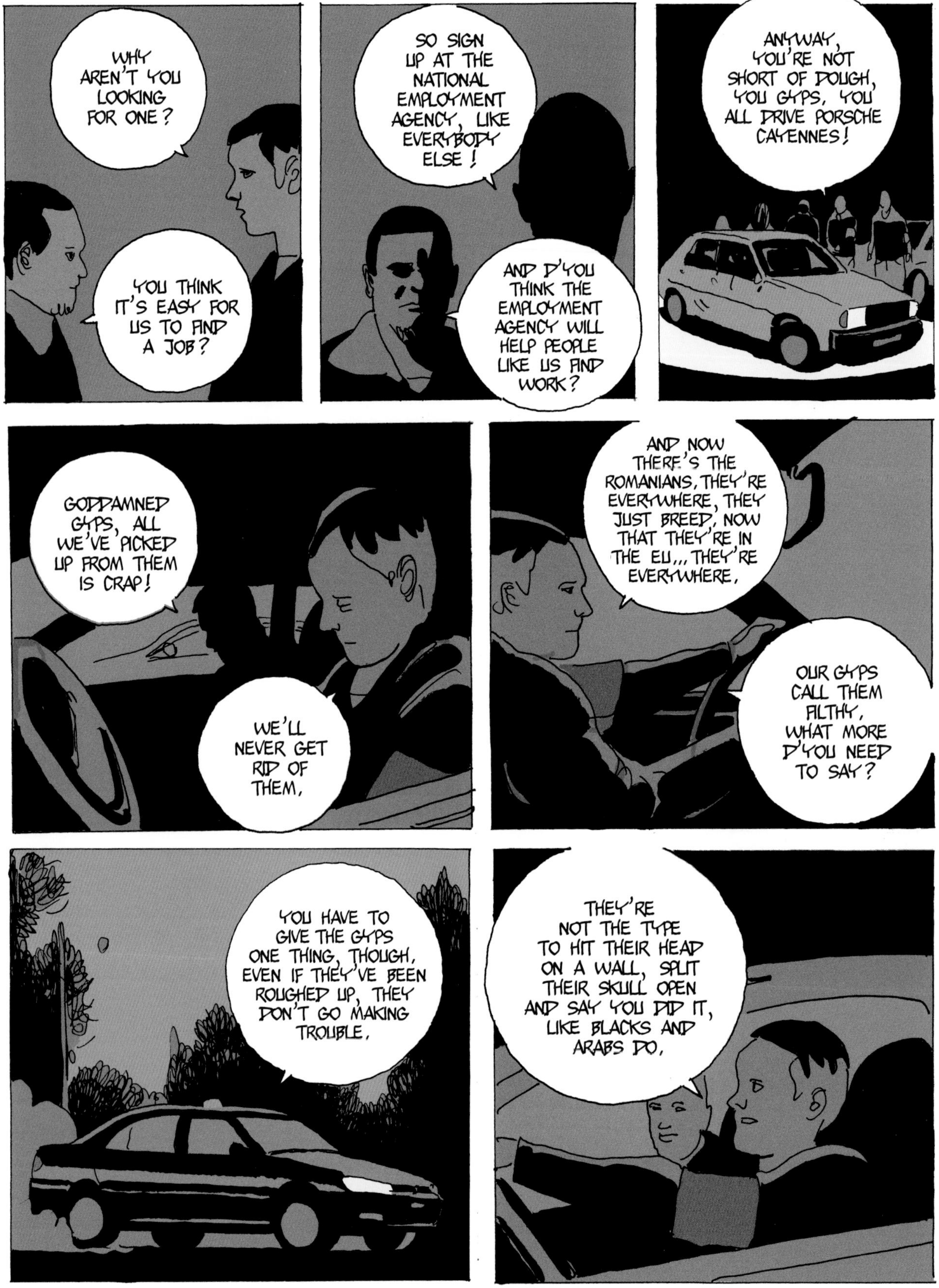
WHY AREN'T YOU LOOKING FOR ONE?
YOU THINK IT'S EASY FOR US TO FIND A JOB?
SO SIGN UP AT THE NATIONAL EMPLOYMENT AGENCY, LIKE EVERYBODY ELSE!
AND D'YOU THINK THE EMPLOYMENT AGENCY WILL HELP PEOPLE LIKE US FIND WORK?
ANYWAY, YOU'RE NOT SHORT OF DOUGH, YOU GYPS, YOU ALL DRIVE PORSCHE CAYENNES!
GODDAMNED GYPS, ALL WE'VE PICKED UP FROM THEM IS CRAP!
WE'LL NEVER GET RID OF THEM.
AND NOW THERE'S THE ROMANIANS, THEY'RE EVERYWHERE, THEY JUST BREED, NOW THAT THEY'RE IN THE EU... THEY'RE EVERYWHERE.
OUR GYPS CALL THEM FILTHY, WHAT MORE D'YOU NEED TO SAY?
YOU HAVE TO GIVE THE GYPS ONE THING, THOUGH, EVEN IF THEY'VE BEEN ROUGHED UP, THEY DON'T GO MAKING TROUBLE.
THEY'RE NOT THE TYPE TO HIT THEIR HEAD ON A WALL, SPLIT THEIR SKULL OPEN AND SAY YOU DID IT, LIKE BLACKS AND ARABS DO.

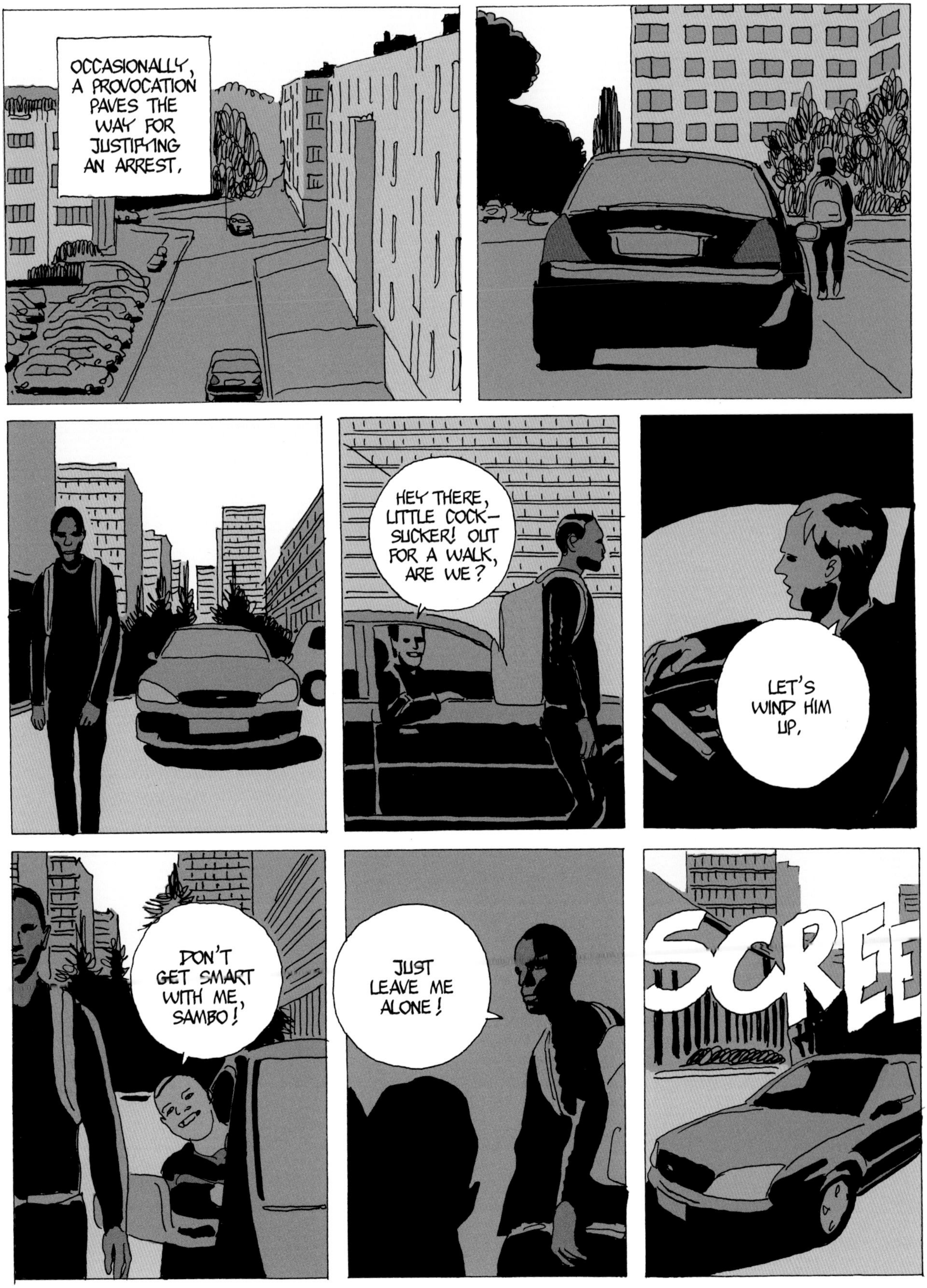

OCCASIONALLY, A PROVOCATION PAVES THE WAY FOR JUSTIFYING AN ARREST.
HEY THERE, LITTLE COCK-SUCKER! OUT FOR A WALK, ARE WE?
LET'S WIND HIM UP.
DON'T GET SMART WITH ME, SAMBO!
JUST LEAVE ME ALONE!
SCREE

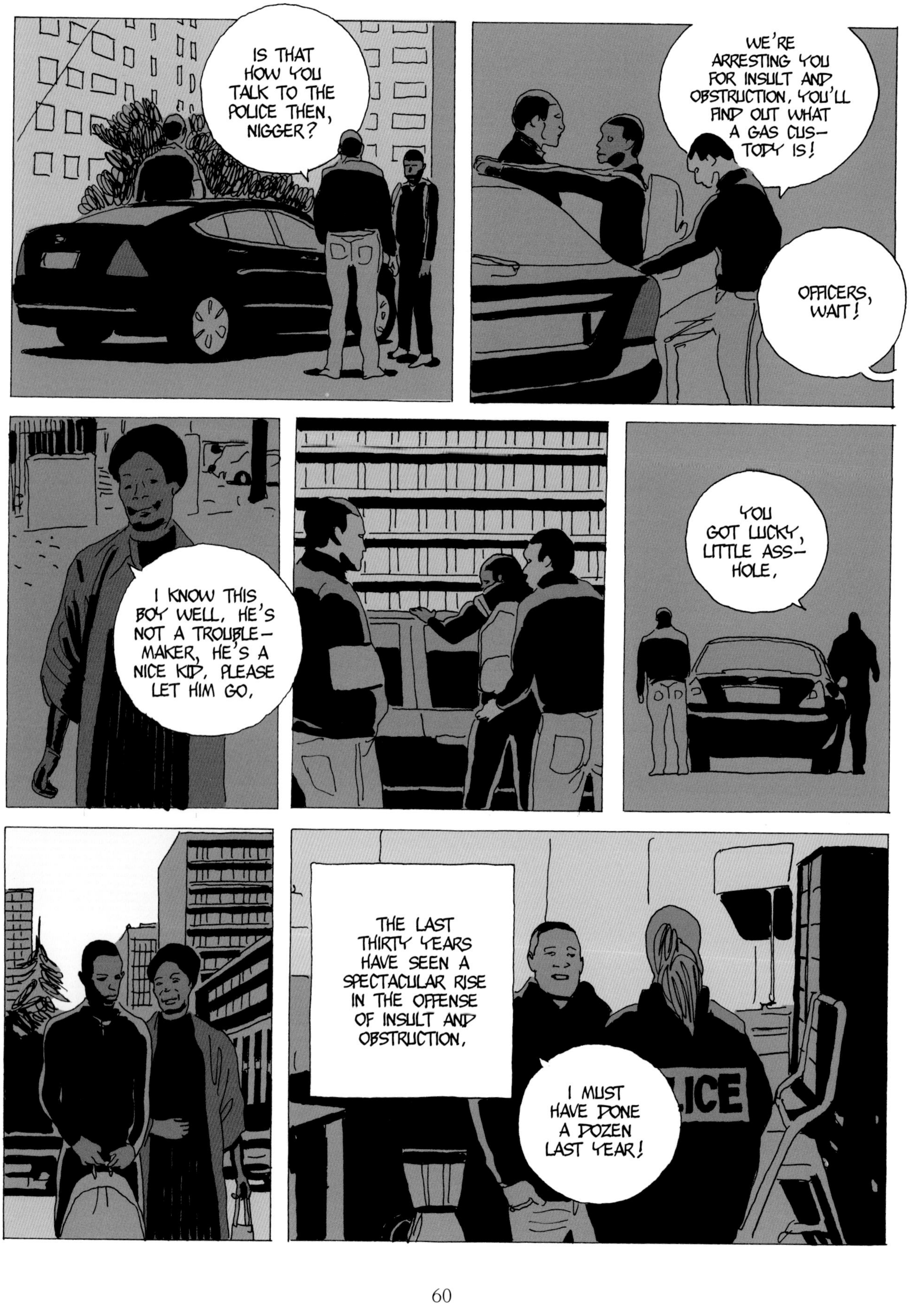

IS THAT HOW YOU TALK TO THE POLICE THEN, NIGGER?
WE'RE ARRESTING YOU FOR INSULT AND OBSTRUCTION. YOU'LL FIND OUT WHAT A GAS CUS-TODY IS!
OFFICERS, WAIT!
I KNOW THIS BOY WELL. HE'S NOT A TROUBLE-MAKER. HE'S A NICE KID. PLEASE LET HIM GO.
YOU GOT LUCKY, LITTLE ASS-HOLE.
THE LAST THIRTY YEARS HAVE SEEN A SPECTACULAR RISE IN THE OFFENSE OF INSULT AND OBSTRUCTION.
I MUST HAVE DONE A DOZEN LAST YEAR!
LICE

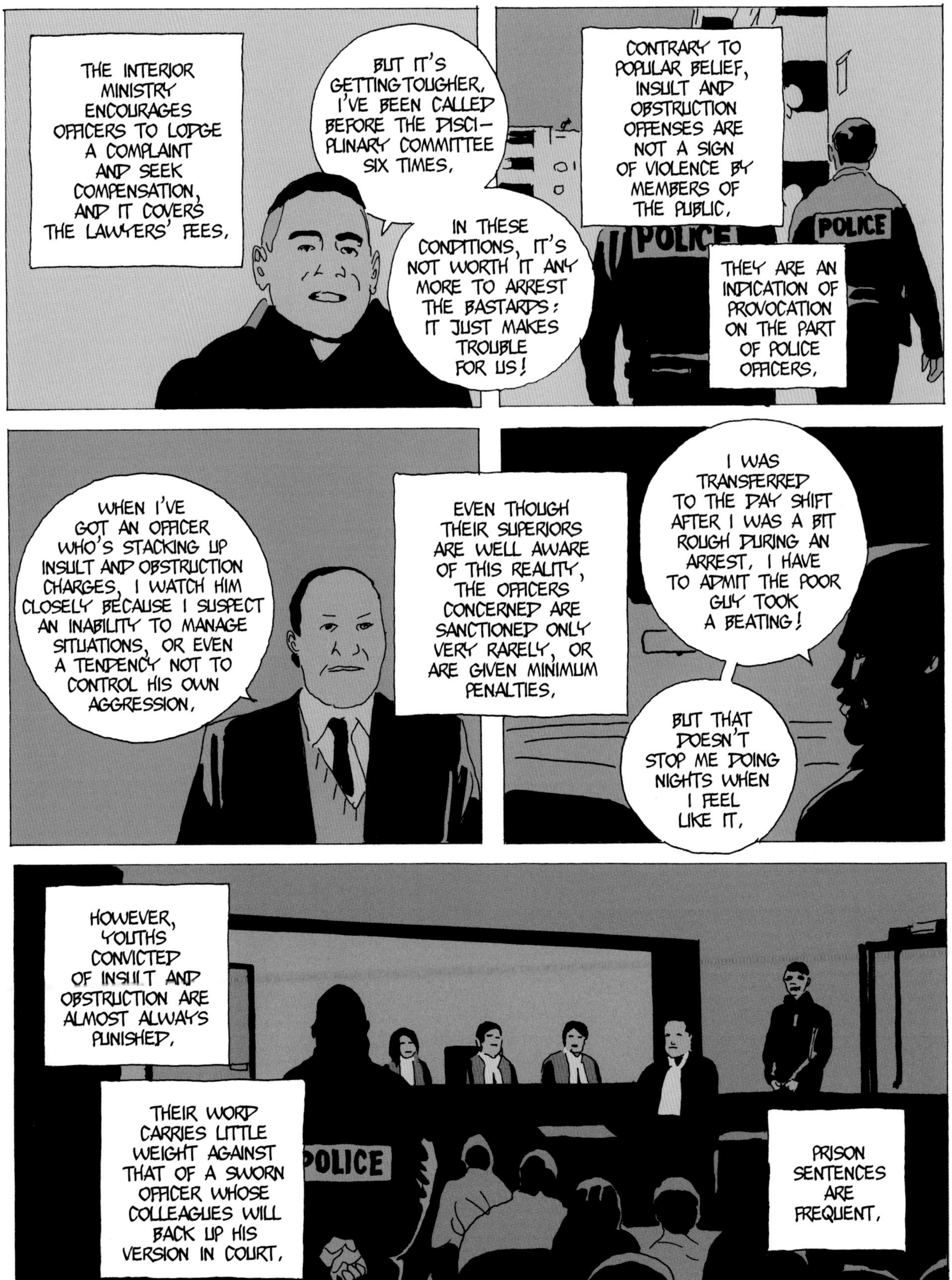
THE INTERIOR MINISTRY ENCOURAGES OFFICERS TO LODGE A COMPLAINT AND SEEK COMPENSATION, AND IT COVERS THE LAWYERS' FEES.
BUT IT'S GETTING TOUGHER, I'VE BEEN CALLED BEFORE THE DISCI-PLINARY COMMITTEE SIX TIMES.
IN THESE CONDITIONS, IT'S NOT WORTH IT ANY MORE TO ARREST THE BASTARDS: IT JUST MAKES TROUBLE FOR US!
CONTRARY TO POPULAR BELIEF, INSULT AND OBSTRUCTION OFFENSES ARE NOT A SIGN OF VIOLENCE BY MEMBERS OF THE PUBLIC.
POLICE
POLICE
THEY ARE AN INDICATION OF PROVOCATION ON THE PART OF POLICE OFFICERS.
WHEN I'VE GOT AN OFFICER WHO'S STACKING UP INSULT AND OBSTRUCTION CHARGES, I WATCH HIM CLOSELY BECAUSE I SUSPECT AN INABILITY TO MANAGE SITUATIONS, OR EVEN A TENDENCY NOT TO CONTROL HIS OWN AGGRESSION.
EVEN THOUGH THEIR SUPERIORS ARE WELL AWARE OF THIS REALITY, THE OFFICERS CONCERNED ARE SANCTIONED ONLY VERY RARELY, OR ARE GIVEN MINIMUM PENALTIES.
I WAS TRANSFERRED TO THE DAY SHIFT AFTER I WAS A BIT ROUGH DURING AN ARREST, I HAVE TO ADMIT THE POOR GUY TOOK A BEATING!
BUT THAT DOESN'T STOP ME DOING NIGHTS WHEN I FEEL LIKE IT.
HOWEVER, YOUTHS CONVICTED OF INSULT AND OBSTRUCTION ARE ALMOST ALWAYS PUNISHED.
THEIR WORD CARRIES LITTLE WEIGHT AGAINST THAT OF A SWORN OFFICER WHOSE COLLEAGUES WILL BACK UP HIS VERSION IN COURT.
POLICE
PRISON SENTENCES ARE FREQUENT.

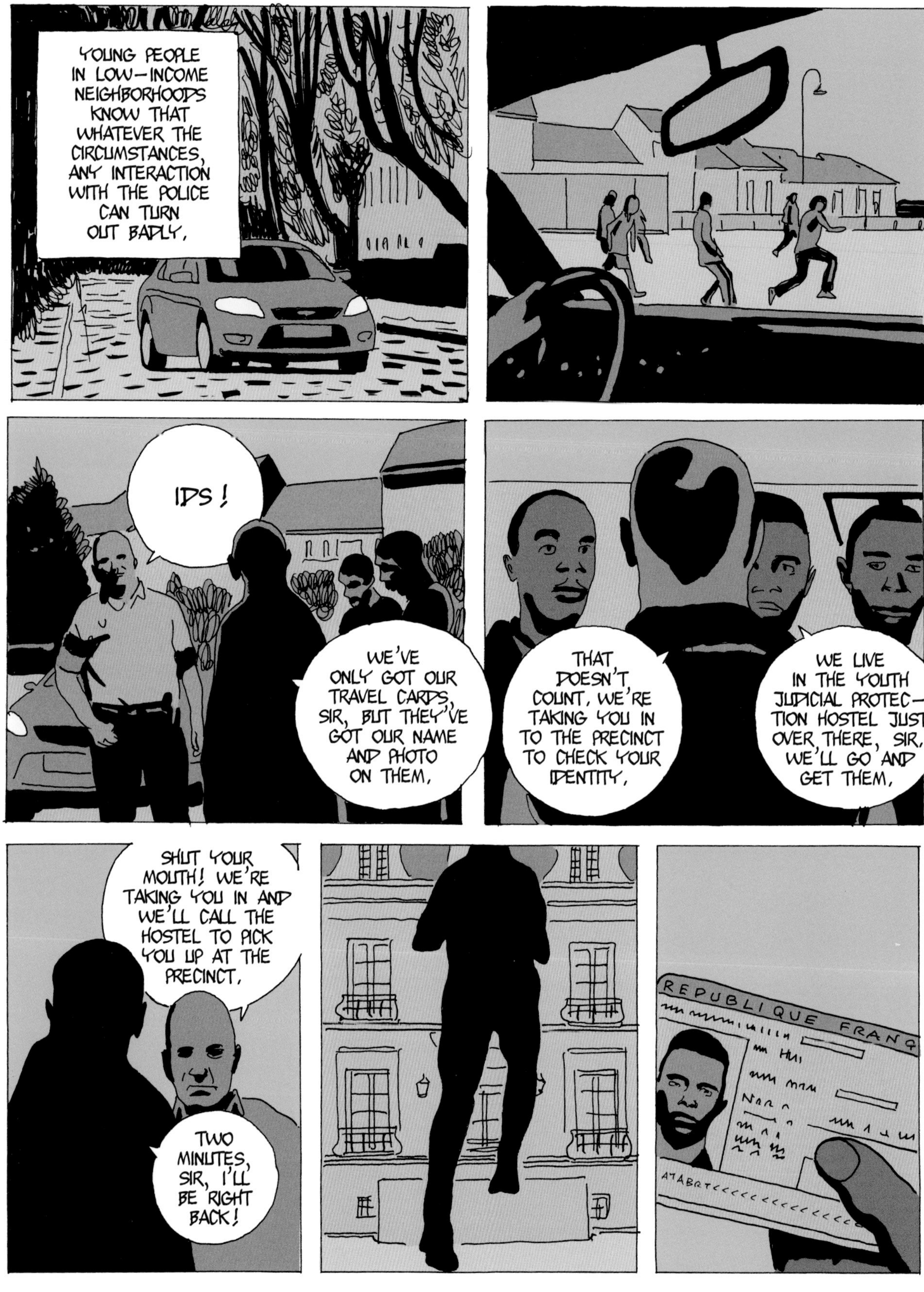
YOUNG PEOPLE IN LOW-INCOME NEIGHBORHOODS KNOW THAT WHATEVER THE CIRCUMSTANCES, ANY INTERACTION WITH THE POLICE CAN TURN OUT BADLY.
IDS!
WE'VE ONLY GOT OUR TRAVEL CARDS, SIR, BUT THEY'VE GOT OUR NAME AND PHOTO ON THEM.
THAT DOESN'T COUNT. WE'RE TAKING YOU IN TO THE PRECINCT TO CHECK YOUR IDENTITY.
WE LIVE IN THE YOUTH JUDICIAL PROTECTION HOSTEL JUST OVER THERE, SIR. WE'LL GO AND GET THEM.
SHUT YOUR MOUTH! WE'RE TAKING YOU IN AND WE'LL CALL THE HOSTEL TO PICK YOU UP AT THE PRECINCT.
TWO MINUTES, SIR, I'LL BE RIGHT BACK!
REPUBLIQUE FRANÇ

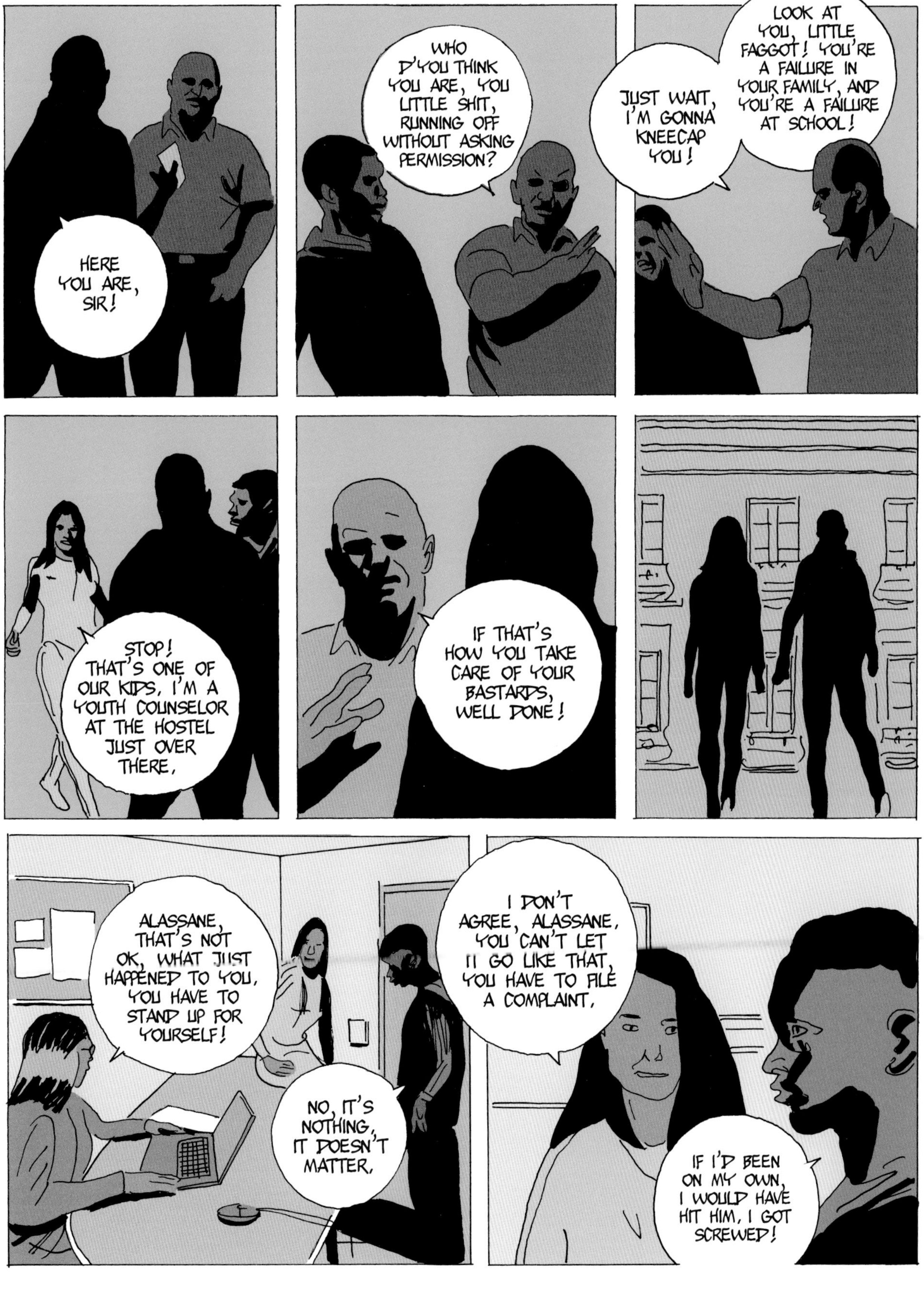
HERE YOU ARE, SIR!
WHO D'YOU THINK YOU ARE, YOU LITTLE SHIT, RUNNING OFF WITHOUT ASKING PERMISSION?
LOOK AT YOU, LITTLE FAGGOT! YOU'RE A FAILURE IN YOUR FAMILY, AND YOU'RE A FAILURE AT SCHOOL!
JUST WAIT, I'M GONNA KNEECAP YOU!
STOP! THAT'S ONE OF OUR KIDS, I'M A YOUTH COUNSELOR AT THE HOSTEL JUST OVER THERE.
IF THAT'S HOW YOU TAKE CARE OF YOUR BASTARDS, WELL DONE!
ALASSANE, THAT'S NOT OK, WHAT JUST HAPPENED TO YOU, YOU HAVE TO STAND UP FOR YOURSELF!
NO, IT'S NOTHING, IT DOESN'T MATTER.
I DON'T AGREE, ALASSANE, YOU CAN'T LET IT GO LIKE THAT, YOU HAVE TO FILE A COMPLAINT.
IF I'D BEEN ON MY OWN, I WOULD HAVE HIT HIM, I GOT SCREWED!

NO, YOU WERE RIGHT TO ACT THE WAY YOU DID, OTHERWISE YOU'D HAVE ENDED UP IN CUSTODY.

BUT IF YOU DON'T SAY ANYTHING ABOUT IT, NOTHING CAN CHANGE.

NO, IT DOESN'T MATTER, IT'S DONE, IT'S OVER.

YOU KNOW, A HUMAN RIGHTS COMMITTEE JUST BROUGHT OUT A REPORT ON POLICE ABUSES AND CALLED FOR THEM TO BE PUNISHED.

THERE'S NO POINT!

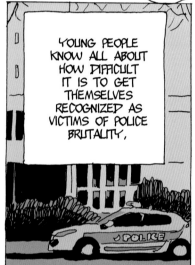

YOUNG PEOPLE KNOW ALL ABOUT HOW DIFFICULT IT IS TO GET THEMSELVES RECOGNIZED AS VICTIMS OF POLICE BRUTALITY.

WERE YOU INVOLVED IN STEALING A BICYCLE WITH TWO OTHER PERSONS AROUND 7:00 P.M. TODAY?

YOU SHOULDN'T TELL LIES! ANYWAY, YOUR ALIBI DOESN'T HOLD WATER.

NO, SIR!

HAVE YOU ANYTHING TO ADD?

YES, SIR, WHY DID THE OFFICER SLAP ME?

WHAT OFFICER?

THE BLACK OFFICER.

THERE WASN'T A BLACK OFFICER.

YES, THERE WAS, HE WAS ON A MOTORBIKE, MY FRIEND'LL CONFIRM IT.

I'M GOING TO READ YOU YOUR STATEMENT AND YOU'RE GOING TO SIGN IT.

64

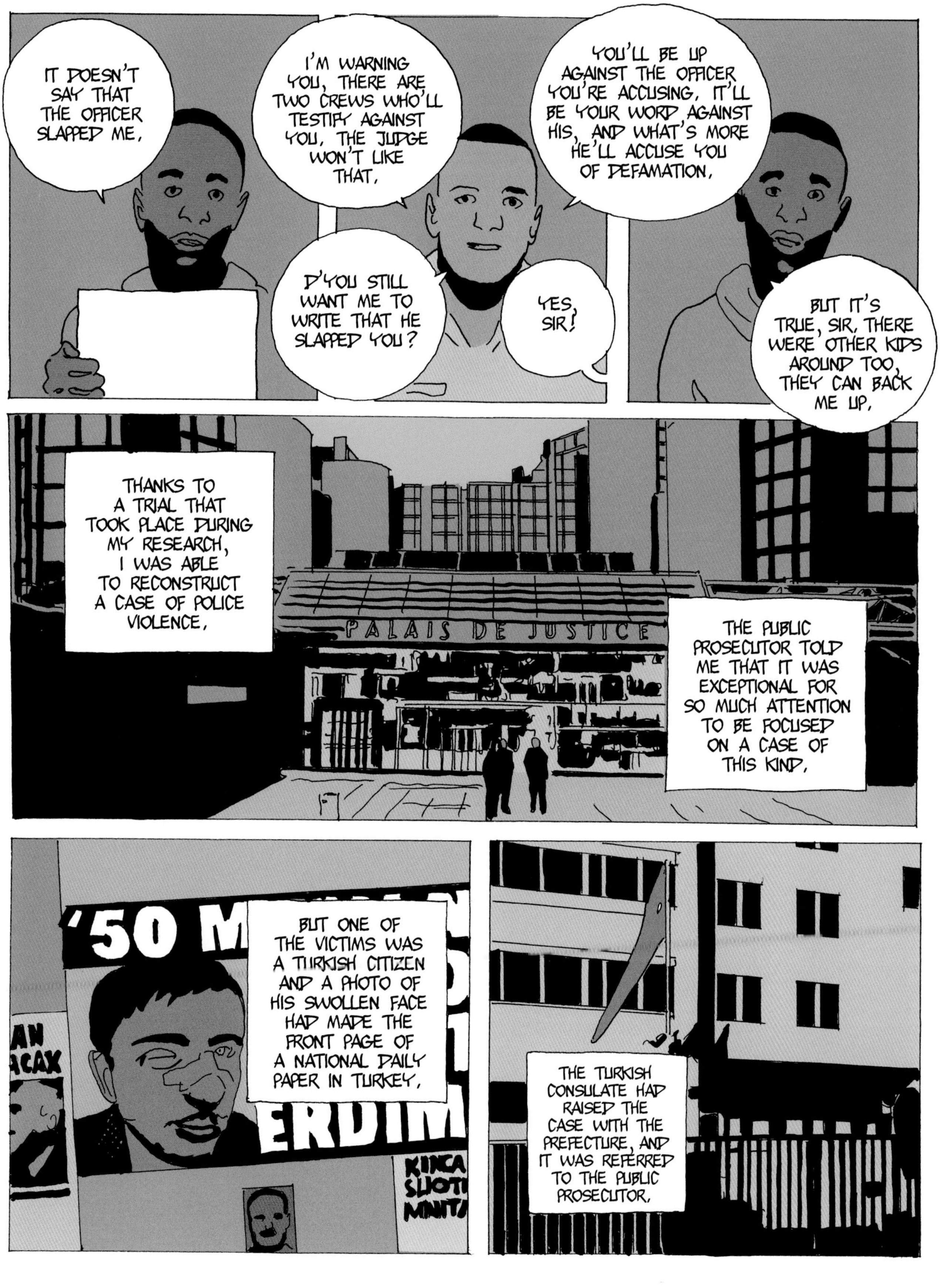

IT DOESN'T SAY THAT THE OFFICER SLAPPED ME.
I'M WARNING YOU, THERE ARE TWO CREWS WHO'LL TESTIFY AGAINST YOU. THE JUDGE WON'T LIKE THAT.
D'YOU STILL WANT ME TO WRITE THAT HE SLAPPED YOU?
YES, SIR!
YOU'LL BE UP AGAINST THE OFFICER YOU'RE ACCUSING. IT'LL BE YOUR WORD AGAINST HIS, AND WHAT'S MORE HE'LL ACCUSE YOU OF DEFAMATION.
BUT IT'S TRUE, SIR, THERE WERE OTHER KIDS AROUND TOO. THEY CAN BACK ME UP.
THANKS TO A TRIAL THAT TOOK PLACE DURING MY RESEARCH, I WAS ABLE TO RECONSTRUCT A CASE OF POLICE VIOLENCE.
PALAIS DE JUSTICE
THE PUBLIC PROSECUTOR TOLD ME THAT IT WAS EXCEPTIONAL FOR SO MUCH ATTENTION TO BE FOCUSED ON A CASE OF THIS KIND.
'50 M
ERDIM
BUT ONE OF THE VICTIMS WAS A TURKISH CITIZEN AND A PHOTO OF HIS SWOLLEN FACE HAD MADE THE FRONT PAGE OF A NATIONAL DAILY PAPER IN TURKEY.
THE TURKISH CONSULATE HAD RAISED THE CASE WITH THE PREFECTURE, AND IT WAS REFERRED TO THE PUBLIC PROSECUTOR.

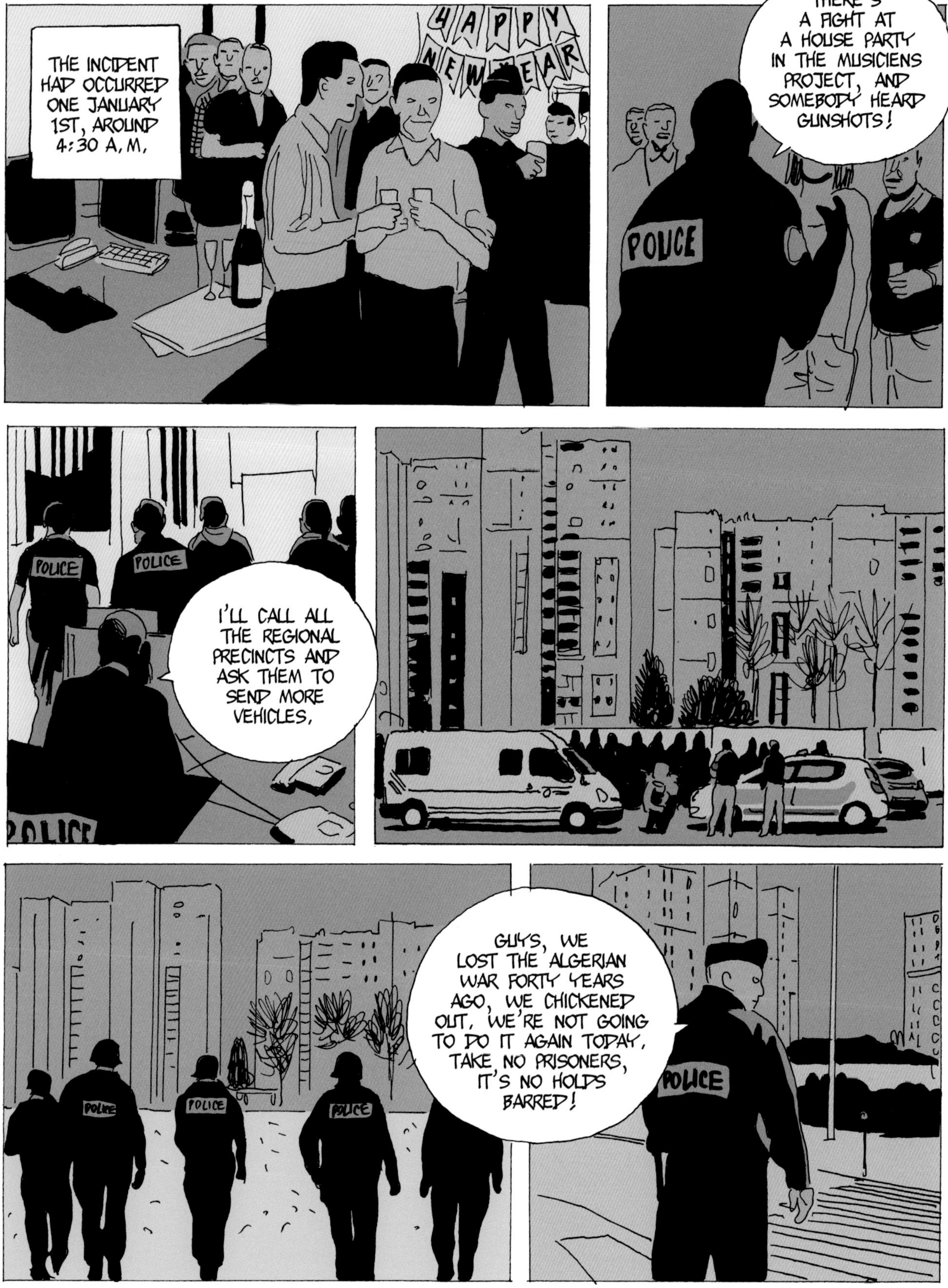

THE INCIDENT HAD OCCURRED ONE JANUARY 1ST, AROUND 4:30 A.M.
HAPPY NEW YEAR
THERE'S A FIGHT AT A HOUSE PARTY IN THE MUSICIENS PROJECT, AND SOMEBODY HEARD GUNSHOTS!
POLICE
I'LL CALL ALL THE REGIONAL PRECINCTS AND ASK THEM TO SEND MORE VEHICLES.
GUYS, WE LOST THE ALGERIAN WAR FORTY YEARS AGO, WE CHICKENED OUT, WE'RE NOT GOING TO DO IT AGAIN TODAY. TAKE NO PRISONERS. IT'S NO HOLDS BARRED!

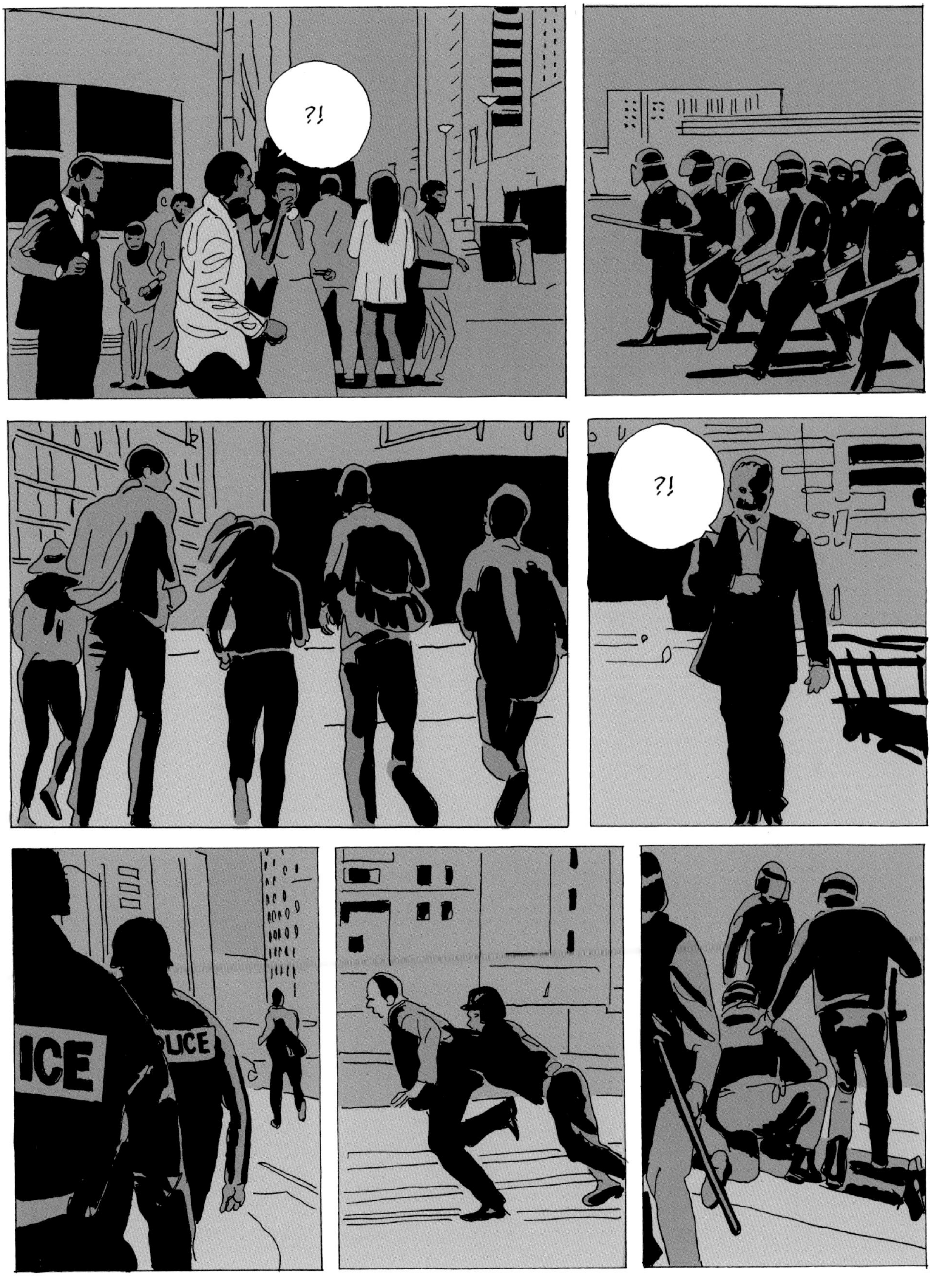
?!
?!
ICE
LICE

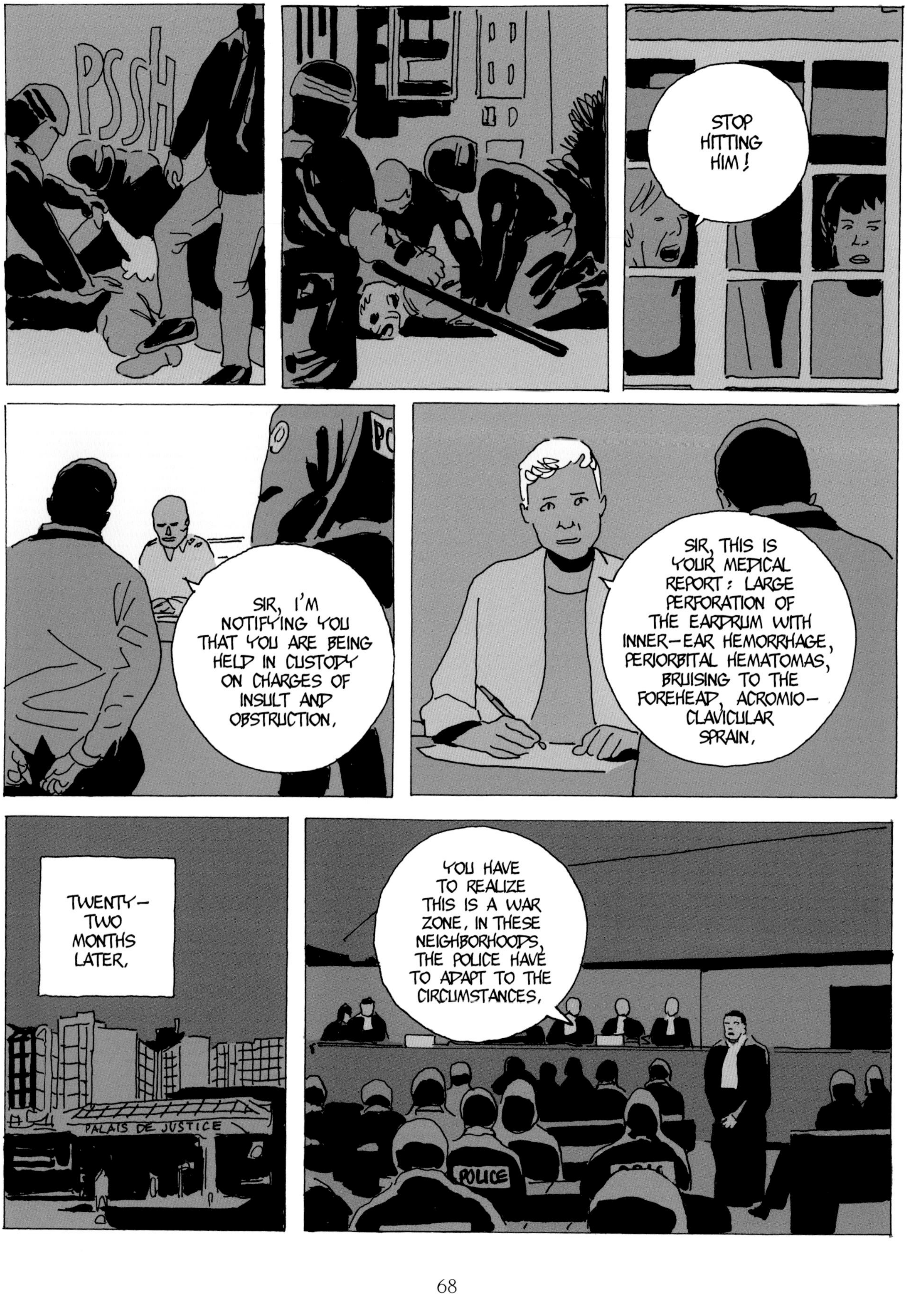
PSSH
STOP HITTING HIM!
SIR, I'M NOTIFYING YOU THAT YOU ARE BEING HELD IN CUSTODY ON CHARGES OF INSULT AND OBSTRUCTION.
SIR, THIS IS YOUR MEDICAL REPORT: LARGE PERFORATION OF THE EARDRUM WITH INNER-EAR HEMORRHAGE, PERIORBITAL HEMATOMAS, BRUISING TO THE FOREHEAD, ACROMIO-CLAVICULAR SPRAIN.
TWENTY-TWO MONTHS LATER.
PALAIS DE JUSTICE
YOU HAVE TO REALIZE THIS IS A WAR ZONE, IN THESE NEIGHBORHOODS. THE POLICE HAVE TO ADAPT TO THE CIRCUMSTANCES.
POLICE

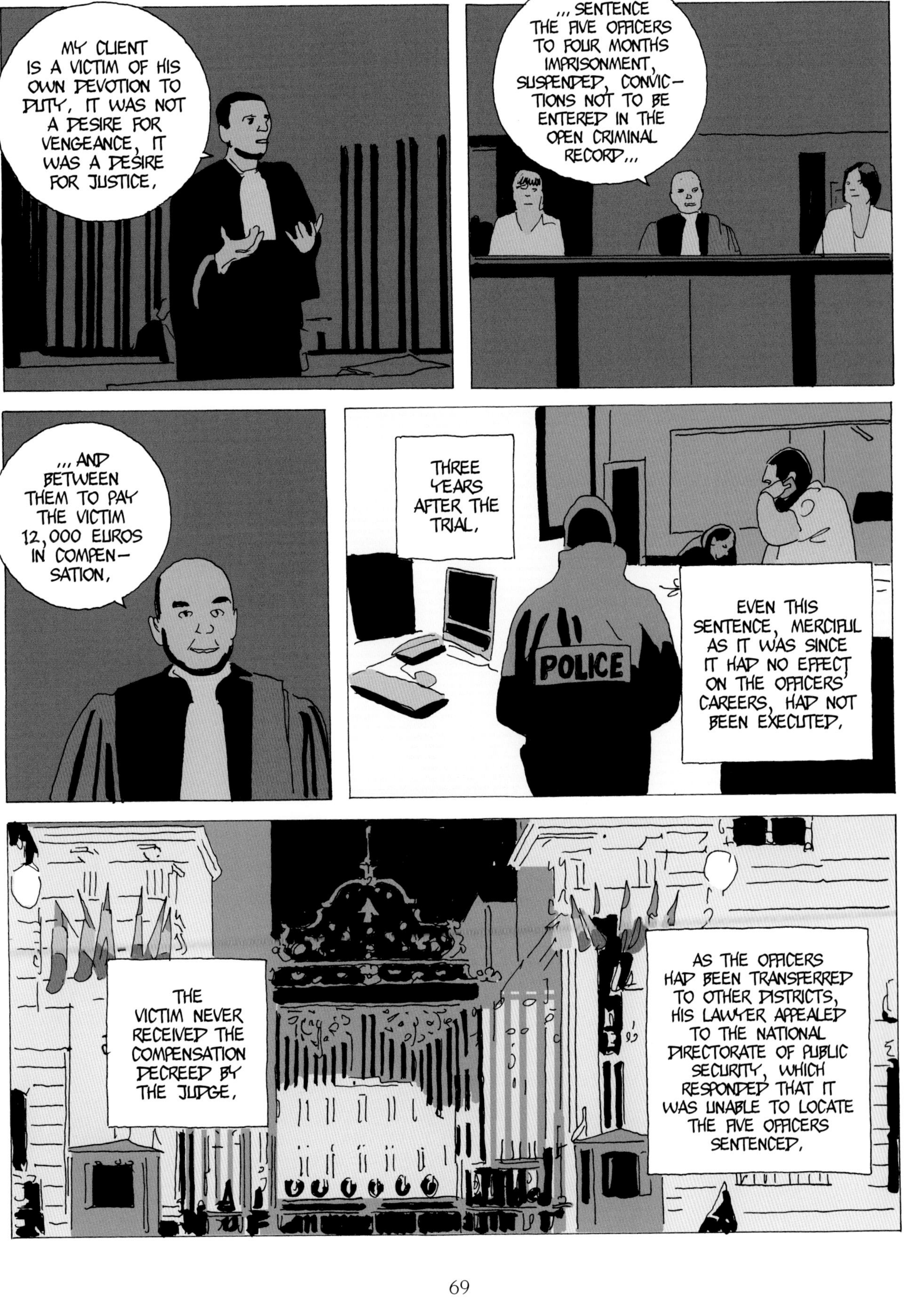
MY CLIENT IS A VICTIM OF HIS OWN DEVOTION TO DUTY. IT WAS NOT A DESIRE FOR VENGEANCE. IT WAS A DESIRE FOR JUSTICE.
... SENTENCE THE FIVE OFFICERS TO FOUR MONTHS IMPRISONMENT, SUSPENDED, CONVICTIONS NOT TO BE ENTERED IN THE OPEN CRIMINAL RECORD...
... AND BETWEEN THEM TO PAY THE VICTIM 12,000 EUROS IN COMPENSATION.
THREE YEARS AFTER THE TRIAL.
POLICE
EVEN THIS SENTENCE, MERCIFUL AS IT WAS SINCE IT HAD NO EFFECT ON THE OFFICERS' CAREERS, HAD NOT BEEN EXECUTED.
THE VICTIM NEVER RECEIVED THE COMPENSATION DECREED BY THE JUDGE.
AS THE OFFICERS HAD BEEN TRANSFERRED TO OTHER DISTRICTS, HIS LAWYER APPEALED TO THE NATIONAL DIRECTORATE OF PUBLIC SECURITY, WHICH RESPONDED THAT IT WAS UNABLE TO LOCATE THE FIVE OFFICERS SENTENCED.

POLICE OFFICERS NEED TO FIND THEIR OWN JUSTIFICATION FOR PRACTICES THAT THEIR SUPERIORS DEEM CONTRARY TO THE ETHICS OF THEIR PROFESSION...

..., AND THAT OUTRAGE CITIZENS WHEN THEY LEARN OF THEM,

HELLO, POLICE?

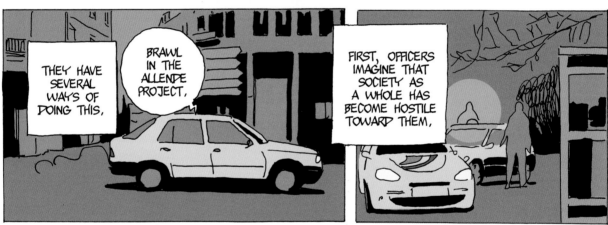

THEY HAVE SEVERAL WAYS OF DOING THIS,

BRAWL IN THE ALLENDE PROJECT,

FIRST, OFFICERS IMAGINE THAT SOCIETY AS A WHOLE HAS BECOME HOSTILE TOWARD THEM,

THIS FEELING HELPS TO STRENGTHEN THEIR TEAM SPIRIT AND THE COHESION OF THEIR CREWS, BELIEVING THEMSELVES ALONE AGAINST THE WORLD...

IT'S ANOTHER HOAX BY THOSE LITTLE ASSHOLES!

..., AND LEGITIMIZES THEIR AGGRESSION IN RETURN,

THERE! IT MUST BE HIM!

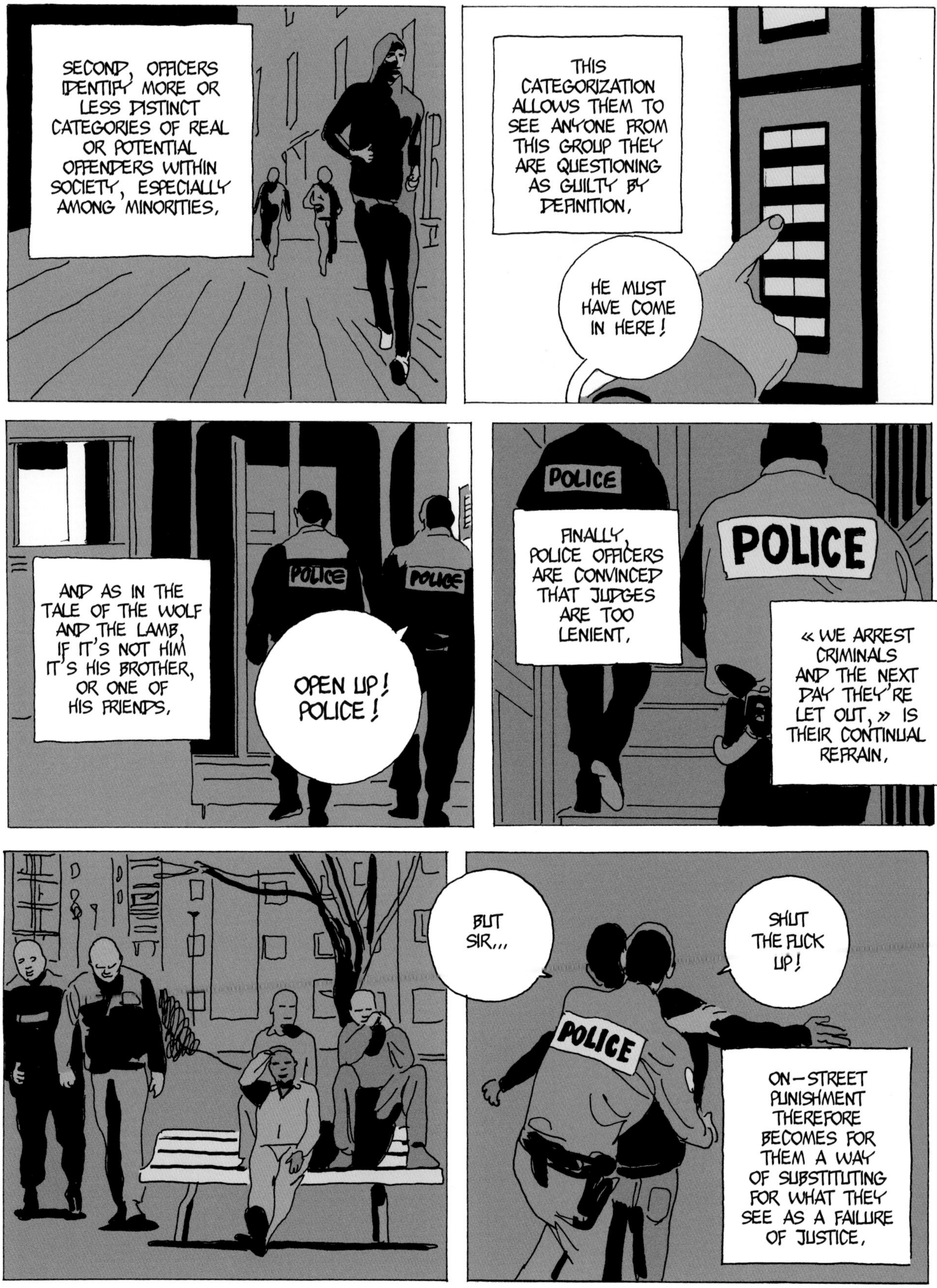
SECOND, OFFICERS IDENTIFY MORE OR LESS DISTINCT CATEGORIES OF REAL OR POTENTIAL OFFENDERS WITHIN SOCIETY, ESPECIALLY AMONG MINORITIES.
THIS CATEGORIZATION ALLOWS THEM TO SEE ANYONE FROM THIS GROUP THEY ARE QUESTIONING AS GUILTY BY DEFINITION.
HE MUST HAVE COME IN HERE!
AND AS IN THE TALE OF THE WOLF AND THE LAMB, IF IT'S NOT HIM IT'S HIS BROTHER, OR ONE OF HIS FRIENDS.
POLICE
POLICE
OPEN UP! POLICE!
POLICE
FINALLY, POLICE OFFICERS ARE CONVINCED THAT JUDGES ARE TOO LENIENT.
POLICE
« WE ARREST CRIMINALS AND THE NEXT DAY THEY'RE LET OUT. » IS THEIR CONTINUAL REFRAIN.
BUT SIR...
SHUT THE FUCK UP!
POLICE
ON-STREET PUNISHMENT THEREFORE BECOMES FOR THEM A WAY OF SUBSTITUTING FOR WHAT THEY SEE AS A FAILURE OF JUSTICE.

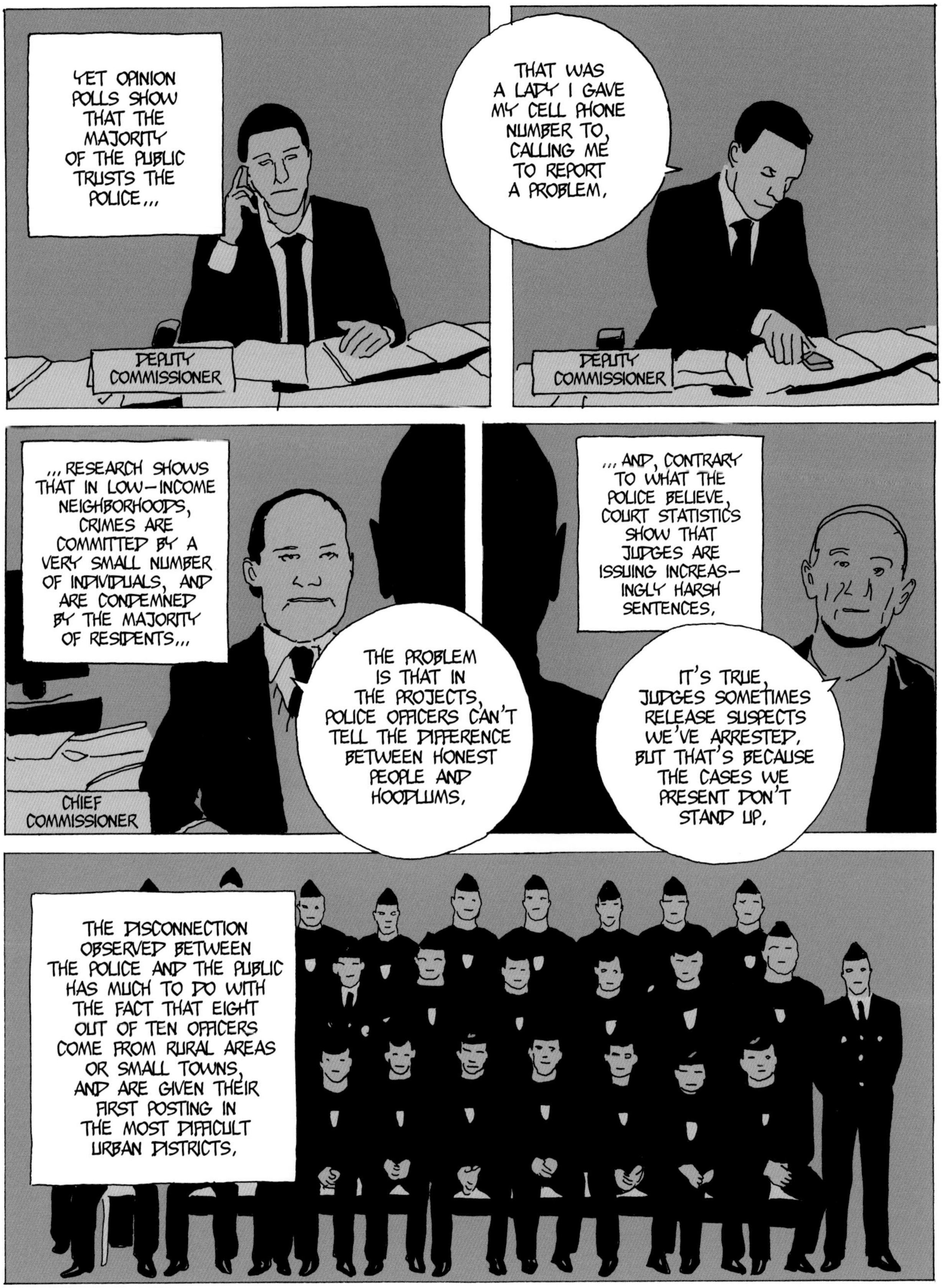
YET OPINION POLLS SHOW THAT THE MAJORITY OF THE PUBLIC TRUSTS THE POLICE...
DEPUTY COMMISSIONER
THAT WAS A LADY I GAVE MY CELL PHONE NUMBER TO, CALLING ME TO REPORT A PROBLEM.
DEPUTY COMMISSIONER
...RESEARCH SHOWS THAT IN LOW-INCOME NEIGHBORHOODS, CRIMES ARE COMMITTED BY A VERY SMALL NUMBER OF INDIVIDUALS, AND ARE CONDEMNED BY THE MAJORITY OF RESIDENTS...
CHIEF COMMISSIONER
THE PROBLEM IS THAT IN THE PROJECTS, POLICE OFFICERS CAN'T TELL THE DIFFERENCE BETWEEN HONEST PEOPLE AND HOODLUMS.
...AND, CONTRARY TO WHAT THE POLICE BELIEVE, COURT STATISTICS SHOW THAT JUDGES ARE ISSUING INCREAS-INGLY HARSH SENTENCES.
IT'S TRUE, JUDGES SOMETIMES RELEASE SUSPECTS WE'VE ARRESTED, BUT THAT'S BECAUSE THE CASES WE PRESENT DON'T STAND UP.
THE DISCONNECTION OBSERVED BETWEEN THE POLICE AND THE PUBLIC HAS MUCH TO DO WITH THE FACT THAT EIGHT OUT OF TEN OFFICERS COME FROM RURAL AREAS OR SMALL TOWNS, AND ARE GIVEN THEIR FIRST POSTING IN THE MOST DIFFICULT URBAN DISTRICTS.

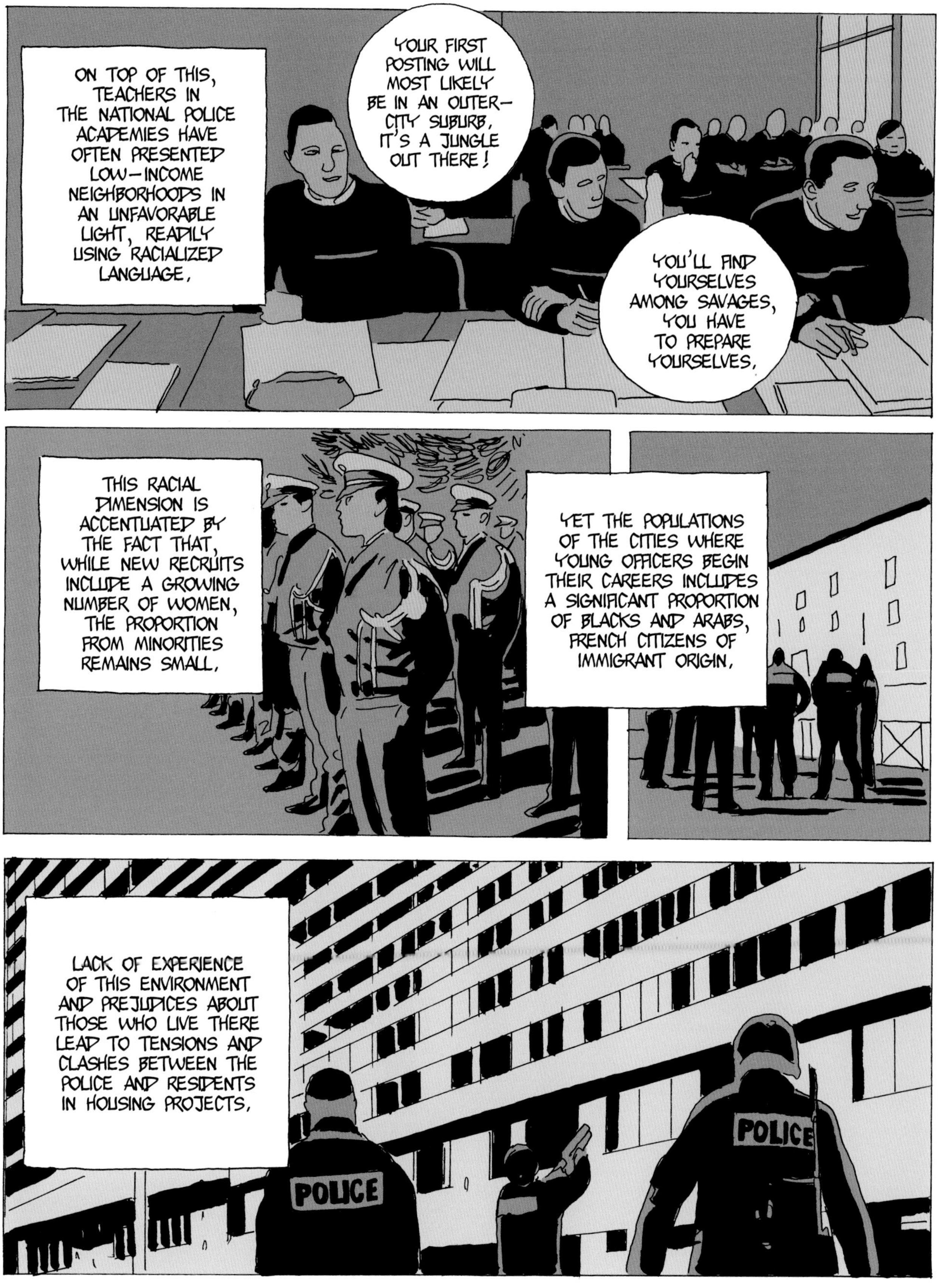
ON TOP OF THIS, TEACHERS IN THE NATIONAL POLICE ACADEMIES HAVE OFTEN PRESENTED LOW-INCOME NEIGHBORHOODS IN AN UNFAVORABLE LIGHT, READILY USING RACIALIZED LANGUAGE.
YOUR FIRST POSTING WILL MOST LIKELY BE IN AN OUTER-CITY SUBURB. IT'S A JUNGLE OUT THERE!
YOU'LL FIND YOURSELVES AMONG SAVAGES. YOU HAVE TO PREPARE YOURSELVES.
THIS RACIAL DIMENSION IS ACCENTUATED BY THE FACT THAT, WHILE NEW RECRUITS INCLUDE A GROWING NUMBER OF WOMEN, THE PROPORTION FROM MINORITIES REMAINS SMALL.
YET THE POPULATIONS OF THE CITIES WHERE YOUNG OFFICERS BEGIN THEIR CAREERS INCLUDES A SIGNIFICANT PROPORTION OF BLACKS AND ARABS, FRENCH CITIZENS OF IMMIGRANT ORIGIN.
LACK OF EXPERIENCE OF THIS ENVIRONMENT AND PREJUDICES ABOUT THOSE WHO LIVE THERE LEAD TO TENSIONS AND CLASHES BETWEEN THE POLICE AND RESIDENTS IN HOUSING PROJECTS.
POLICE
POLICE

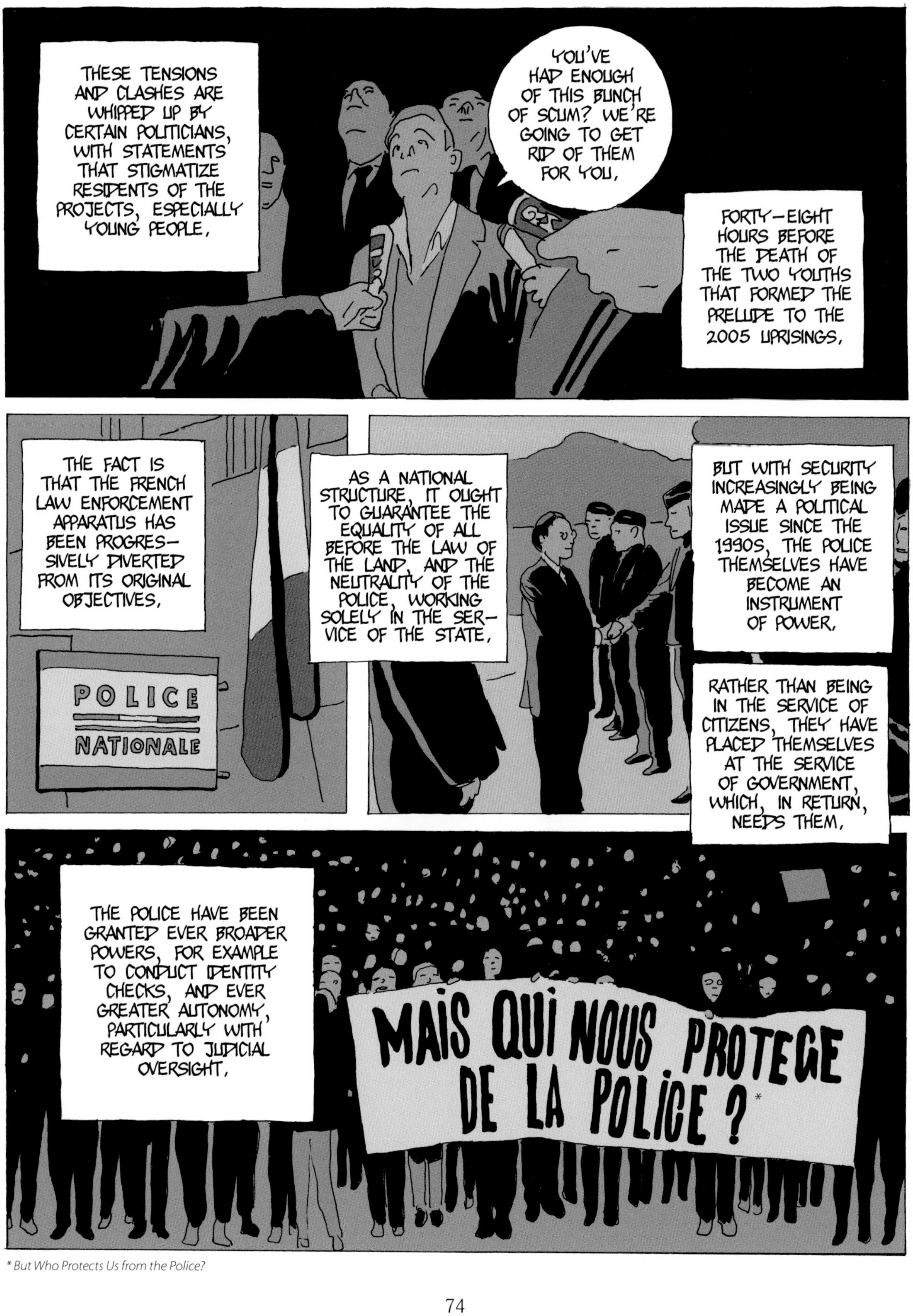
THESE TENSIONS AND CLASHES ARE WHIPPED UP BY CERTAIN POLITICIANS, WITH STATEMENTS THAT STIGMATIZE RESIDENTS OF THE PROJECTS, ESPECIALLY YOUNG PEOPLE.
YOU'VE HAD ENOUGH OF THIS BUNCH OF SCUM? WE'RE GOING TO GET RID OF THEM FOR YOU.
FORTY-EIGHT HOURS BEFORE THE DEATH OF THE TWO YOUTHS THAT FORMED THE PRELUDE TO THE 2005 UPRISINGS.
THE FACT IS THAT THE FRENCH LAW ENFORCEMENT APPARATUS HAS BEEN PROGRES-SIVELY DIVERTED FROM ITS ORIGINAL OBJECTIVES.
POLICE NATIONALE
AS A NATIONAL STRUCTURE, IT OUGHT TO GUARANTEE THE EQUALITY OF ALL BEFORE THE LAW OF THE LAND, AND THE NEUTRALITY OF THE POLICE, WORKING SOLELY IN THE SER-VICE OF THE STATE.
BUT WITH SECURITY INCREASINGLY BEING MADE A POLITICAL ISSUE SINCE THE 1990S, THE POLICE THEMSELVES HAVE BECOME AN INSTRUMENT OF POWER.
RATHER THAN BEING IN THE SERVICE OF CITIZENS, THEY HAVE PLACED THEMSELVES AT THE SERVICE OF GOVERNMENT, WHICH, IN RETURN, NEEDS THEM.
THE POLICE HAVE BEEN GRANTED EVER BROADER POWERS, FOR EXAMPLE TO CONDUCT IDENTITY CHECKS, AND EVER GREATER AUTONOMY, PARTICULARLY WITH REGARD TO JUDICIAL OVERSIGHT.
MAIS QUI NOUS PROTEGE DE LA POLICE ?*

* *But Who Protects Us from the Police?*

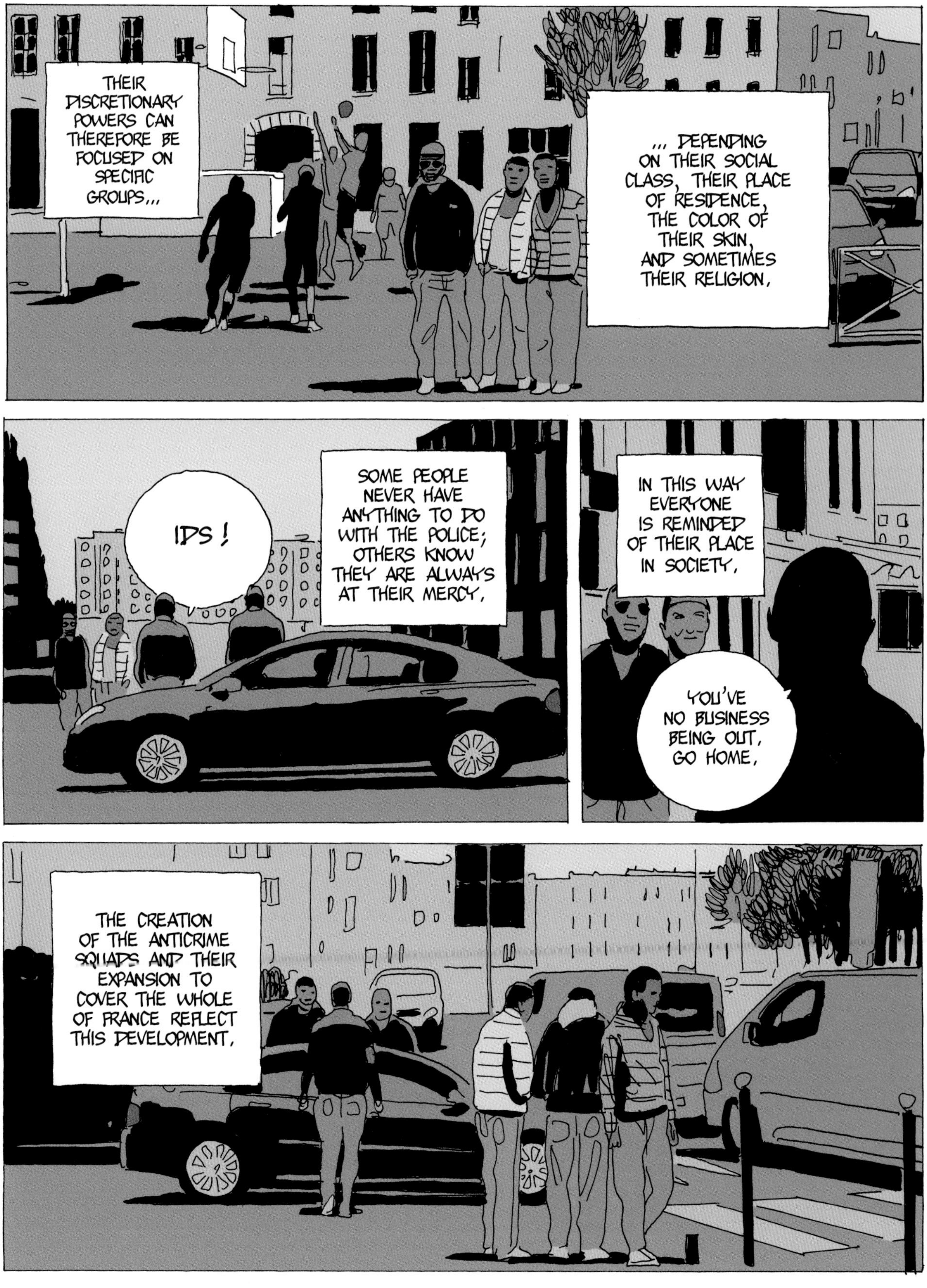
THEIR DISCRETIONARY POWERS CAN THEREFORE BE FOCUSED ON SPECIFIC GROUPS...
... DEPENDING ON THEIR SOCIAL CLASS, THEIR PLACE OF RESIDENCE, THE COLOR OF THEIR SKIN, AND SOMETIMES THEIR RELIGION.
IDS!
SOME PEOPLE NEVER HAVE ANYTHING TO DO WITH THE POLICE; OTHERS KNOW THEY ARE ALWAYS AT THEIR MERCY.
IN THIS WAY EVERYONE IS REMINDED OF THEIR PLACE IN SOCIETY.
YOU'VE NO BUSINESS BEING OUT. GO HOME.
THE CREATION OF THE ANTICRIME SQUADS AND THEIR EXPANSION TO COVER THE WHOLE OF FRANCE REFLECT THIS DEVELOPMENT.

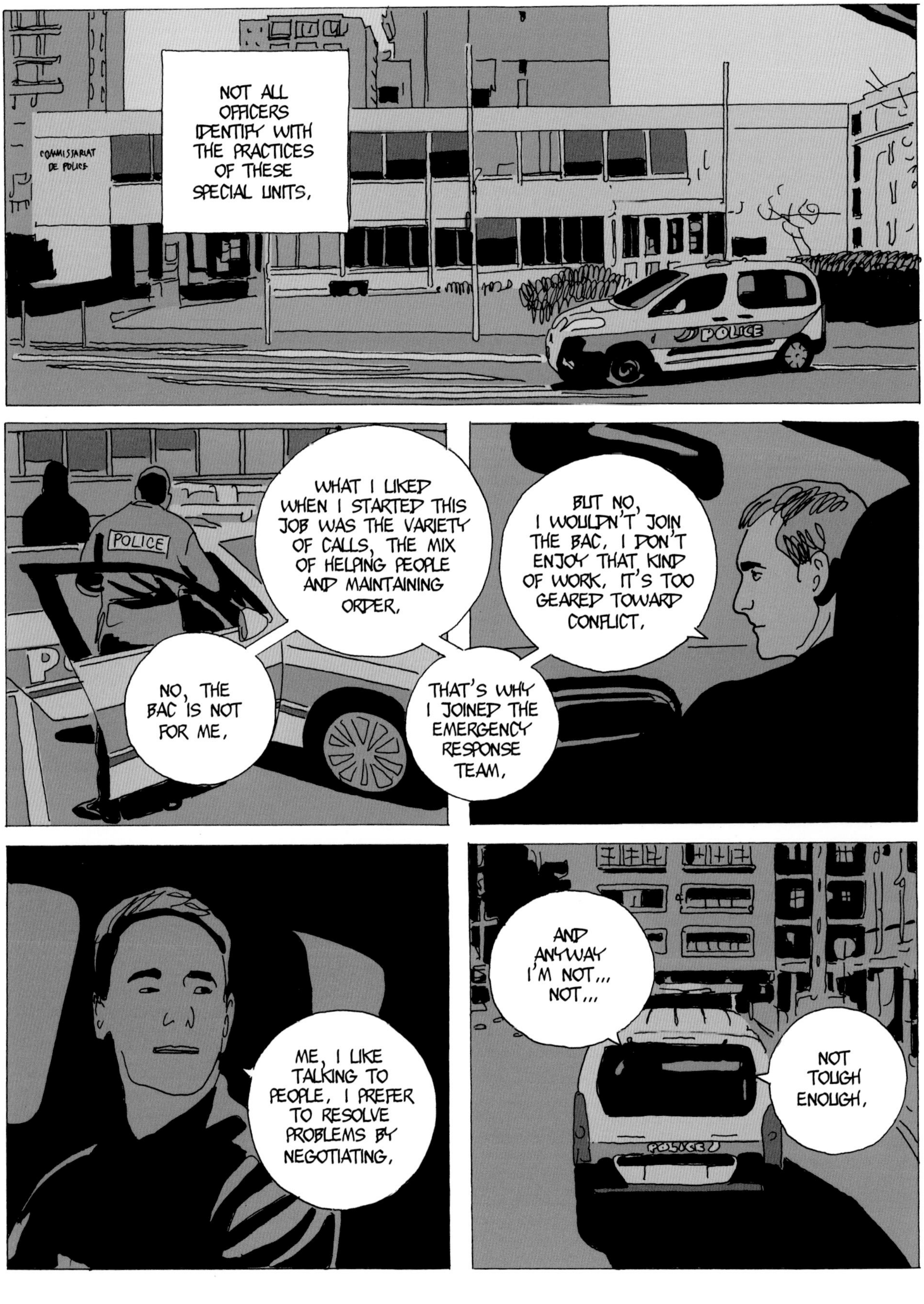
COMMISSARIAT DE POLICE
NOT ALL OFFICERS IDENTIFY WITH THE PRACTICES OF THESE SPECIAL UNITS,
POLICE
POLICE
WHAT I LIKED WHEN I STARTED THIS JOB WAS THE VARIETY OF CALLS, THE MIX OF HELPING PEOPLE AND MAINTAINING ORDER,
NO, THE BAC IS NOT FOR ME,
BUT NO, I WOULDN'T JOIN THE BAC, I DON'T ENJOY THAT KIND OF WORK, IT'S TOO GEARED TOWARD CONFLICT,
THAT'S WHY I JOINED THE EMERGENCY RESPONSE TEAM,
ME, I LIKE TALKING TO PEOPLE, I PREFER TO RESOLVE PROBLEMS BY NEGOTIATING,
AND ANYWAY I'M NOT... NOT...
NOT TOUGH ENOUGH,

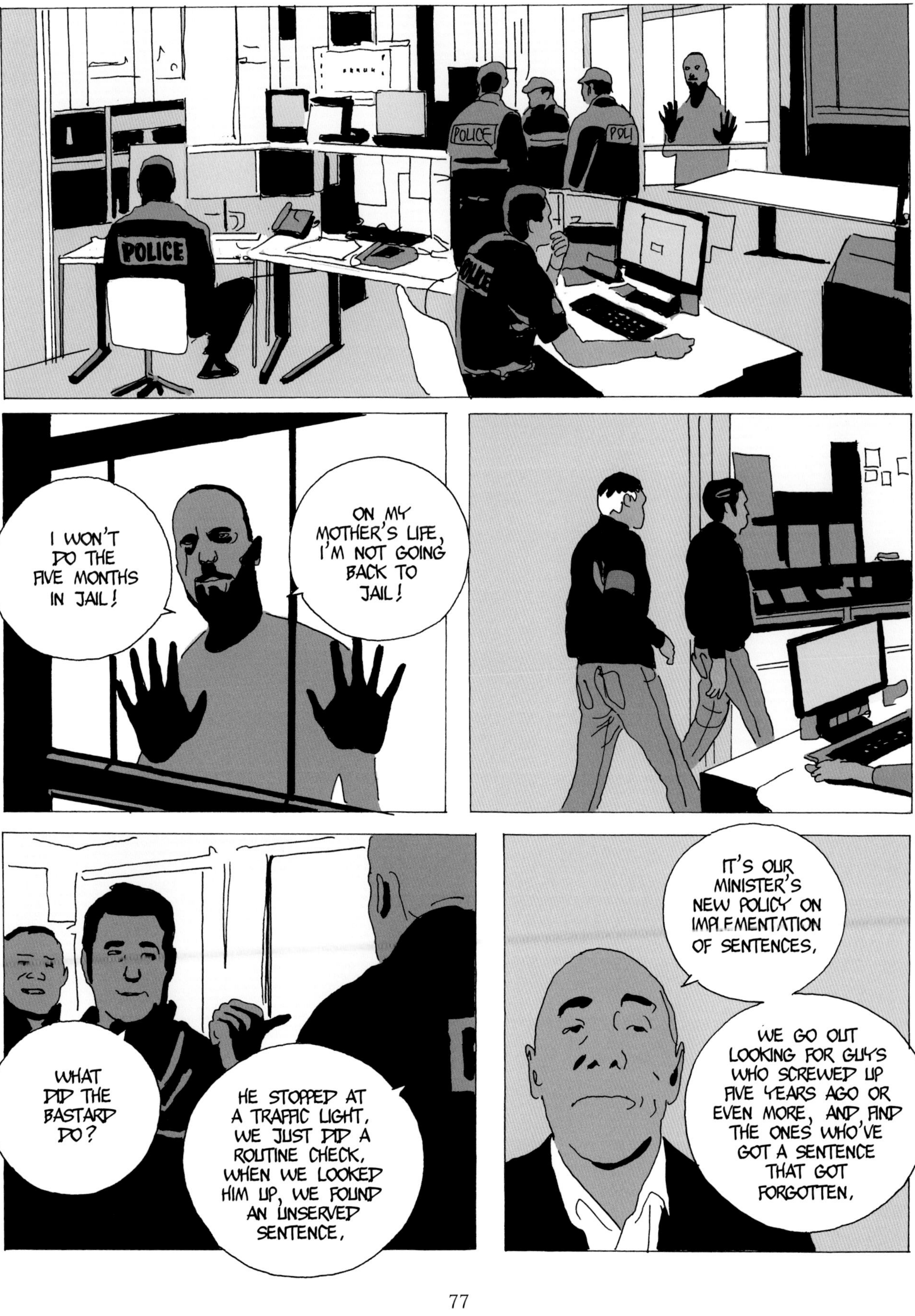
POLICE
POLICE
POLI
POLICE
I WON'T DO THE FIVE MONTHS IN JAIL!
ON MY MOTHER'S LIFE, I'M NOT GOING BACK TO JAIL!
WHAT DID THE BASTARD DO?
HE STOPPED AT A TRAFFIC LIGHT, WE JUST DID A ROUTINE CHECK, WHEN WE LOOKED HIM UP, WE FOUND AN UNSERVED SENTENCE.
IT'S OUR MINISTER'S NEW POLICY ON IMPLEMENTATION OF SENTENCES.
WE GO OUT LOOKING FOR GUYS WHO SCREWED UP FIVE YEARS AGO OR EVEN MORE, AND FIND THE ONES WHO'VE GOT A SENTENCE THAT GOT FORGOTTEN.

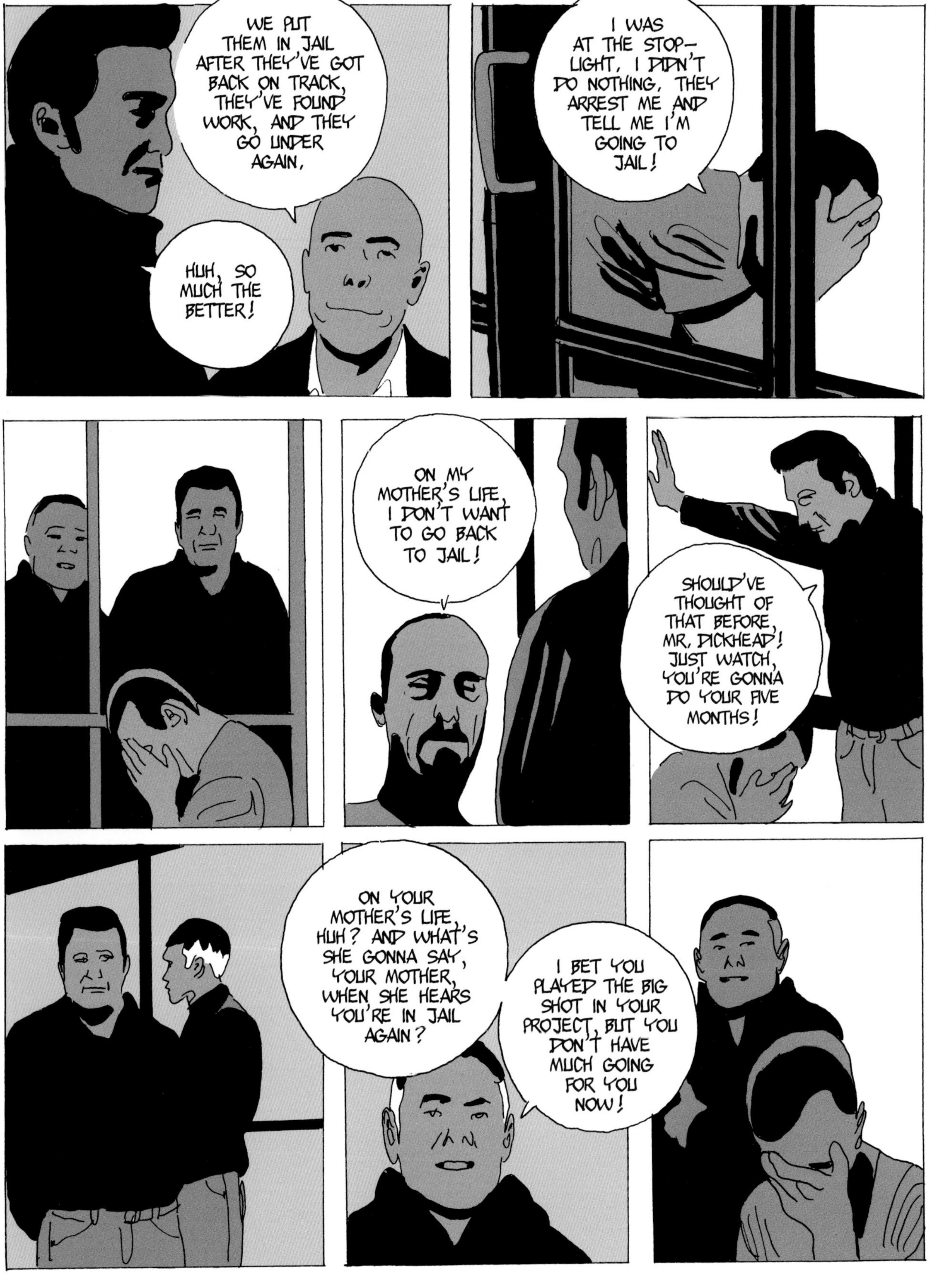
WE PUT THEM IN JAIL AFTER THEY'VE GOT BACK ON TRACK, THEY'VE FOUND WORK, AND THEY GO UNDER AGAIN.
HUH, SO MUCH THE BETTER!
I WAS AT THE STOP-LIGHT, I DIDN'T DO NOTHING, THEY ARREST ME AND TELL ME I'M GOING TO JAIL!
ON MY MOTHER'S LIFE, I DON'T WANT TO GO BACK TO JAIL!
SHOULD'VE THOUGHT OF THAT BEFORE, MR. DICKHEAD! JUST WATCH, YOU'RE GONNA DO YOUR FIVE MONTHS!
ON YOUR MOTHER'S LIFE, HUH? AND WHAT'S SHE GONNA SAY, YOUR MOTHER, WHEN SHE HEARS YOU'RE IN JAIL AGAIN?
I BET YOU PLAYED THE BIG SHOT IN YOUR PROJECT, BUT YOU DON'T HAVE MUCH GOING FOR YOU NOW!

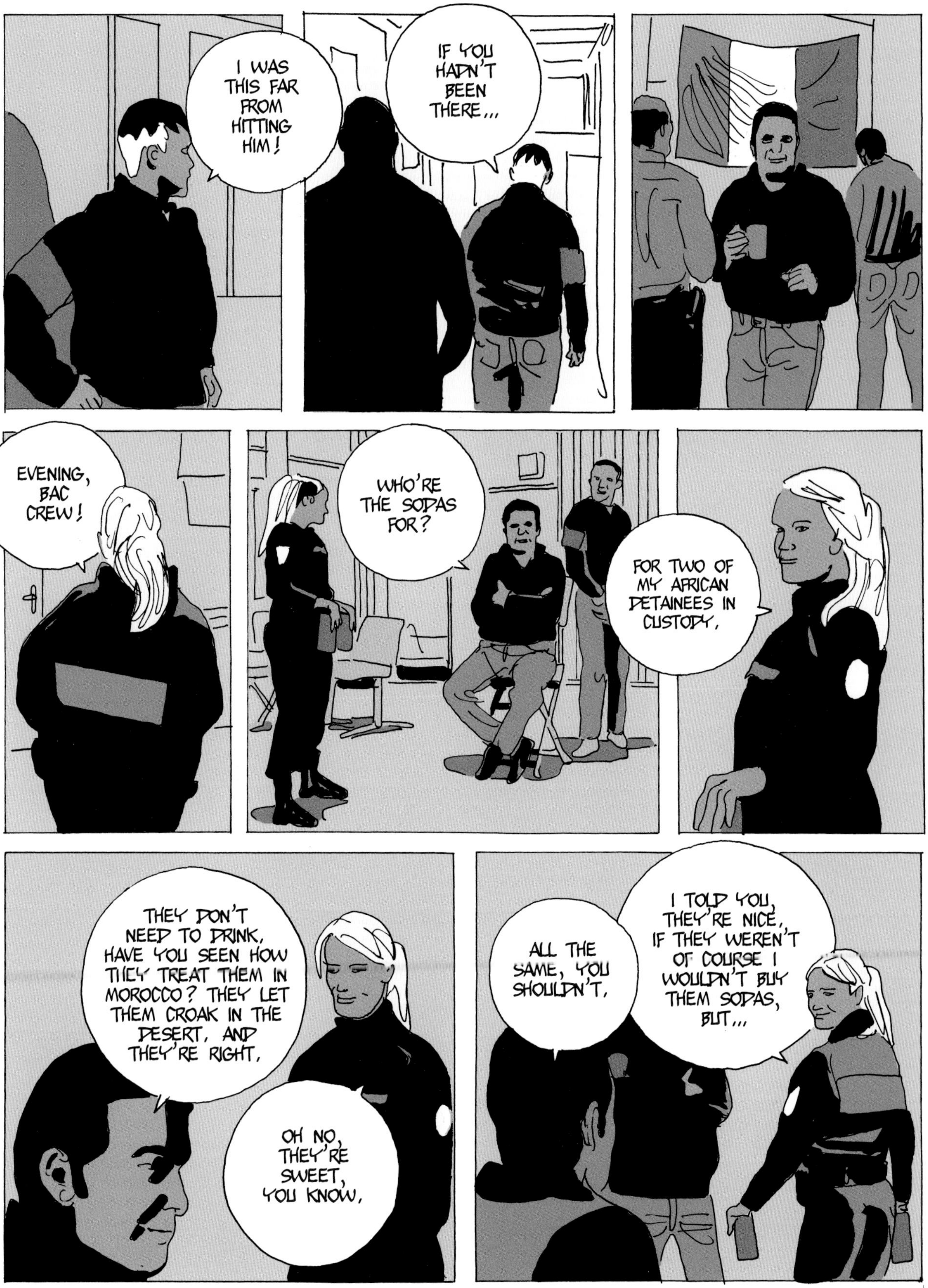
I WAS THIS FAR FROM HITTING HIM!
IF YOU HADN'T BEEN THERE...
EVENING, BAC CREW!
WHO'RE THE SODAS FOR?
FOR TWO OF MY AFRICAN DETAINEES IN CUSTODY.
THEY DON'T NEED TO DRINK, HAVE YOU SEEN HOW THEY TREAT THEM IN MOROCCO? THEY LET THEM CROAK IN THE DESERT, AND THEY'RE RIGHT.
OH NO, THEY'RE SWEET, YOU KNOW.
ALL THE SAME, YOU SHOULDN'T.
I TOLD YOU, THEY'RE NICE. IF THEY WEREN'T OF COURSE I WOULDN'T BUY THEM SODAS, BUT...

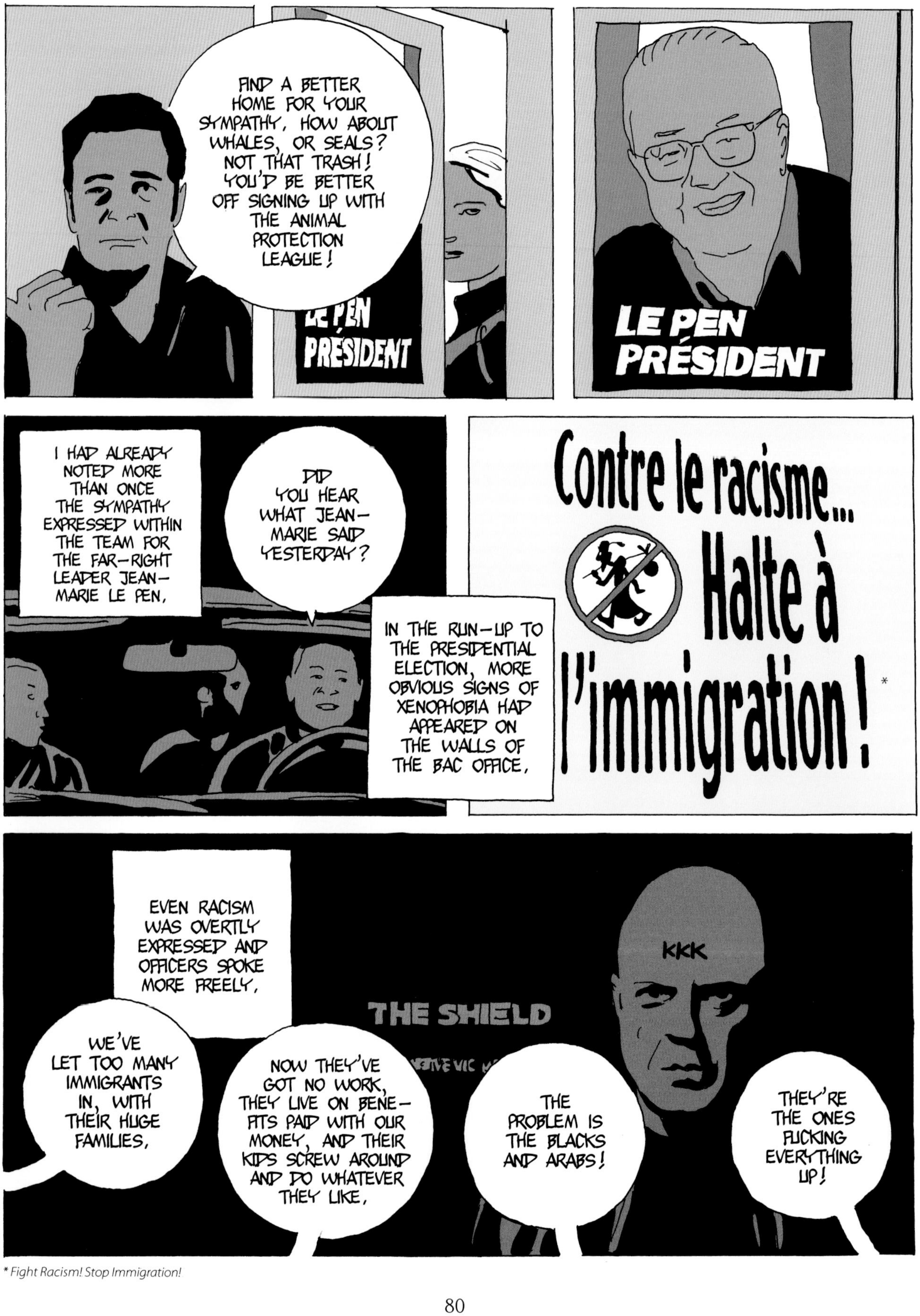
FIND A BETTER HOME FOR YOUR SYMPATHY, HOW ABOUT WHALES, OR SEALS? NOT THAT TRASH! YOU'D BE BETTER OFF SIGNING UP WITH THE ANIMAL PROTECTION LEAGUE!
LE PEN PRÉSIDENT
LE PEN PRÉSIDENT
I HAD ALREADY NOTED MORE THAN ONCE THE SYMPATHY EXPRESSED WITHIN THE TEAM FOR THE FAR-RIGHT LEADER JEAN-MARIE LE PEN,
DID YOU HEAR WHAT JEAN-MARIE SAID YESTERDAY?
IN THE RUN-UP TO THE PRESIDENTIAL ELECTION, MORE OBVIOUS SIGNS OF XENOPHOBIA HAD APPEARED ON THE WALLS OF THE BAC OFFICE,
Contre le racisme... Halte à l'immigration! *
EVEN RACISM WAS OVERTLY EXPRESSED AND OFFICERS SPOKE MORE FREELY,
KKK
THE SHIELD
WE'VE LET TOO MANY IMMIGRANTS IN, WITH THEIR HUGE FAMILIES,
NOW THEY'VE GOT NO WORK, THEY LIVE ON BENE-FITS PAID WITH OUR MONEY, AND THEIR KIDS SCREW AROUND AND DO WHATEVER THEY LIKE,
THE PROBLEM IS THE BLACKS AND ARABS!
THEY'RE THE ONES FUCKING EVERYTHING UP!

* *Fight Racism! Stop Immigration!*

SOME OFFICERS ALTERED WHAT THEY WORE, AND WOULD STROLL THROUGH THE PROJECTS SPORTING BLACK T-SHIRTS THAT UNAMBIGUOUSLY DISPLAYED THE EMBLEMS OF THEIR AFFINITIES,

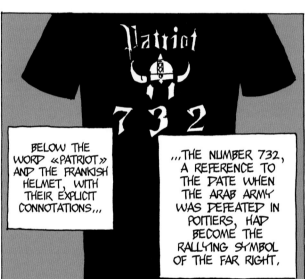

Patriot
732

BELOW THE WORD «PATRIOT» AND THE FRANKISH HELMET, WITH THEIR EXPLICIT CONNOTATIONS,,,

,,,THE NUMBER 732, A REFERENCE TO THE DATE WHEN THE ARAB ARMY WAS DEFEATED IN POITIERS, HAD BECOME THE RALLYING SYMBOL OF THE FAR RIGHT,

B.A.K*
Brigade Anti Keuf

THE POLICE ADMINIS-TRATION HAD REFERRED A T-SHIRT MANUFAC-TURER, WHO HAD MADE SHIRTS THAT IRONICALLY SUBVERTED THE ANTI-CRIME SQUAD'S ACRO-NYM, TO THE PUBLIC PROSECUTOR, AND HAD HIM CONVICTED OF INSULTING THE POLICE,,,

,,, BUT CONVERSELY SHOWED GREAT LENIENCY TOWARD THOSE OF ITS OFFICERS WHO DISPLAYED THEIR HOSTILE VIEWS ON IMMIGRANTS AND MINORITIES TO THE PUBLIC,

IT'S TRUE, I'VE ALSO NOTICED IT, ALMOST ALL OF OUR RIGHT-WING AND FAR-RIGHT OFFICERS ARE IN THE BAC, BUT I DON'T KNOW WHY,

THE IDEOLOGY PROUDLY DISPLAYED BY THE MAJORITY OF ITS MEMBERS MIGHT HAVE SUGGESTED THIS SQUAD WAS AN EXCEPTION, HAD IT NOT BEEN FOR A POLL A FEW YEARS LATER,,,

,,,THAT REVEALED THAT IN THE REGIONAL ELECTIONS, MORE THAN HALF OF LAW ENFORCEMENT OFFICERS HAD VOTED FOR THE FAR-RIGHT PARTY: DOUBLE THE NATIONAL AVERAGE,

POLICE

* BAK, or Anti-Cop Squad, is a parody of BAC, the Anti-Crime Squad.

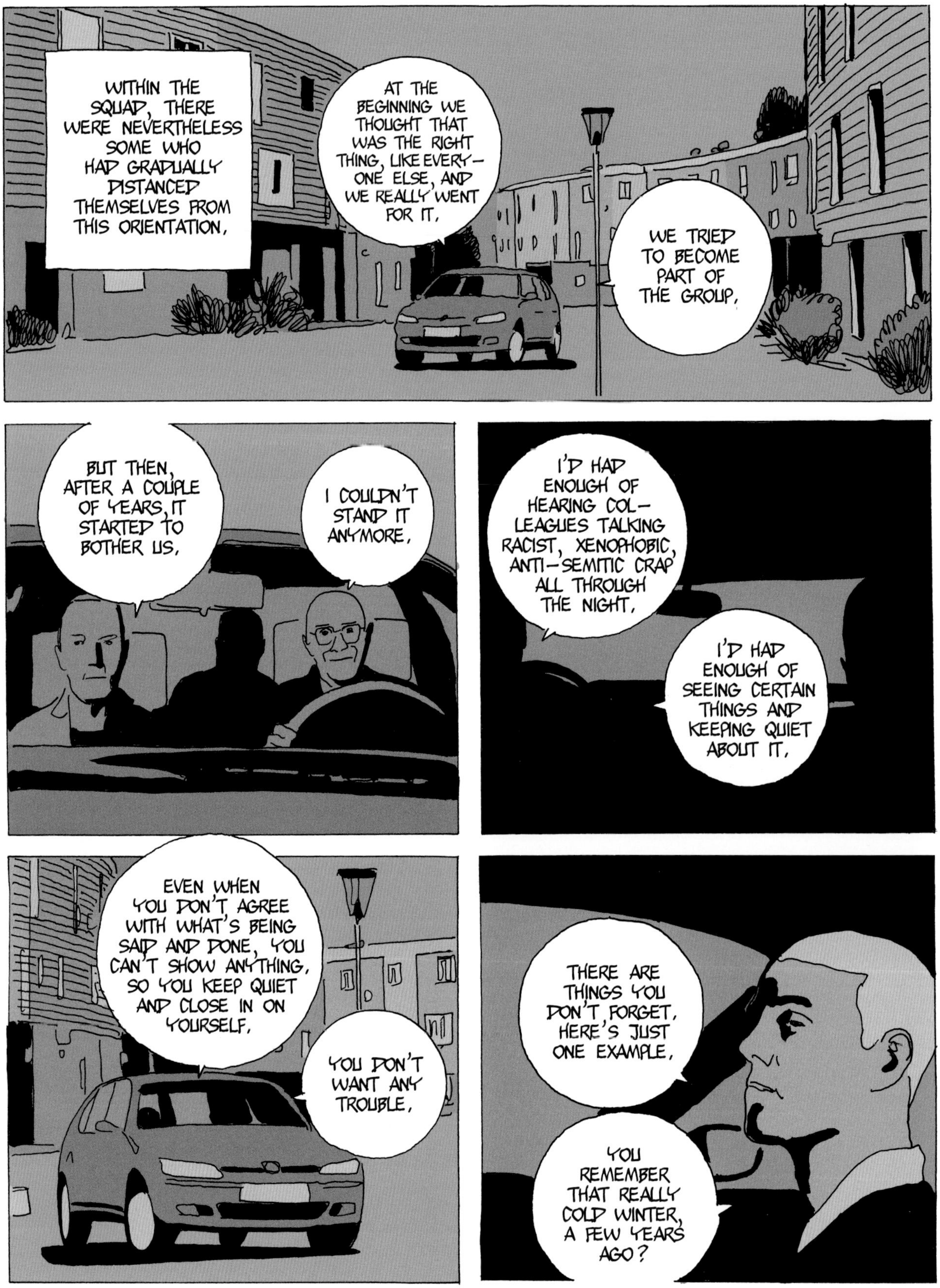
WITHIN THE SQUAD, THERE WERE NEVERTHELESS SOME WHO HAD GRADUALLY DISTANCED THEMSELVES FROM THIS ORIENTATION.
AT THE BEGINNING WE THOUGHT THAT WAS THE RIGHT THING, LIKE EVERY-ONE ELSE, AND WE REALLY WENT FOR IT.
WE TRIED TO BECOME PART OF THE GROUP.
BUT THEN, AFTER A COUPLE OF YEARS, IT STARTED TO BOTHER US.
I COULDN'T STAND IT ANYMORE.
I'D HAD ENOUGH OF HEARING COL-LEAGUES TALKING RACIST, XENOPHOBIC, ANTI-SEMITIC CRAP ALL THROUGH THE NIGHT.
I'D HAD ENOUGH OF SEEING CERTAIN THINGS AND KEEPING QUIET ABOUT IT.
EVEN WHEN YOU DON'T AGREE WITH WHAT'S BEING SAID AND DONE, YOU CAN'T SHOW ANYTHING, SO YOU KEEP QUIET AND CLOSE IN ON YOURSELF.
YOU DON'T WANT ANY TROUBLE.
THERE ARE THINGS YOU DON'T FORGET. HERE'S JUST ONE EXAMPLE.
YOU REMEMBER THAT REALLY COLD WINTER, A FEW YEARS AGO?

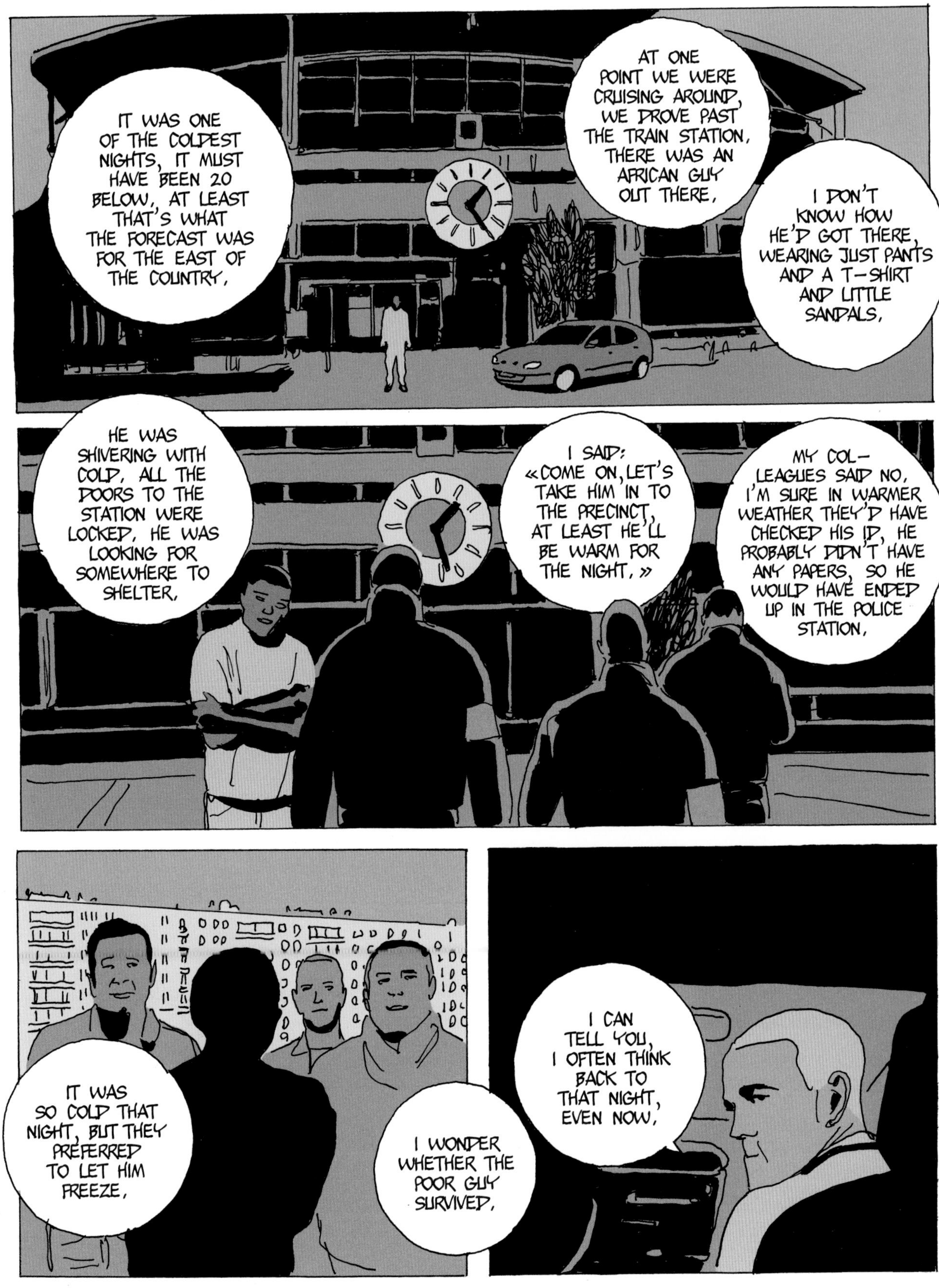
IT WAS ONE OF THE COLDEST NIGHTS, IT MUST HAVE BEEN 20 BELOW, AT LEAST THAT'S WHAT THE FORECAST WAS FOR THE EAST OF THE COUNTRY.
AT ONE POINT WE WERE CRUISING AROUND, WE DROVE PAST THE TRAIN STATION, THERE WAS AN AFRICAN GUY OUT THERE.
I DON'T KNOW HOW HE'D GOT THERE, WEARING JUST PANTS AND A T-SHIRT AND LITTLE SANDALS.
HE WAS SHIVERING WITH COLD, ALL THE DOORS TO THE STATION WERE LOCKED, HE WAS LOOKING FOR SOMEWHERE TO SHELTER.
I SAID: «COME ON, LET'S TAKE HIM IN TO THE PRECINCT, AT LEAST HE'LL BE WARM FOR THE NIGHT.»
MY COL-LEAGUES SAID NO. I'M SURE IN WARMER WEATHER THEY'D HAVE CHECKED HIS ID, HE PROBABLY DIDN'T HAVE ANY PAPERS, SO HE WOULD HAVE ENDED UP IN THE POLICE STATION.
IT WAS SO COLD THAT NIGHT, BUT THEY PREFERRED TO LET HIM FREEZE.
I WONDER WHETHER THE POOR GUY SURVIVED.
I CAN TELL YOU, I OFTEN THINK BACK TO THAT NIGHT, EVEN NOW.

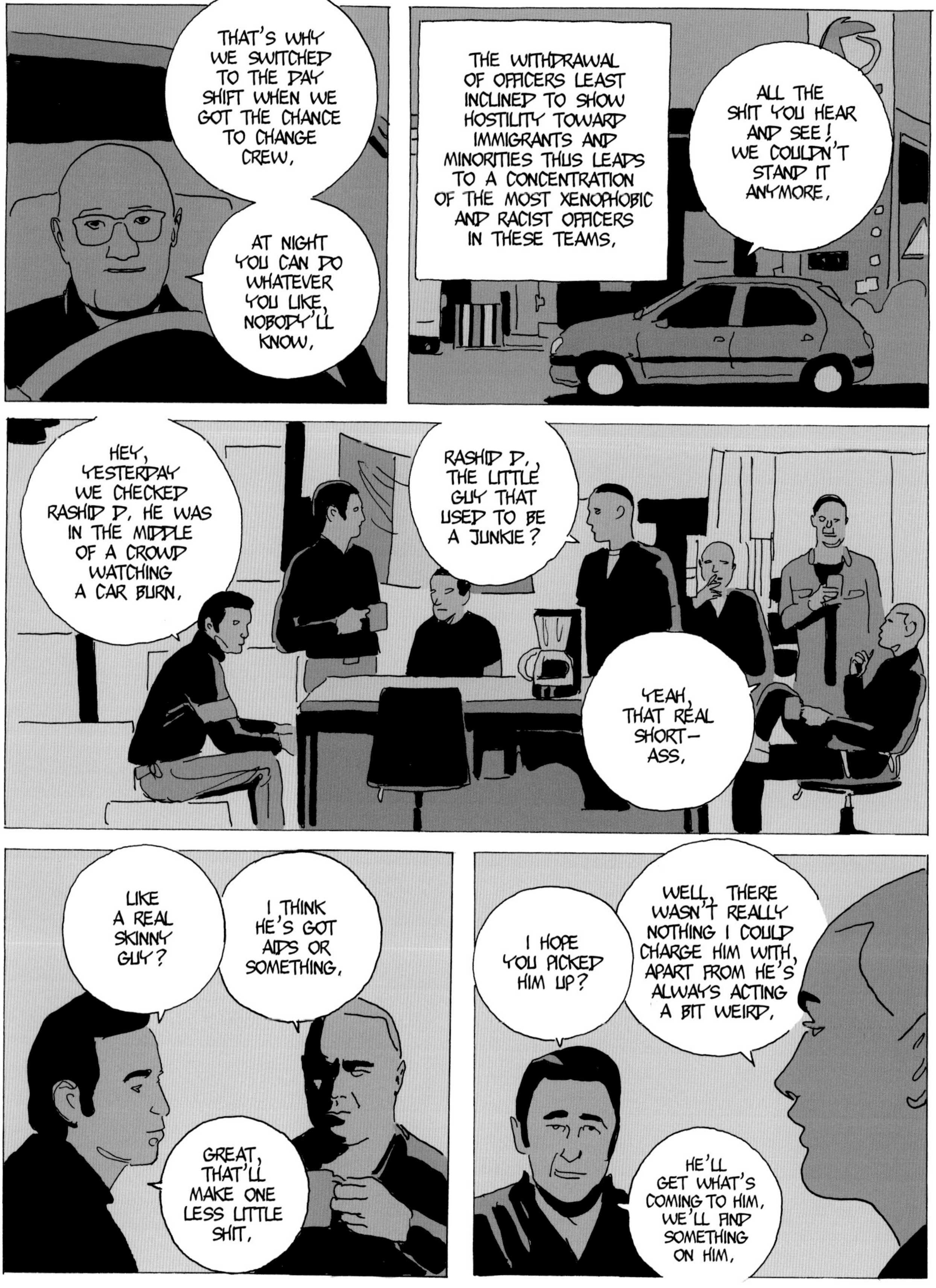

THAT'S WHY WE SWITCHED TO THE DAY SHIFT WHEN WE GOT THE CHANCE TO CHANGE CREW.
AT NIGHT YOU CAN DO WHATEVER YOU LIKE, NOBODY'LL KNOW.
THE WITHDRAWAL OF OFFICERS LEAST INCLINED TO SHOW HOSTILITY TOWARD IMMIGRANTS AND MINORITIES THUS LEADS TO A CONCENTRATION OF THE MOST XENOPHOBIC AND RACIST OFFICERS IN THESE TEAMS.
ALL THE SHIT YOU HEAR AND SEE! WE COULDN'T STAND IT ANYMORE.
HEY, YESTERDAY WE CHECKED RASHID D. HE WAS IN THE MIDDLE OF A CROWD WATCHING A CAR BURN.
RASHID D., THE LITTLE GUY THAT USED TO BE A JUNKIE?
YEAH, THAT REAL SHORT-ASS.
LIKE A REAL SKINNY GUY?
I THINK HE'S GOT AIDS OR SOMETHING.
GREAT, THAT'LL MAKE ONE LESS LITTLE SHIT.
I HOPE YOU PICKED HIM UP?
WELL, THERE WASN'T REALLY NOTHING I COULD CHARGE HIM WITH, APART FROM HE'S ALWAYS ACTING A BIT WEIRD.
HE'LL GET WHAT'S COMING TO HIM. WE'LL FIND SOMETHING ON HIM.

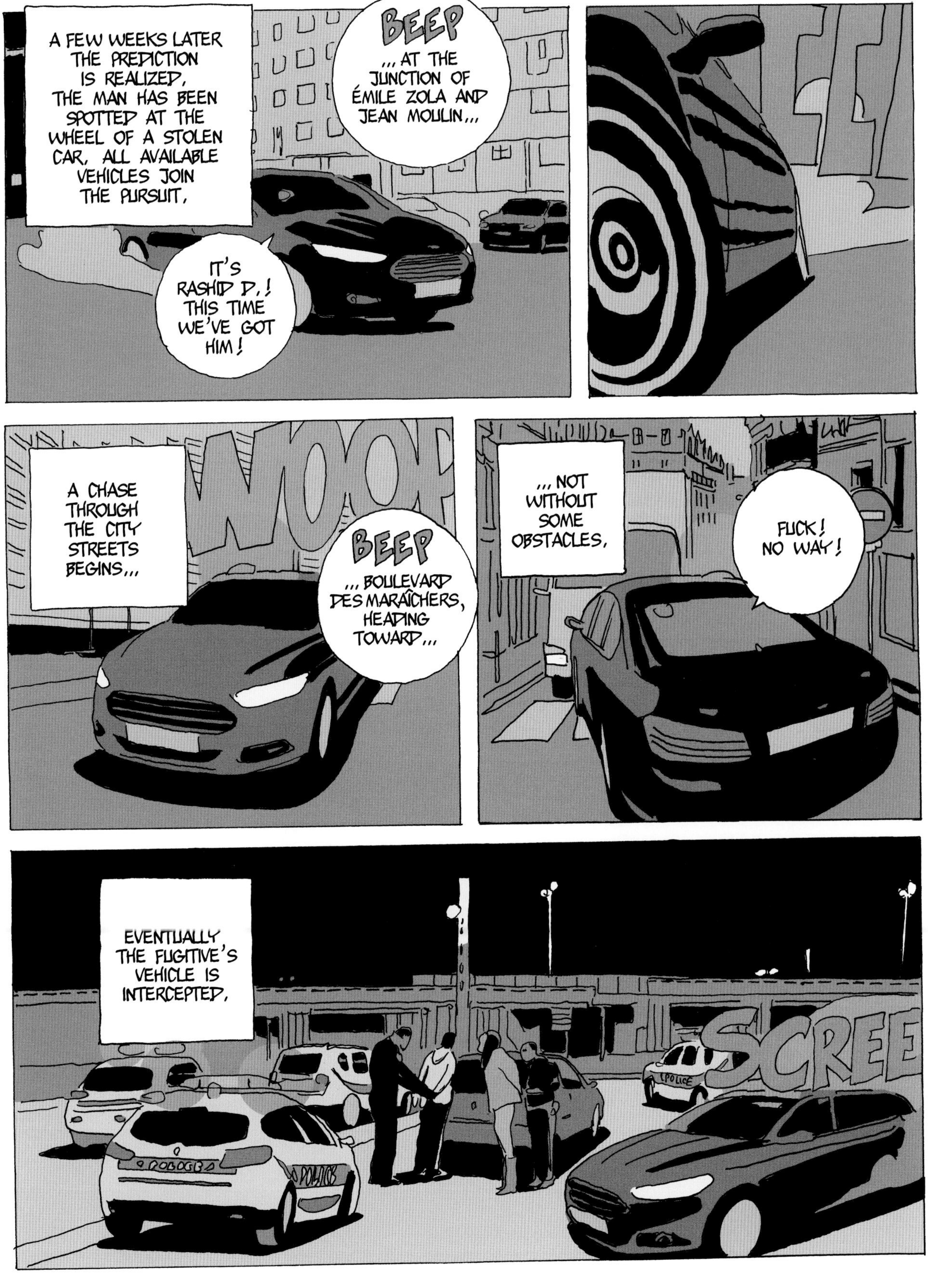
A FEW WEEKS LATER THE PREDICTION IS REALIZED, THE MAN HAS BEEN SPOTTED AT THE WHEEL OF A STOLEN CAR, ALL AVAILABLE VEHICLES JOIN THE PURSUIT.
BEEP
... AT THE JUNCTION OF ÉMILE ZOLA AND JEAN MOULIN...
IT'S RASHID D.! THIS TIME WE'VE GOT HIM!
WOOP
A CHASE THROUGH THE CITY STREETS BEGINS...
BEEP
... BOULEVARD DES MARAÎCHERS, HEADING TOWARD...
... NOT WITHOUT SOME OBSTACLES.
FUCK! NO WAY!
EVENTUALLY THE FUGITIVE'S VEHICLE IS INTERCEPTED.
SCREE
POLICE
POLICE

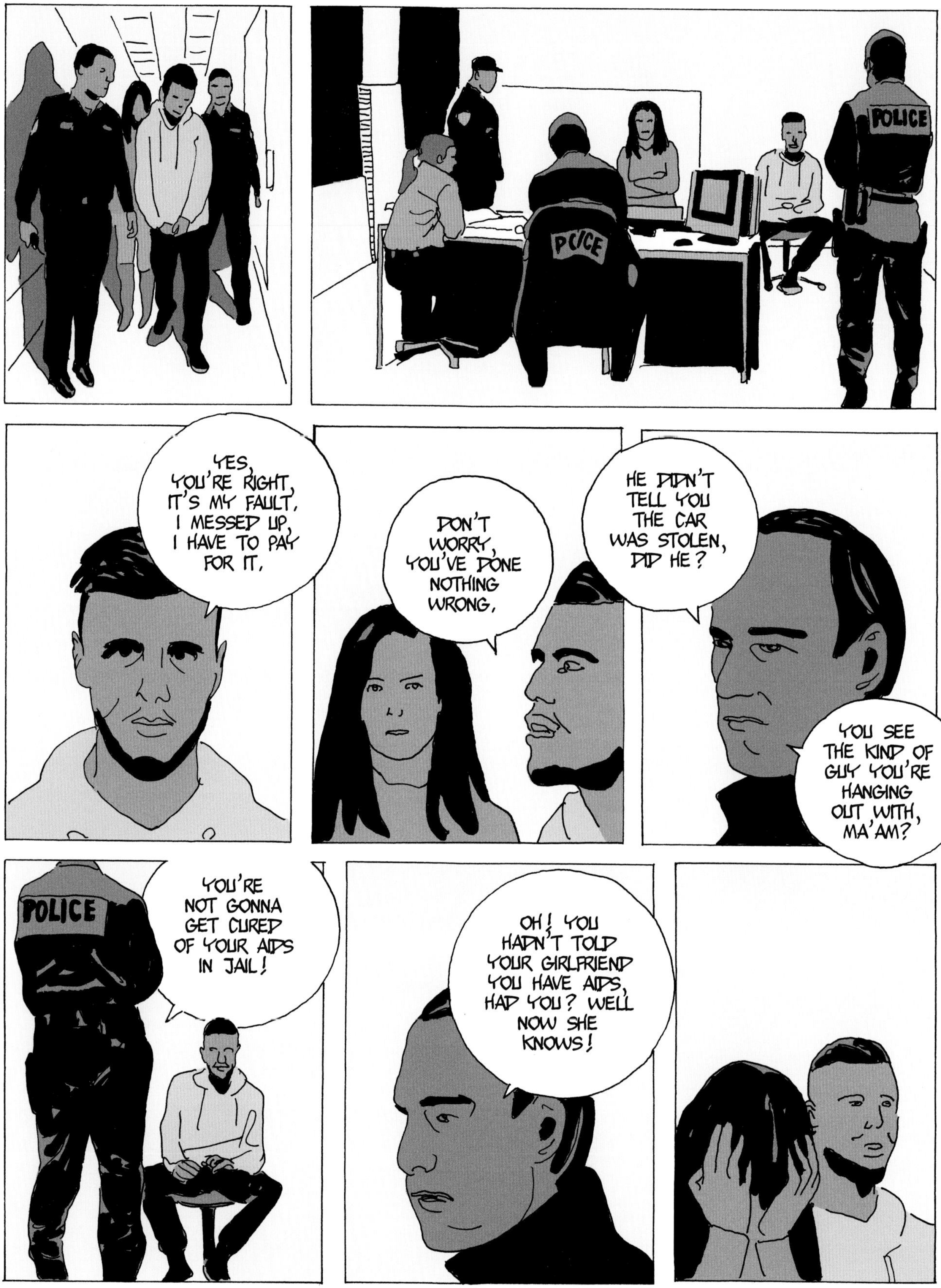
POLICE
POLICE
YES, YOU'RE RIGHT, IT'S MY FAULT, I MESSED UP, I HAVE TO PAY FOR IT.
DON'T WORRY, YOU'VE DONE NOTHING WRONG.
HE DIDN'T TELL YOU THE CAR WAS STOLEN, DID HE?
YOU SEE THE KIND OF GUY YOU'RE HANGING OUT WITH, MA'AM?
POLICE
YOU'RE NOT GONNA GET CURED OF YOUR AIDS IN JAIL!
OH! YOU HADN'T TOLD YOUR GIRLFRIEND YOU HAVE AIDS, HAD YOU? WELL NOW SHE KNOWS!

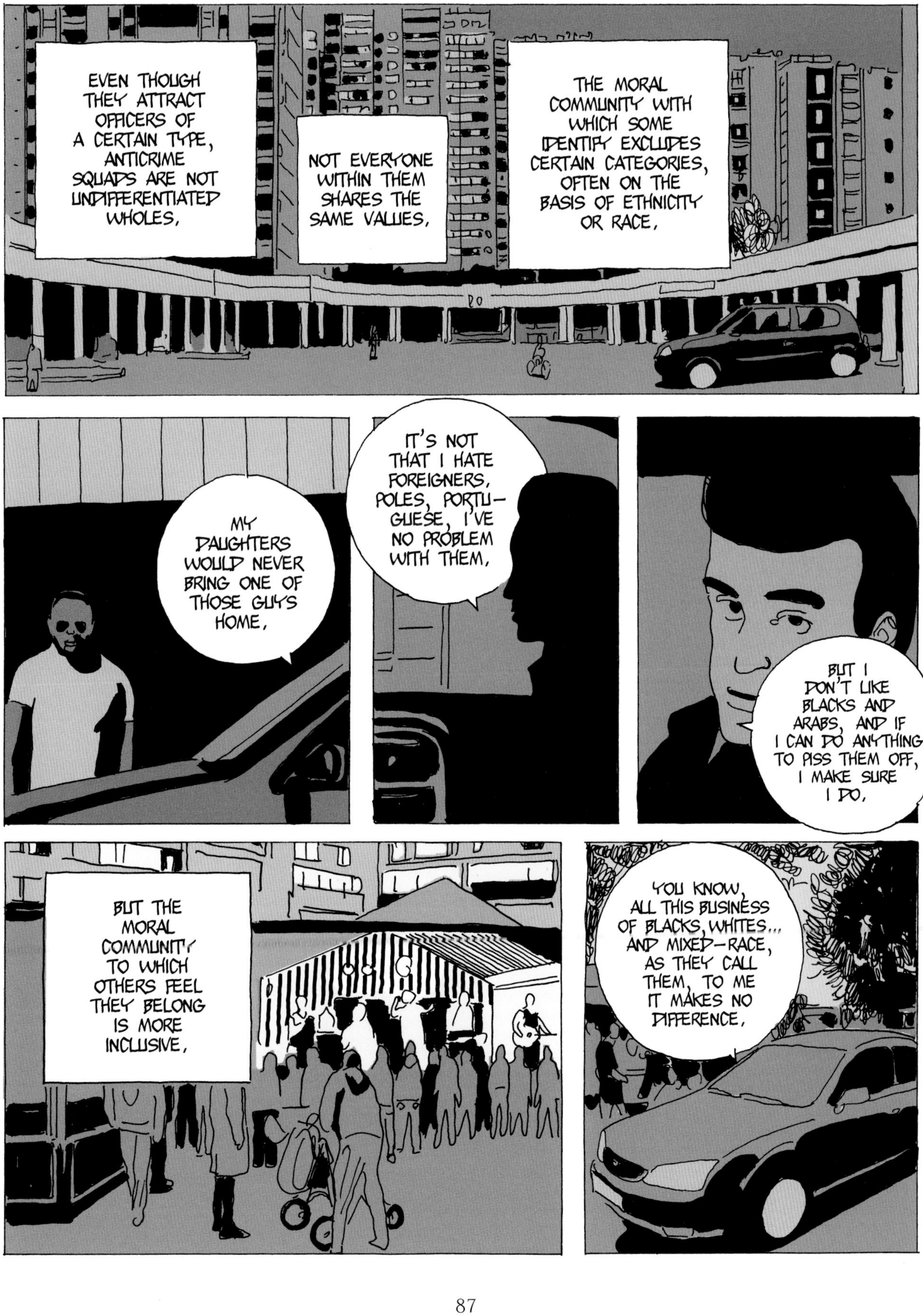
EVEN THOUGH THEY ATTRACT OFFICERS OF A CERTAIN TYPE, ANTICRIME SQUADS ARE NOT UNDIFFERENTIATED WHOLES.
NOT EVERYONE WITHIN THEM SHARES THE SAME VALUES.
THE MORAL COMMUNITY WITH WHICH SOME IDENTIFY EXCLUDES CERTAIN CATEGORIES, OFTEN ON THE BASIS OF ETHNICITY OR RACE.
MY DAUGHTERS WOULD NEVER BRING ONE OF THOSE GUYS HOME.
IT'S NOT THAT I HATE FOREIGNERS, POLES, PORTU-GUESE, I'VE NO PROBLEM WITH THEM.
BUT I DON'T LIKE BLACKS AND ARABS, AND IF I CAN DO ANYTHING TO PISS THEM OFF, I MAKE SURE I DO.
BUT THE MORAL COMMUNITY TO WHICH OTHERS FEEL THEY BELONG IS MORE INCLUSIVE.
YOU KNOW, ALL THIS BUSINESS OF BLACKS, WHITES... AND MIXED-RACE, AS THEY CALL THEM, TO ME IT MAKES NO DIFFERENCE.

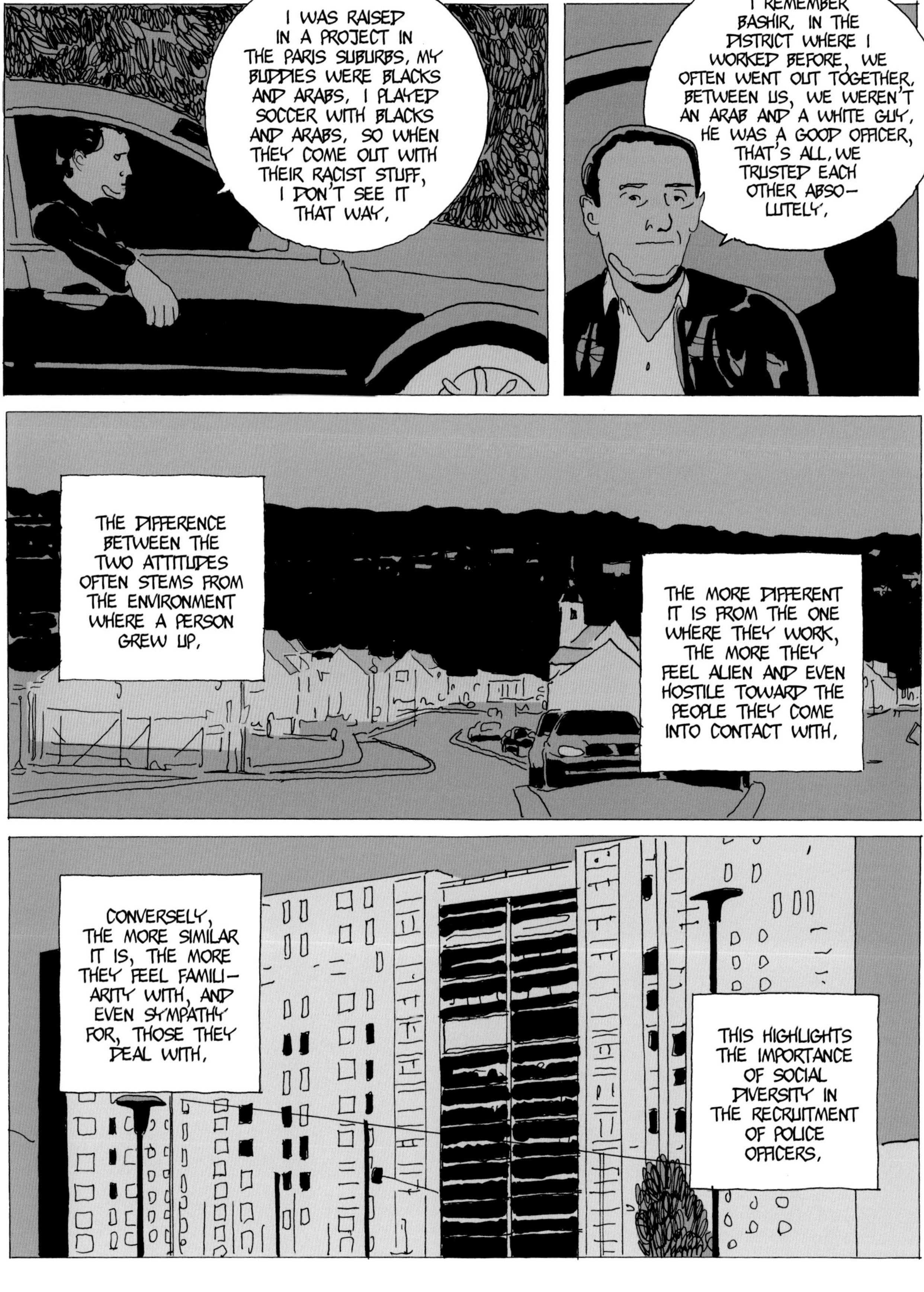

I WAS RAISED IN A PROJECT IN THE PARIS SUBURBS, MY BUDDIES WERE BLACKS AND ARABS, I PLAYED SOCCER WITH BLACKS AND ARABS, SO WHEN THEY COME OUT WITH THEIR RACIST STUFF, I DON'T SEE IT THAT WAY.
I REMEMBER BASHIR, IN THE DISTRICT WHERE I WORKED BEFORE, WE OFTEN WENT OUT TOGETHER. BETWEEN US, WE WEREN'T AN ARAB AND A WHITE GUY, HE WAS A GOOD OFFICER, THAT'S ALL. WE TRUSTED EACH OTHER ABSO-LUTELY.
THE DIFFERENCE BETWEEN THE TWO ATTITUDES OFTEN STEMS FROM THE ENVIRONMENT WHERE A PERSON GREW UP.
THE MORE DIFFERENT IT IS FROM THE ONE WHERE THEY WORK, THE MORE THEY FEEL ALIEN AND EVEN HOSTILE TOWARD THE PEOPLE THEY COME INTO CONTACT WITH.
CONVERSELY, THE MORE SIMILAR IT IS, THE MORE THEY FEEL FAMILI-ARITY WITH, AND EVEN SYMPATHY FOR, THOSE THEY DEAL WITH.
THIS HIGHLIGHTS THE IMPORTANCE OF SOCIAL DIVERSITY IN THE RECRUITMENT OF POLICE OFFICERS.

FOR A LONG TIME, TWO MAJOR MODELS OF POLICING CONTRASTED WITH EACH OTHER,

IN THE UNITED KINGDOM IT WAS THE «BOBBY», UNARMED, OFTEN A BEAT OFFICER, WELL INTEGRATED INTO HIS COMMUNITY AND RESPECTED FOR HIS SENSE OF CIVIC DUTY,

IN THE UNITED STATES IT WAS THE «COP», ALWAYS ARMED, PATROLLING IN A CAR, WITH A LIMITED RELATIONSHIP WITH THE PUBLIC, AND FEARED FOR HIS BRUTALITY AND HIS RACISM,

THIS IS THE MODEL THAT HAS BECOME ESTABLISHED ALMOST EVERYWHERE IN THE WORLD,

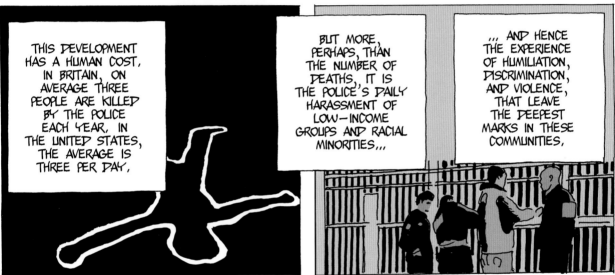

THIS DEVELOPMENT HAS A HUMAN COST, IN BRITAIN, ON AVERAGE THREE PEOPLE ARE KILLED BY THE POLICE EACH YEAR, IN THE UNITED STATES, THE AVERAGE IS THREE PER DAY,

BUT MORE, PERHAPS, THAN THE NUMBER OF DEATHS, IT IS THE POLICE'S DAILY HARASSMENT OF LOW-INCOME GROUPS AND RACIAL MINORITIES,,,

,,, AND HENCE THE EXPERIENCE OF HUMILIATION, DISCRIMINATION, AND VIOLENCE, THAT LEAVE THE DEEPEST MARKS IN THESE COMMUNITIES,

FRANCE IS NO EXCEPTION TO THIS DEVELOPMENT, FRENCH POLICE ARE INCREASINGLY HEAVILY ARMED AND ARE MOVING FURTHER AND FURTHER FROM THE COMMUNITY, FOCUSING THEIR ACTIVITY ON THE GROUPS MOST AFFECTED BY SOCIAL INEQUALITY,

NAK LA BIC*

* Tag playing on words: FACK the BUC.

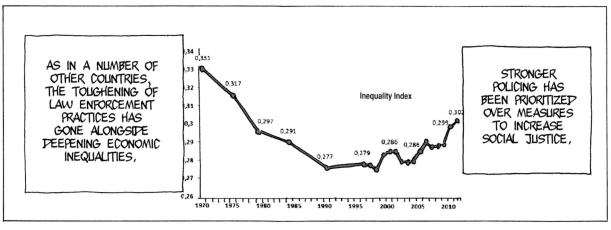

AS IN A NUMBER OF OTHER COUNTRIES, THE TOUGHENING OF LAW ENFORCEMENT PRACTICES HAS GONE ALONGSIDE DEEPENING ECONOMIC INEQUALITIES,

Inequality Index

STRONGER POLICING HAS BEEN PRIORITIZED OVER MEASURES TO INCREASE SOCIAL JUSTICE,

THE ANTICRIME SQUADS' MODE OF INTERVENTION IS THUS ALSO INDICATIVE OF THE POLITICAL RESPONSE TO WORSENING INEQUALITY: A SLIPPAGE FROM THE SOCIAL STATE TOWARD THE PENAL STATE,

«ONE CAN NEVER DISCOVER ANY SUFFICIENT REASON FOR EVERYTHING COMING ABOUT AS IT HAS, IT MIGHT JUST AS WELL HAVE TURNED OUT DIFFERENTLY, »

«WHAT IS EVEN MORE PECULIAR IS THAT MOST PEOPLE DO NOT EVEN NOTICE IT, »

— ROBERT MUSIL

90

EPILOGUE

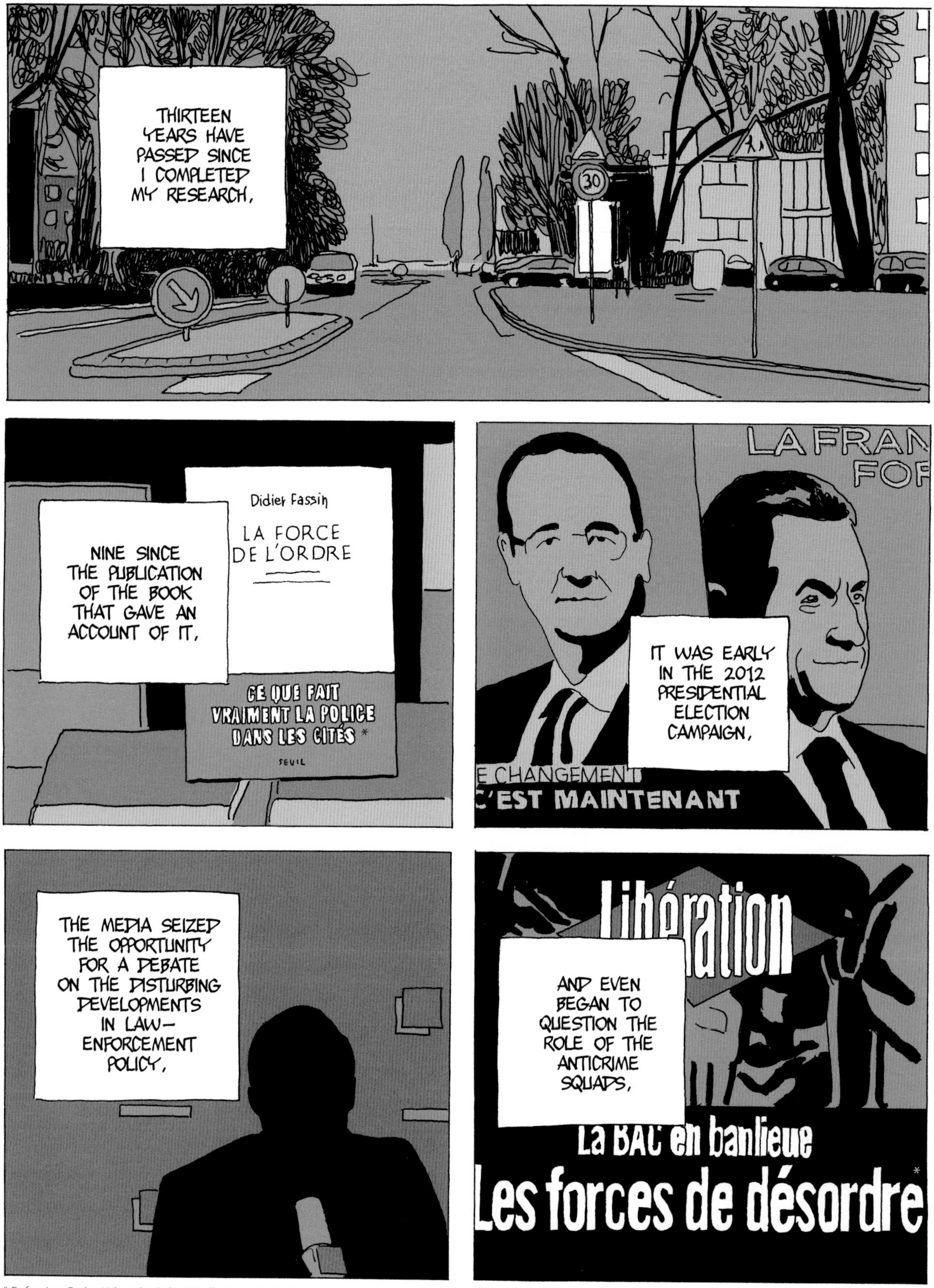
THIRTEEN YEARS HAVE PASSED SINCE I COMPLETED MY RESEARCH,
30
NINE SINCE THE PUBLICATION OF THE BOOK THAT GAVE AN ACCOUNT OF IT,
Didier Fassin
LA FORCE DE L'ORDRE
CE QUE FAIT VRAIMENT LA POLICE DANS LES CITÉS *
SEUIL
LA FRAN
FOR
IT WAS EARLY IN THE 2012 PRESIDENTIAL ELECTION CAMPAIGN,
E CHANGEMENT
C'EST MAINTENANT
THE MEDIA SEIZED THE OPPORTUNITY FOR A DEBATE ON THE DISTURBING DEVELOPMENTS IN LAW-ENFORCEMENT POLICY,
AND EVEN BEGAN TO QUESTION THE ROLE OF THE ANTICRIME SQUADS,
La BAC en banlieue
Les forces de désordre *

* *Enforcing Order: What the Police Really Do in the Projects*

* *The BAC in the Outer Cities: Enforcing Disorder*

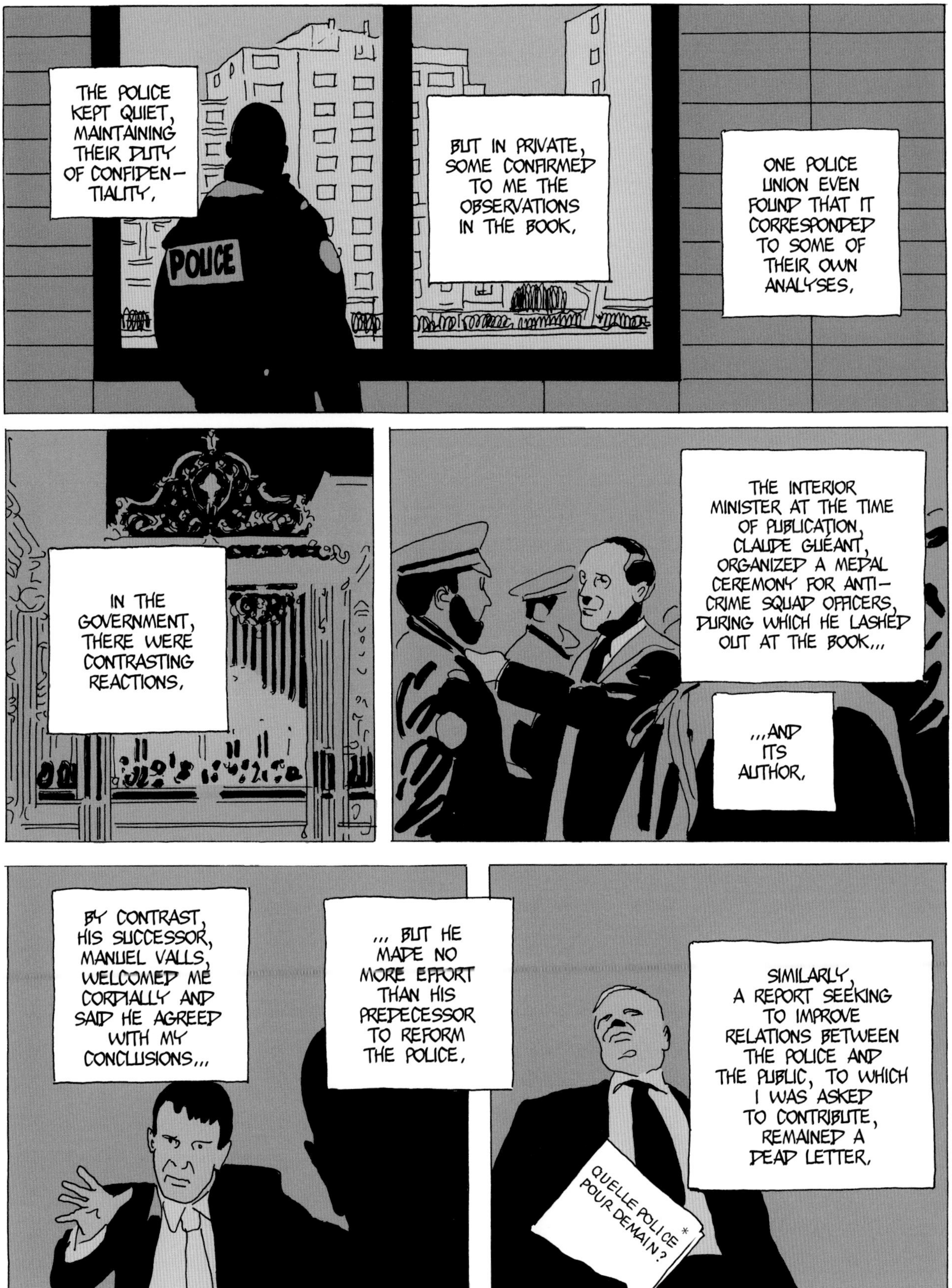
THE POLICE KEPT QUIET, MAINTAINING THEIR DUTY OF CONFIDEN-TIALITY,
POLICE
BUT IN PRIVATE, SOME CONFIRMED TO ME THE OBSERVATIONS IN THE BOOK,
ONE POLICE UNION EVEN FOUND THAT IT CORRESPONDED TO SOME OF THEIR OWN ANALYSES,
IN THE GOVERNMENT, THERE WERE CONTRASTING REACTIONS,
THE INTERIOR MINISTER AT THE TIME OF PUBLICATION, CLAUDE GUÉANT, ORGANIZED A MEDAL CEREMONY FOR ANTI-CRIME SQUAD OFFICERS, DURING WHICH HE LASHED OUT AT THE BOOK,,,
,,,AND ITS AUTHOR,
BY CONTRAST, HIS SUCCESSOR, MANUEL VALLS, WELCOMED ME CORDIALLY AND SAID HE AGREED WITH MY CONCLUSIONS,,,
,,, BUT HE MADE NO MORE EFFORT THAN HIS PREDECESSOR TO REFORM THE POLICE,
SIMILARLY, A REPORT SEEKING TO IMPROVE RELATIONS BETWEEN THE POLICE AND THE PUBLIC, TO WHICH I WAS ASKED TO CONTRIBUTE, REMAINED A DEAD LETTER,
QUELLE POLICE POUR DEMAIN? *

* *What Police for the Future?*

IN THE YEARS THAT FOLLOWED, POLICE PRACTICES REMAINED ESSENTIALLY THE SAME AS THOSE I HAD OBSERVED,

THE IDENTITY CHECK CERTIFICATE THAT HAD BEEN PROMISED IN THE PRESIDENTIAL CAMPAIGN WAS NEVER INTRODUCED,

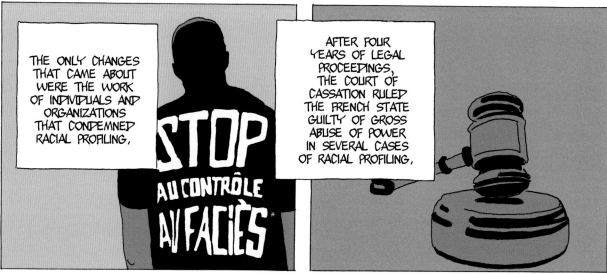

THE ONLY CHANGES THAT CAME ABOUT WERE THE WORK OF INDIVIDUALS AND ORGANIZATIONS THAT CONDEMNED RACIAL PROFILING,

STOP AU CONTRÔLE AU FACIÈS*

AFTER FOUR YEARS OF LEGAL PROCEEDINGS, THE COURT OF CASSATION RULED THE FRENCH STATE GUILTY OF GROSS ABUSE OF POWER IN SEVERAL CASES OF RACIAL PROFILING,

YET THE FOLLOWING YEAR THE INDEPENDENT DEFENDER OF RIGHTS SHOWED THAT YOUNG BLACKS AND ARABS WERE STILL TWENTY TIMES MORE LIKELY TO BE STOPPED AND FRISKED THAN THE REST OF THE POPULATION,

KEVIN - AGE 15 CHECKED 5 TIMES IN MONTEREAU (DEPT. 77)

STAN - AGE 38 CHECKED 0 TIMES DOUBLE STANDARDS?

* End Racial Profiling

THE LITANY OF VIOLENCE AGAINST YOUTHS FROM THE PROJECTS ALSO CONTINUED,

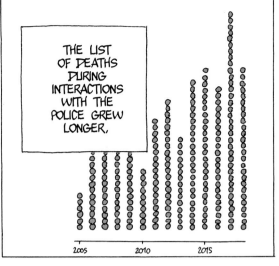

THE LIST OF DEATHS DURING INTERACTIONS WITH THE POLICE GREW LONGER,

2005   2010   2015

A JUDGE PLACED AN OFFICER UNDER INVESTIGATION FOR RAPE AFTER AN IDENTITY CHECK DURING WHICH HE CAUSED SERIOUS RECTAL INJURIES WITH HIS BATON TO A YOUNG MAN OF CONGOLESE ORIGIN,

BUT IT REMAINED RARE FOR LAW ENFORCEMENT OFFICERS TO BE CONVICTED, EVEN IN CASES OF DEATH,

LA POLICE TUE ET VIOLE*

MAIS QUE FAIT L'ÉTAT?*

GRASSROOTS CAMPAIGNS, OFTEN LED BY THE SISTERS OF VICTIMS, MOBILIZED THROUGHOUT THE COUNTRY,

JUSTICE ET DIGNITÉ

STOP À L'IMPUNITÉ POLICIÈRE

* Police = Killers and Rapists   * What's the Government Doing?

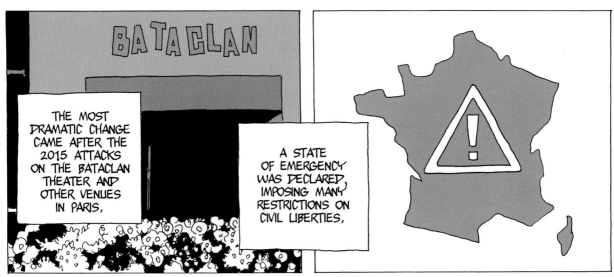

THE MOST DRAMATIC CHANGE CAME AFTER THE 2015 ATTACKS ON THE BATACLAN THEATER AND OTHER VENUES IN PARIS,

A STATE OF EMERGENCY WAS DECLARED, IMPOSING MANY RESTRICTIONS ON CIVIL LIBERTIES,

POLICE WERE GIVEN GREATER POWERS TO SEARCH PREMISES,,,

,,, AND FOR IDENTITY CHECKS, WHICH COULD NOW BE MADE PURELY ON GROUNDS OF PHYSICAL APPEARANCE,

THESE PRACTICES WERE FOCUSED ON MUSLIMS AND THOSE ASSUMED TO BE MUSLIM,

ALTHOUGH THEY WERE ACKNOWLEDGED TO BE INEFFECTIVE, THEY GAVE MUCH OF THE POPULATION, WHO DID NOT SUFFER UNDER THE NEW RESTRICTIONS, THE FEELING OF BEING PROTECTED,

THE SITUATION WAS THUS RIPE FOR PASSING LAWS THAT BROADENED THE CONDITIONS FOR POLICE USE OF WEAPONS AND THE DEFINITION OF LEGITIMATE SELF-DEFENSE,

THE STATE OF EMERGENCY WAS MAINTAINED FOR NEARLY TWO YEARS, WHEN IT WAS LIFTED, A BILL THAT REINSTATED ITS MAIN PROVISIONS WAS SIGNED INTO LAW BY THE PRESIDENT,

WHAT WAS SUPPOSED TO BE THE EXCEPTION HAS NOW BECOME THE RULE,

SINCE THEN, REPRESSION HAS AFFECTED NOT ONLY LOW—INCOME NEIGHBORHOODS, BUT ALSO MIGRANTS AND REFUGEES,,,

,,,WHILE THE CRIMINALIZATION OF SOLIDARITY ACTIONS AIMS TO INTIMIDATE HUMANITARIAN AND HUMAN RIGHTS ACTIVISTS,

VIOLENCE IS ALSO BECOMING ROUTINE AT DEMONSTRATIONS, WITH THE USE OF NEW WEAPONS,,,

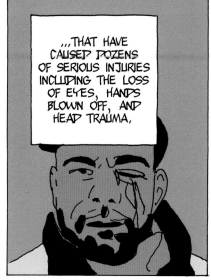

,,,THAT HAVE CAUSED DOZENS OF SERIOUS INJURIES INCLUDING THE LOSS OF EYES, HANDS BLOWN OFF, AND HEAD TRAUMA,

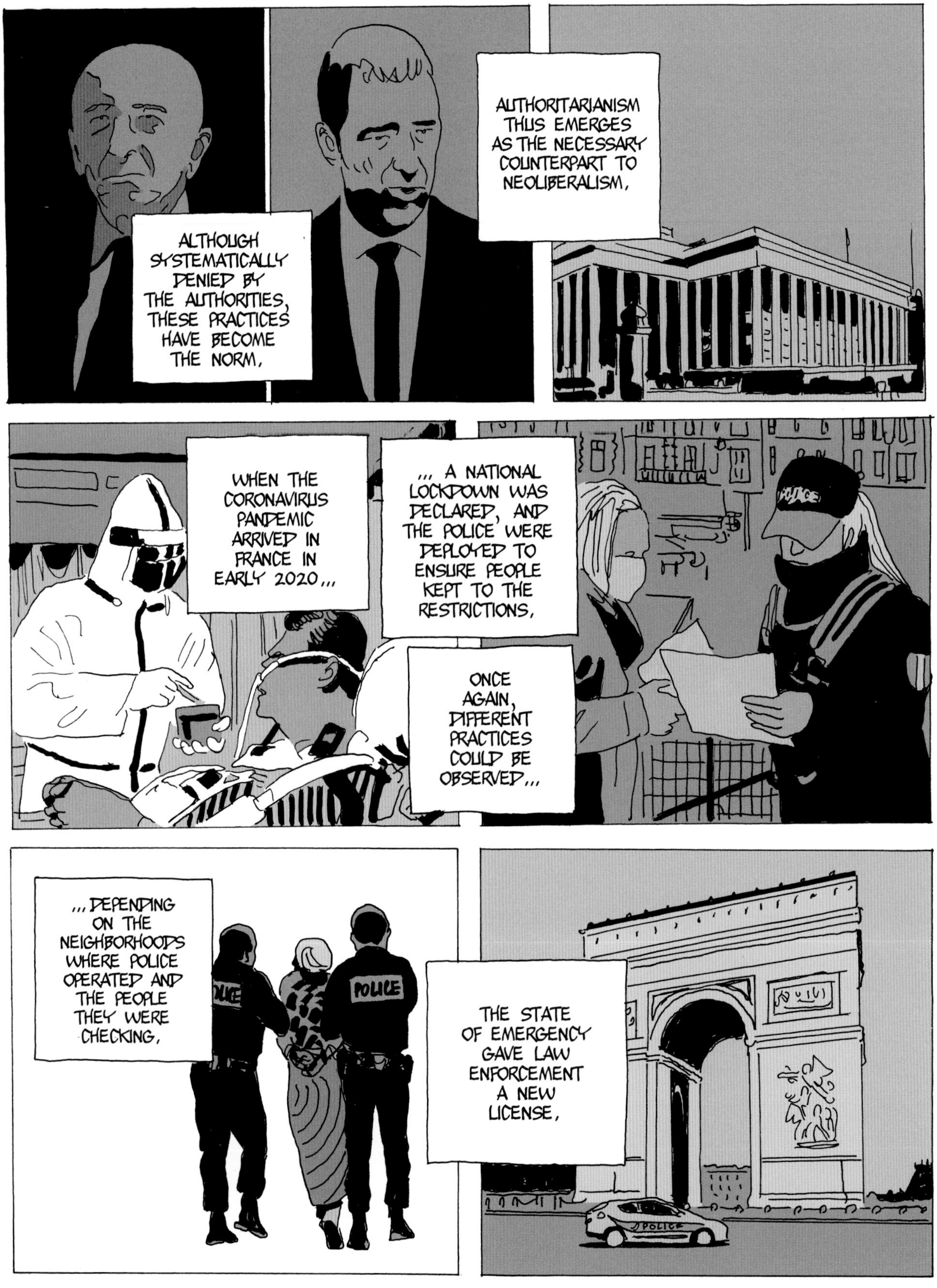
ALTHOUGH SYSTEMATICALLY DENIED BY THE AUTHORITIES, THESE PRACTICES HAVE BECOME THE NORM.
AUTHORITARIANISM THUS EMERGES AS THE NECESSARY COUNTERPART TO NEOLIBERALISM.
WHEN THE CORONAVIRUS PANDEMIC ARRIVED IN FRANCE IN EARLY 2020...
... A NATIONAL LOCKDOWN WAS DECLARED, AND THE POLICE WERE DEPLOYED TO ENSURE PEOPLE KEPT TO THE RESTRICTIONS.
ONCE AGAIN, DIFFERENT PRACTICES COULD BE OBSERVED...
...DEPENDING ON THE NEIGHBORHOODS WHERE POLICE OPERATED AND THE PEOPLE THEY WERE CHECKING.
POLICE
THE STATE OF EMERGENCY GAVE LAW ENFORCEMENT A NEW LICENSE.
POLICE

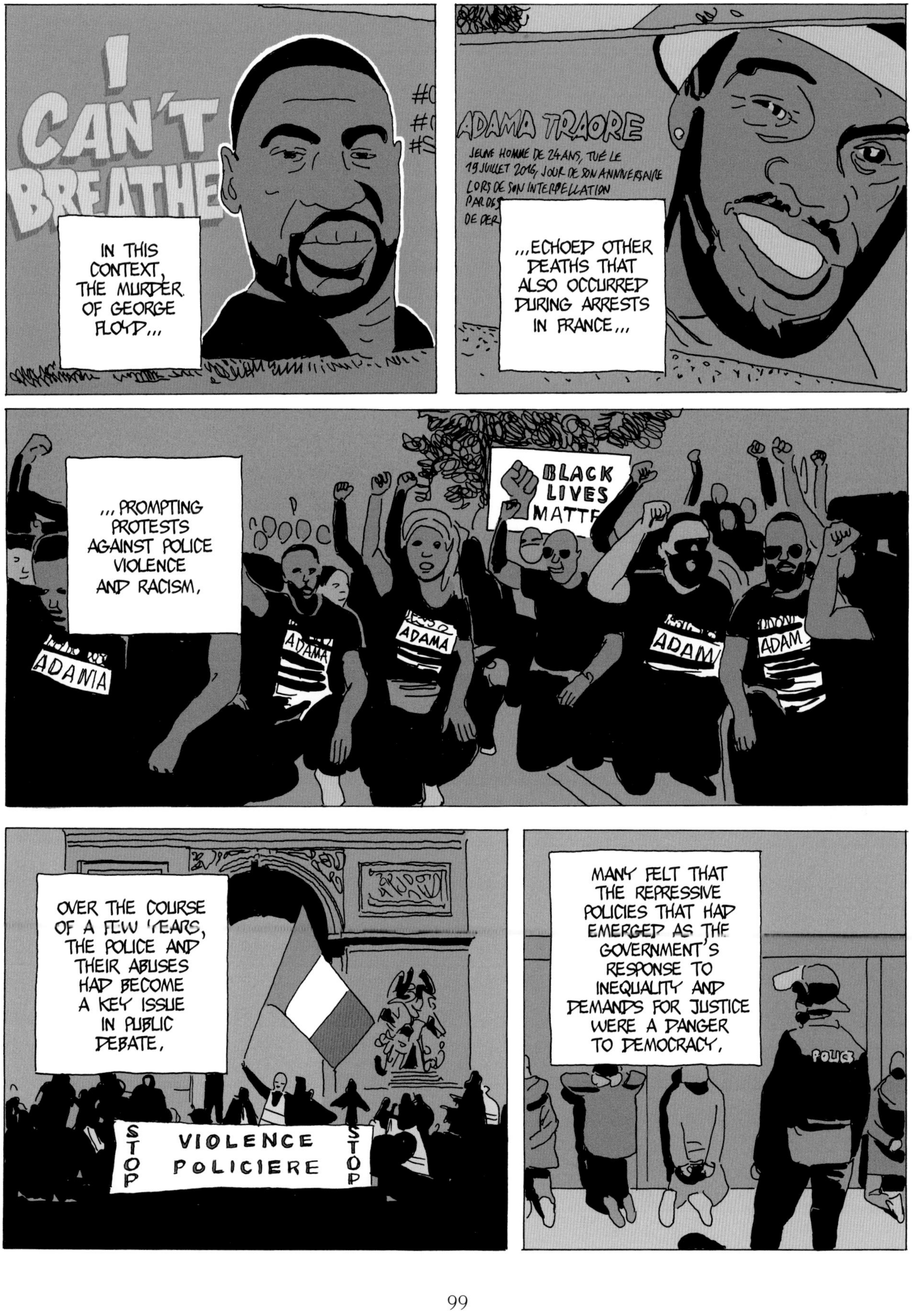
I CAN'T BREATHE
IN THIS CONTEXT, THE MURDER OF GEORGE FLOYD...
ADAMA TRAORE
JEUNE HOMME DE 24 ANS, TUÉ LE
19 JUILLET 2016, JOUR DE SON ANNIVERSAIRE
LORS DE SON INTERPELLATION
...ECHOED OTHER DEATHS THAT ALSO OCCURRED DURING ARRESTS IN FRANCE...
...PROMPTING PROTESTS AGAINST POLICE VIOLENCE AND RACISM.
BLACK LIVES MATTE
ADAMA
ADAMA
ADAMA
ADAM
ADAM
OVER THE COURSE OF A FEW YEARS, THE POLICE AND THEIR ABUSES HAD BECOME A KEY ISSUE IN PUBLIC DEBATE.
STOP VIOLENCE POLICIERE STOP
MANY FELT THAT THE REPRESSIVE POLICIES THAT HAD EMERGED AS THE GOVERNMENT'S RESPONSE TO INEQUALITY AND DEMANDS FOR JUSTICE WERE A DANGER TO DEMOCRACY.

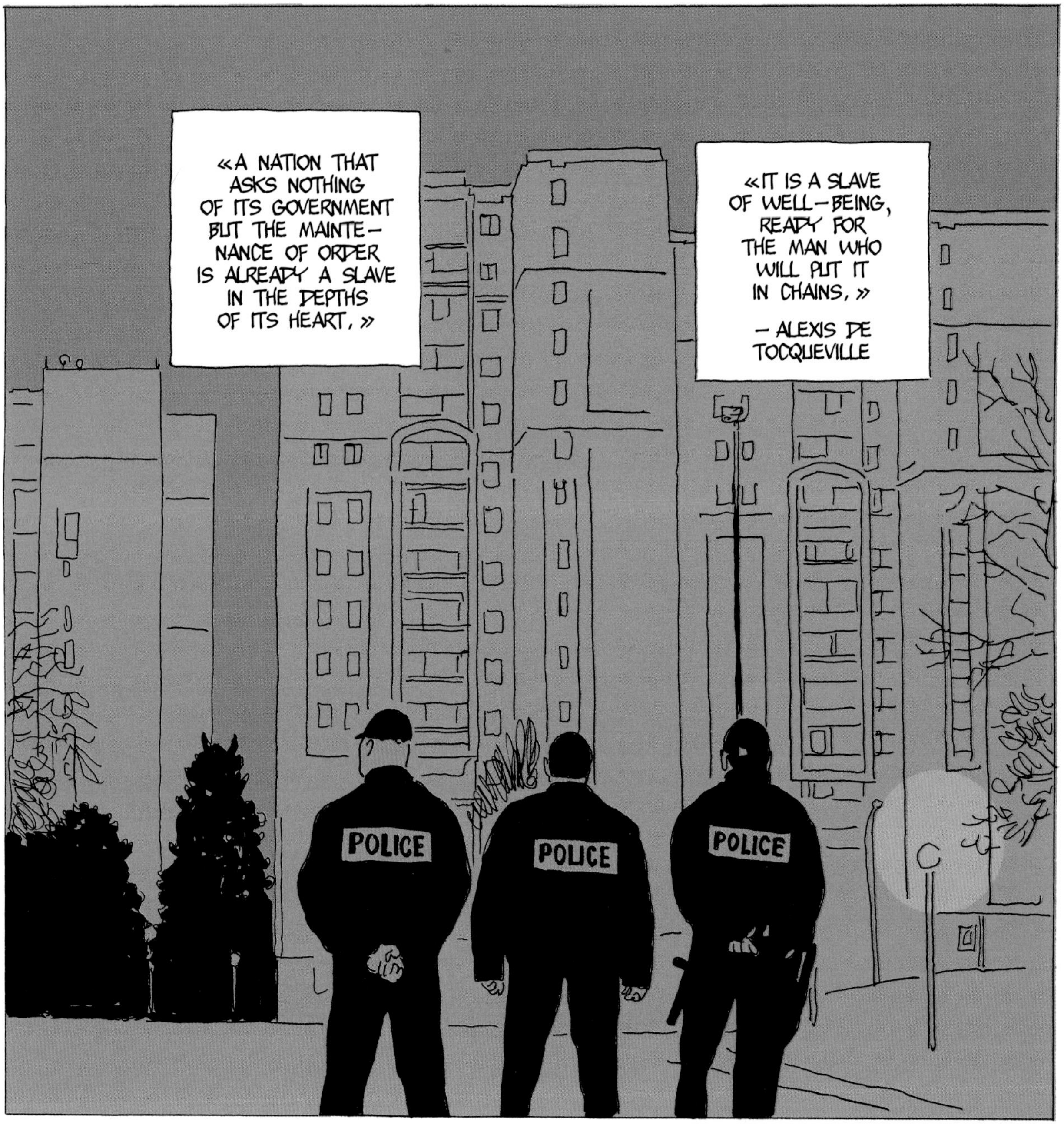
«A NATION THAT ASKS NOTHING OF ITS GOVERNMENT BUT THE MAINTE-NANCE OF ORDER IS ALREADY A SLAVE IN THE DEPTHS OF ITS HEART.»
«IT IS A SLAVE OF WELL-BEING, READY FOR THE MAN WHO WILL PUT IT IN CHAINS.»
– ALEXIS DE TOCQUEVILLE
POLICE
POLICE
POLICE

DIDIER FASSIN
FRÉDÉRIC DEBOMY
JAKE RAYNAL